Raincheck

Marlo Lanz

BLACK ROSE
writing™

ISBN: 978-1-61296-908-4
PUBLISHED BY BLACK ROSE WRITING
www.blackrosewriting.com

Printed in the United States of America
Suggested Retail Price (SRP) $18.95

Raincheck is printed in Garamond Premier Pro

Thank you to all of my girlfriends who've read one – or more – versions of *Raincheck*. A special thanks to Dorothy, my fellow aspiring author, who has both edited my story and commiserated along our writing journey. And to my BFF, Lisa, who has read each and every version of *Raincheck*, without complaining. So appreciated.

To my kids, Tristan, Charlize and Kye - know that you can make anything happen if you try hard enough.

Raincheck

Chapter 1 ~ Liv

An old saying goes that hind-sight is twenty-twenty. And right now, I totally get it. Because if I had any foresight, I would have finished my last term paper over the weekend instead of procrastinating. Instead of watching an Anne of Green Gables movie marathon, going out for supper, taking a spin class, and having a nap. You know one of those delicious, right in the middle of the day, time wasting naps? Yup, I had one of those too.

Because if I'd finished that damn paper, I wouldn't have had to stay up all night then rush to the University this morning to hand it in.

And I wouldn't be late now.

Glancing at my phone, I checked the time and ignored another text message from Gabe, my best guy friend and room-mate.

I was so late. He was definitely going to kill me!

I tried to move faster, but this stupid duffle bag weighed more than I did. More hind-sight. If I'd packed last night – instead of stressing over that fricken paper - Gabe could have taken my duffle this morning and I wouldn't have had to haul it across town on the bus.

Note to self – smarten the fuck up.

I had five years of University behind me so it wasn't like I didn't know better. Because I did. And I was usually good at completing my course work ahead of schedule. Or I wouldn't have earned a spot in one of the most coveted Master's programs in the country.

Although right now, I was sick of classes and writing papers. I just wanted to focus on my actual thesis. And have some fun this summer. Which is the exact reason I was tagging along with Gabe.

His band Diesel would be opening for Raincheck's North American Summer Tour and, according to Gabe, Raincheck was THE band out right now. So this tour was a giant deal. It could literally jump start Diesel's entire career. And I'd be there to watch it happen.

If they hadn't left already. Shit!

. . . . .

"Baby Doll!" Gabe called, waving at me as I hurried toward the concert hall where we were supposed to meet half an hour ago. OK, according to his latest text, thirty-nine minutes ago. "I was starting to panic. Where've you been?"

He closed the distance between us wrapping me in a giant hug, his solid six-foot frame engulfing my entire five feet, four inches.

"Sorry Gabe," I muttered shifting the weight of my giant duffle bag from one shoulder to the other when my feet hit solid ground again. "I told you this morning that I had to hand in my last paper."

Gabe reached over, using his thumb and forefinger to slide my sunglasses up onto my head. His pale blue eyes finding mine. "And let me guess, you just finished the paper, oh about," he looked down purposefully at his watch, "an hour ago?"

I scrunched up my nose as Gabe shook his head in reproach.

"Hour and a half ago. You forgot travel time from the University to the concert hall you know." I glanced at the historic brick building where Diesel had played last night with Raincheck. The first concert of their tour. Too bad I had to miss it.

Damn paper.

"We're pulling out any minute Liv, you almost missed the bus," Gabe chastised. "Are you deliberately trying to stress me out today?"

"Of course not. The printer jammed so things took longer than I expected."

"And why am I not surprised?" He shook his head again. "Well, at least you're here now."

"Good things come to those who wait," I joked, hoping to ease the tension on Gabe's face. Hating myself for adding to his stress. Today was important to him and so far I'd only made it worse.

Great friend, yup, that's me.

"I've spent the last five years waiting for you," Gabe returned, his expression softening. "I just need to confirm a few details with Allison the tour manager. Why don't you go and get settled on the bus. It's parked in the back of the building, second from the end. Put your stuff in the bunk farthest back – that's where we'll be sleeping," he added wiggling his eyebrows suggestively.

And things were back to normal. Gabe loved to tease me about us getting together – so to speak.

"As if," I groaned. I gave Gabe my signature goofball grin, showing as many teeth as possible before heading around the side of the building. A shiver of excitement crawling up my spine.

Gabe and I met five years ago when I lived in residence with his younger sister Laina, our other room-mate and my best friend. Already in his third year, and knowing how wild his sister could be, Gabe ended up hanging out with us. A lot. To Laina's complete irritation. Until she figured out that hanging around with Gabe, meant hanging around his really hot friends. Then the tables turned, and Gabe became the exasperated one.

With three younger sisters, however, I always appreciated the way that Gabe watched over us. Scaring creepy guys away at the bar, making sure we got home safe, and even fixing things around our shoe-box sized apartment. Things that my sisters never could, or would, do.

"One, two." I counted eagerly, looking at the line of four huge tour buses. With a bit of effort, I yanked open the door and stepped up into luxury. This bus was a hundred times nicer than our two-bedroom apartment. Which both excited and depressed me.

I moved through the mahogany kitchen slash eating area towards the middle of the bus where two sets of bunks nestled into the wall. "And this is home," I declared pulling back the bottom curtain of the last compartment. "Mmm not too shabby." The built in flat screen TV and plush mattress caught my eye in the dark paneled sleeping compartment.

Today was finally getting better.

I shoved my bag into the storage space underneath the bunk and sank onto the mattress, fatigue overwhelming my body. The all nighter I'd just pulled catching up with me.

· · · · ·

"Hey! Hey! Wake up!"

I leapt up, cracking my head against the top of the bunk as a deep, angry voice ripped through my sleep. A pair of intense brown eyes glared down at me as I struggled to get my brain started. The guy looked familiar, really familiar, but my sleep-deprived brain just couldn't place him. I rubbed at the spot where my head had met metal feeling self-conscious.

"Hey chick, get your ass out of my bed and off my bus before I call the cops! I know what you're hoping for and it's not going to happen."

"I, umm, I," I muttered incoherently, working to make sense of what was happening.

"Forget this," the guy growled grabbing my arm, dragging me out of the sleeping compartment.

"Get your hands off me!" I squeaked, ripping my arm out of his grasp. Disoriented, I stumbled backwards frantically looking for an escape route as he grabbed at me again. I could only see one way off the bus and, of course, it was behind this lunatic. This very large lunatic. Gabe was six feet tall and well built and this guy was even bigger. I was going to be toast in about a minute if I didn't get out of here.

As he lunged at me again, a surge of adrenaline filled my body and I kicked hard, digging the heel of my boot into his thigh. With a horrific scream the guy crumpled over, falling onto the floor. Seeing my chance, I scrambled over him and out of the bus, running full speed back towards the building. Towards Gabe, my safety.

"Gabe!" I screamed dodging around people and into his arms. "There's a lunatic on the bus. He, he tried to attack me," I stuttered. My heart racing a million miles a minute as I clung to Gabe's broad chest.

"Oh my God, Liv – are you alright?" Gabe gasped, taking my face gently between his hands, surveying for damage. "Christ, you're bleeding!"

Lightly, I touched my fingers to the throbbing spot on the top of my forehead feeling something warm and sticky ooze over my skin. I looked down at the red stain on my fingertips. For some weird reason, the sight of blood never bothered me – except when it was my own. Like now. I could feel the acid in my stomach begin to churn.

"I'll kill him!" Gabe exploded, vibrating with anger. His knuckles turning white as his hands clenched into tight fists. "Liv you stay here. Brian take care of her! Will, Liam, you guys come with me."

I watched the guys march towards the tour bus as if they were going into battle. A sickening feeling spreading through my stomach. And I wasn't sure if that feeling had more to do with the blood or straight up fear. Because, although I knew that I was safe now, and that Gabe could handle himself, something still felt very wrong.

"Sit down Liv, let me have a look at your head," Brian commanded, taking my hand and leading me to the nearby curb.

"It's fine. I just hit it on the top of the bunk bed when that lunatic woke me up."

"He woke you up?" Brian questioned, fishing a tissue out of the pocket of his board shorts.

"Owe that hurts!" I protested as he pressed the Kleenex against my forehead. "Please tell me that tissue is clean?"

"Just sit still and tell me what happened," he ordered, clamping his free hand around my shoulder to keep me still.

"I fell asleep and the next thing I knew this maniac was screaming at me to get off his bus. Then he literally yanked me from the bunk muttering something about this isn't going to happen. It was a total - real life – nightmare!" I stared into Brian's soft brown eyes as the scene replayed in my mind. A shudder cut through my body as the realization of what could have happened washed over me.

"Then what?" Brian asked, gently pulling the tissue away so that he could study my forehead.

"Then I kicked him as hard as I could and got off the fricken bus!"

A tall, lanky guy sat down on my other side. "Hi, I'm Dave."

"Liv," I replied, forcing a weak smile.

Awesome, an audience. Just what I was hoping for as Brian administered his version of first aid with a – more than likely - used Kleenex.

"I'm the guitarist for Raincheck," he elaborated. "How's your head?"

Guitarist for Raincheck. Even better. Way to make a first impression Liv.

"It's fine. Right doc, I'm gonna live?" I looked at Brian for confirmation.

"I think she's gonna make it. Don't worry this is just par for the course with Liv. This girl is walking trouble," Brian told Dave with a chuckle. "Remind me to tell you some Liv stories while we're on tour. Trust me, you can't make up the shit that happens to her."

"You keep those stories to yourself mister," I snapped.

Dave grinned as I shot Brian the evil eye, wishing he was wrong. Unfortunately, if something weird was going to happen and I was anywhere in the vicinity, it would happen to me. Like when the door-handle of a bathroom at UBC snapped off, trapping me inside for over an hour. It had been four months since that freak incident and I still hadn't lived it down.

"So this guy was yelling at you to get off his bus?" Dave asked with open curiosity.

"Yep, a real nut job. I hope for his sake that he's long gone, cause Gabe is gonna – kick – his - ass."

And I was good with that. Jerk, scared the shit out of me.

"Just for interest sake, what did this nut job look like?" Dave probed.

I could see he was trying to hold back a smile.

Very weird.

"He was really tall, taller than Gabe and built solid, like a rugby player or something. His hair and eyes were dark." I paused as the guy's face flashed before my eyes. Forever scorched in my memory. "I'll never forget his eyes as long as I live. They were so intense and angry. The way that he looked at me still gives me chills. I seriously think he's certifiable."

"And was his hair short on the sides and longer on top, sort of done up in a pompadour?" Dave confirmed no longer able to contain his smile, his bright blue eyes lit up like a kid's on Christmas morning.

"You know him?" The sickening feeling in my stomach began to spread like wild fire throughout the rest of my body. I stared at Dave, waiting for his answer.

"Maybe," he replied slowly, deliberately, prolonging my torment. "Which bus were you on again?"

"Second from the front – Gabe's bus," I answered, cringing in horror as Dave let out a loud chuckle.

"Our bus is second from the BACK Liv!" Brian cut in, his voice at least two octaves higher than normal. "Oh no, what have you done?! Please tell me she didn't?" he begged Dave.

Dave began laughing hysterically, making my stomach drop into my toes.

"What? What did I do?" I demanded, leaping up. I glanced down at Brian who looked absolutely sick, then at Dave, who was almost crying with laughter.

"That wasn't our bus Liv, it was Raincheck's bus! And the guy you assaulted is their front man - Ty Benson!" Brian's face looked pale in spite of his olive toned skin.

"Oh crap, that's why he looked so familiar," I muttered sitting down again between Brian and Dave before my knees gave out. "I can't believe I didn't know who he was. I, um, think I might have hurt him," I added quietly, my eyes glued to the sidewalk.

Shit! This was so bad. Gabe would have been better off if I had missed the bus.

When Diesel was first being considered as the opening act for Raincheck's summer tour, Gabe told me that Ty Benson had a reputation for being an ass. He liked to get what he wanted, when he wanted it. So if he wanted Gabe gone, then Gabe would be gone – and it would be all my fault! I felt like throwing up.

'Please don't let me have ruined this for Gabe', I silently prayed.

"There's no way you could've hurt Ty. He's like six-foot four and two hundred and forty pounds. You're what, five-foot nothing and maybe weigh a buck ten. Don't worry about it," Dave soothed, lightly patting my back.

"But I think I really might have," I muttered, sinking lower by the second.

"Seriously don't worry about it Liv, Ty's tough. I'm sure that nothing you did would damage the beast. Trust me."

"You call him the beast?" I asked.

Dave nodded, amusement evident on his face. "The name fits his build and temper," he explained, tucking one side of his chin length blond hair behind an ear. "You don't want to be around Ty when he's mad."

"Awesome," I replied dejectedly. "Maybe I should just go home. I don't want to ruin things for you guys. Tell Gabe to call me." I started to get up but Brian grabbed my arm, pulling me back down beside him.

"No way sister, not unless you talk to Gabe first. You know he'll flip out if he comes back and you're gone. And I'M NOT dealing with that."

"You two are brother and sister?" Dave asked, his eyes bouncing from my face to Brian's then back again.

I shook my head. "Nope, fortunately for me we're just friends."

Brian grinned, wrapping his arm around my shoulder.

"You only wish that you were my sister," Brian retaliated. "I'd be an awesome big brother. Much better than Gabe, if I do say so myself."

"You can't possibly be Gabe's sister," Dave stated, confusion evident on his face as his eyes swept over my face again. "Brian I can see, but you and Gabe look nothing alike."

True enough, Gabe was very blond, very fair and had liquid blue eyes. I was the exact opposite.

"Liv's definitely NOT his sister," Brian chuckled. "Wait till you meet his sister Laina, she's totally hot."

I rolled my eyes at him. "Thanks Bri."

Realization, then remorse, crossed Brian face. "Sorry Liv, I didn't mean to imply. I, I, mean, you're hot too."

"Brian's just desperate to get into Laina's pants," I explained to Dave.

"I wouldn't exactly say desperate, just interested," Brian added pulling his arm from around my shoulders as I eyed him skeptically. "What? Laina's my perfect woman."

I shook my head. Some guys would never learn. Brian had been chasing Laina for three years already. Everyone, including Laina, had told him that it would never happen but Brian was proving to be an eternal optimist - or glutton for punishment - depending on how you looked at it.

"Liv," a familiar voice beckoned. I looked up to see Gabe standing alone by the building. I hadn't noticed until now, but most of the other people were gone. "Liv," he called again.

"Oh shit," I muttered to Brian. "Nice meeting you Dave, hope your tour is good. Because I don't think I'll be seeing you again," I added under my breath. I studied Gabe's face as I slowly slunk towards him. He didn't look happy.

"Geez Liv, you kicked the shit out of Ty Benson!" Gabe said raking a hand through his short hair. "He can barely walk and man is he pissed."

I stood numb staring up at Gabe, praying that I hadn't ruined this for him.

"Just tell me that I didn't blow it for you, please Gabe. I'm so sorry," I apologized, my eyes becoming misty. "I'll leave and then Ty won't be so mad. I'm sure he'll forget all about it. Better yet, tell him that you kicked me off the tour. That'll make the lunatic happy."

Gabe reached over, brushing a strand of chestnut hair from my face. "Oh Liv, what am I going to do with you?" he questioned, his voice low and husky. "I couldn't care less about 'that lunatic' or the tour, I'm just thankful that he didn't hurt you." A lopsided grin appeared on his face, easing my anxiety just a little. "Cause then I'd have to kill him and start a jailhouse rock band!" Gabe chuckled, using his index fingers to push up the sides of my down drawn mouth. "Oh cheer up Liv, after I explained that you're MY GIRLFRIEND," he said slowly, nodding his head, "and had mixed up the buses, Ty wasn't AS mad. He just said to make sure that you don't come near him," big pause, "for the entire tour."

"You told him that I'm your girlfriend?" I questioned.

"It just popped into my head and since we're sharing a hotel room during the tour, it makes sense. But more importantly, it appeased the big man. So," he drawled, "now that you're my girlfriend, I think we need to discuss all of the fringe benefits that I haven't been receiving. Things are gonna be changing this summer Baby Doll, we've got lost time to make up for." A huge grin lit up Gabe's face.

"If you didn't think of me as your little sister, I'd almost worry," I retorted, a giant weight lifting off my shoulders. "As long as I didn't get you kicked off the tour I guess I can pretend to be your girlfriend," I agreed, adding in gagging sounds for effect, "and stay away from that egomaniac for the next four months."

I forced my mouth into a grimace while Gabe's smile widened. Although I'd never admit it, pretending to be Gabe's girlfriend for the summer wouldn't be the worst thing in the world. After all he was sweet and completely hot and the best guy I knew, hands down.

"That's my girl. Now let's go and get you on the right bus, everyone is pretty much loaded and ready to go."

Gabe threaded his fingers in between mine, leading me towards the second tour bus – from the end.

Chapter 2 ~ Ty

I followed her. Well actually, I guessed that she'd be here. In this very coffee shop. Right now. Working on her Master's thesis. Not that it was hard to tell where she'd be. Like most women, she was predictable. Whenever the guys from Diesel were setting up at a concert hall, she'd slip away to a local coffee shop with her computer. Although we'd been on the road for a good three weeks, it had only taken me a few days to figure her out.

Like I said – predictable.

The weird thing was that I hadn't intended to follow her. I was planning on heading to the concert hall to help with sound check. But when I saw her leaving the hotel, I just couldn't help myself. After wolfing down the rest of my breakfast, I headed out of the restaurant. Turning left instead of right. Walking straight towards the Starbucks two blocks down, knowing she'd be there.

And here she was. Sitting at a table a few feet away, immersed in her work, completely oblivious to the fact that I was watching her.

Objectively speaking, she was pretty. Long, dark hair, hazel eyes, nice figure. But nothing overly special. Nothing that should make me want to come here. Want to watch her. Like some kind of creepy stalker. Which begged the question, why was I here?

Great question.

And one that I didn't exactly have an answer for. Other than there must be something seriously wrong with me. Following another guy's girlfriend around was insane. And it wasn't me. I didn't follow chicks, they followed me.

I should definitely leave. Yup. If I had any sense at all, I'd leave right now before she catches me staring at her.

. . . . .

Five minutes later I stood by the condiment station, relentlessly stirring my coffee and watching her. Still. Willing her to look up and see me. Giving me the excuse that I needed to walk over and talk to her.

OK Ty, you've officially lost it.

I needed to leave. Right now. Or. Maybe. I should just go over and say a quick hello and then leave?

With five long strides, and zero thought, I closed the distance between us.

"I never would have figured you for a leopard print thong type of girl. You come off as more angelic - you know white lace panties, cotton undershirts," I blurted out.

Oh fuck! Where did that come from?

I was planning to open with a casual, 'hey, how's it going?' Or a good ole, 'fancy meeting you here.'

Liv's hands stilled on the laptop keyboard and I could see her body tense up. Drawing in a huge breath, she looked up at me with those hazel eyes.

"What makes you think that I have leopard print underwear?" she asked, her voice filled with apprehension.

"Well that's what was in your bag, so I just assumed they're yours? Unless they belong to your boyfriend?" The words just fell out of my mouth. I was acting like a complete ass, but I couldn't help it.

Past stopping and rational thought, I sat down at the tiny table as Liv gave me the once over. It was obvious that she wasn't thrilled to see me. That she didn't want me here. But right now I didn't care. I just wanted, or maybe even needed, a few minutes alone with her. Just her. Just me. I needed her to say something stupid or giggle like a high school girl or fawn over me. That's all it would take. Then I could leave and get back to business.

"You went through my bag?" she demanded, locking her eyes to mine.

My thoughts shifted back to the very first day when she'd accidentally fallen asleep on my bus, in my bunk. She'd left her bag behind when she took off and I might have had a quick peek through it. Tiny, lacey thongs, each with a matching bra flashed through my mind, making my cock twitch.

I took a long sip from the paper cup, trying to regain my self-control.

Getting a giant boner wasn't going to help the situation.

"Well it was under MY bunk and I didn't know who it belonged to. What was I supposed to do?" Contrived innocence dripped from my voice and I had to stifle a laugh as her face began to turn various shades of pink.

"My underwear was at the very bottom of the bag, which means that you looked through everything!" Liv exclaimed, clearly starting to unravel.

I shrugged nonchalantly, watching her intently. Trying to hide the fact that I was loving every moment. Making her angry was the most fun I'd had in a long time. And it got my mind off her skimpy underwear.

"I like your pjs – very, um, grandmotherly. EXACTLY what I expected," I pushed as she seethed.

"I'd ask what you mean by that, but I really don't care," Liv snapped. "Look, I have work to do." She focused on the computer, ignoring me, driving me to antagonize her even more.

"So your boyfriend is into the nun look? Well, whatever turns his crank. If you were my girlfriend I'd want you to wear those leopard print panties to bed. And nothing else," I added suggestively when she looked up in surprise, which quickly transformed into anger. "Or maybe you and your boyfriend are saving yourselves until you get married? Funny thing is that you two rarely seem to hold hands or whatever. Actually come to think of it, I've seen very little of the whatever," I mused, looking up at the ceiling, pretending to be deep in thought. "Trouble in paradise? Come on, you can tell me."

I leaned forward on the table, studying Liv's face as I waited for an answer. Her lips pressed together into a thin line and I could tell that she was on the verge of losing it. Women never reacted to me this way. Which made our little encounter even more interesting. A smile crept onto my lips and, to my happiness, made her vibrate even more.

"First of all, you know that my boyfriend has a name!" she almost spat. "It's Gabe. Feel free to use it. Second, our relationship is none of your business, but just for the record we love each other. He's one of my best friends," she added between gritted teeth.

"Hmm that's an interesting thing to say. Your boyfriend is ONE of your best friends. Never heard anyone's girlfriend say that before, usually it's my boyfriend IS my best friend or my everything or something else equally lame." I stared at her expectantly, anticipating an epic eruption.

Drawing in a huge breath, Liv's expression smoothed and she actually smiled at me.

What the fuck?

"Ty, I'm sure that you have better things to do than sit here with me. And I've got work to do. So thanks for the chat and have a super great day." She gave me this goofy, all teeth grin before staring down at her computer.

I couldn't help myself, I burst into laughter. Just when I thought she was going to start screaming, she does a one eighty and instead smiles like the Cheshire Cat on crack. Maybe she wasn't so predictable. A little nutty perhaps, but definitely not predictable.

We sat in silence with Liv's eyes fixed on her laptop and my eyes fixed on her. Realizing that she was set on ignoring me, a twinge of evil overrode my better judgment. Sliding my chair next to hers I leaned in, pressing my body tightly, intimately, against hers as I looked at the computer screen.

"I see that, what exactly are you working on? Hmm, interesting," I commented taking the liberty of slowly scrolling down the page.

Liv leaned her body as far back into her seat as possible, attempting to put some space in between us.

This was getting more amusing by the second. I had to bite the inside of my lip to stop from laughing.

"You finished yet? I really need to get some work done," she hissed, obviously upset that I was invading her personal space. I shifted closer, eliminating the tiny space she'd managed to create between us.

"Very interesting," I muttered, reading over her thesis summary, totally ignoring her demand. "I wouldn't mind reading your entire thesis when you're finished." Her mouth dropped open in shock. "Based on this, I'm assuming it has something to do with violence, brain stimulation and mental illness?" She merely nodded. Her eyes narrowed before fixing on mine. "Master's thesis in neuropsychology, I'm guessing?"

"You're familiar with neuropsych?" she asked skeptically. I sat motionless, waiting as her gaze slowly, methodically, swept over the tattooed sleeves covering each of my arms, then down my vintage Metallica t-shirt and fitted jeans. Making it obvious that she thought I was nothing more than just a brainless asshole with a guitar.

She'd clearly underestimated me. And I loved it. Now the ball was in my court.

"Well," I answered slowly, knowing that she was hanging on my every word.

This is what I was used to. What I expected from women. Home court advantage – Ty!

"I did my Master's in forensic psychology," I continued, feeling cocky, "but there are definite similarities between the two. Actually, I'm hoping to start my PhD after this tour finishes. I was accepted last September but with the new record coming out I had to push it back a year. Who's your advisor?"

Her mouth dropped open again in sheer surprise and I couldn't help but chuckle. She sat there for several moments just staring at me. Her mouth would open, as if she was going to say something, then slam shut again.

Entertainment at its finest. Right here.

"Bet you didn't peg me for a college man?" I asked with amusement when she remained mute. "I went to UBC too. Started before my music career took off. My Dad was adamant that I get an education to fall back on. For when my band tanked."

I realized that my last sentence sounded overtly cynical but I couldn't help it. The relationship I had with my father was anything but supportive. More like a dictatorship where I was a low ranking member of his regime. I rarely spoke to Phillip, as my sister and I called him, these days and if I had to guess, I'd say that both of us were fine with that. He'd re-married a few years ago and his new wife preferred to think that he never had any sort of personal life before her. You know kids, ex-wife, house, dog.

"Your Dad wasn't supportive of your music?" Liv finally responded. "But you're so talented, I mean you play the guitar, drums, piano, and write the most amazing songs. You're very talented," Liv repeated while her cheeks flushed.

So she was a fan. I knew it!

"That was my Mom's influence. She's a high school music teacher." I paused for a moment, studying her face. "How do you know which instruments I play?" I asked, not bothering to mask the satisfaction in my voice.

"I've heard the guys talk and seen bits and pieces of your show." Liv quickly explained, the pink in her cheeks deepening.

"Hmm. What else do you know about me?" My eyes searched hers intimately and I couldn't help but lean in even closer. I could almost hear her heart thumping as we stared at each other.

Breaking eye contact, Liv tried to shift away. Not that it was possible.

She was sandwiched in between me and the wall. And I wasn't going anywhere.

"Not much," she finally mumbled.

"Really?" I asked, making sure that she could hear the cynicism in my voice.

"Really," she stated, angling her chin up. "I hate to burst your bubble rock star, but not everyone is into your music. Some of us actually prefer to read."

Touche! The girl was feisty.

Liv peered down at her laptop, clearly done with our conversation. But I definitely wasn't. I wanted to say something that would antagonize her, so she'd look at me again with those hazel eyes flashing. But my mind was a blank. Or rather, my mind was waylaid with how good she smelled. Like a combination of flowers and citrus.

Maybe I was the one who needed some space?

That or I was going to be in serious danger of burying my face in her hair.

Easy man.

Mustering up enough willpower, I stood then slowly began sauntering away from the table. Glancing back, I expected to see those eyes watching me but they were still trained on her laptop.

Damn! I couldn't get a handle on her.

This was something new for me. Usually I could predict what people would do, especially woman.

· · · · ·

"I got you a slice of lemon loaf and another peppermint tea with honey," I said, setting the items on the table. Liv jumped at the interruption and I couldn't help but chuckle. "Sorry, I didn't mean to scare you."

Just a few more minutes, then I'll leave, I reminded myself. Waiting in line had given me time for a mental pep-talk. There was absolutely no reason I couldn't talk to her like a normal, rational human being. Right?

Right!

"Umm thanks," she muttered obviously taken off guard. "I thought you'd left."

"Just went to get us a snack. You were concentrating so hard that I thought you could use some nourishment."

Liv glanced down at the loaf cake and steaming paper cup, before quickly pushing the chair I'd vacated away from hers. Amusement filled me as I sat down, fighting the urge to slide it back over.

"Thanks, that was really nice of you. How did you know that I like lemon loaf and peppermint tea with honey?" She studied my face with trepidation and I almost felt bad for ambushing her. Again.

"Doesn't take a genius. You order the same thing at every coffee house we go to," I answered with a grin. "So you never told me who your advisor is?"

"Purdon," Liv returned breaking a piece off the lemon loaf.

"Ouch." I grimaced. "He's tough. I had him for a few classes."

She nodded in shared understanding, popping another piece of lemon loaf into her mouth.

It was nice to see a woman actually eat. I was used to being around women, like my ex, who'd calorie count and obsess over every little thing that went near her mouth.

Every not so little thing too. No lie.

Liv's lips pressed together as she ate another piece of loaf, making a soft mmm noise. Something about the way that she enjoyed her food was almost erotic. It made me want to lean across the tiny table and press my mouth against hers. Hoping. Wanting. To hear that same mmm sound emanate from the back of her throat as my tongue pushed in between her lips. My cock twitched at that thought.

For Christ sake Ty! This was not even in the realm of making normal conversation.

I seriously needed to get laid if just the sight of Liv eating was turning me on. Admittedly it had been a while, a long while, but I'd been handling my self-imposed celibacy just fine, before.

Before what?

My eyes swept across Liv's face again. It didn't make sense. This couldn't be a reaction to her or because of her. She made that low mmm sound again and my cock hardened.

Or could it?

"He was hard but fair. Definitely made you work for your mark. What do you think of him as an advisor?" I asked, trying to get my mind off of her mouth. And what she could do to me with that mouth. My cock strained against the tight fabric of my pants, making me squirm in my seat.

Shit! Get your mind out of the gutter, man.

"I'm trying not to be so quick to judge. You know give him the benefit of the doubt and all," she answered with a frown. "But so far, he scares the shit out of me."

A grin snuck across Liv's lips.

"In that case you better get back to work," I said motioning to her computer. "I won't disturb you anymore."

I grabbed the newspaper from the adjacent table and began leafing through it, trying not to look over at Liv. I wanted to say something else. I wanted to talk to her, but the fear that I'd make a jack-ass out of myself, or possibly come in my pants, glued my mouth shut. Instead, I pretended to be interested in the newspaper even though the words where nothing more than a black blur.

Chapter 3 ~ Liv

I stepped out of the tour bus and spotted my favorite guy by the concert hall talking with the singer from Kismet. Another band scheduled to play at the concert tonight.

The expression on Gabe's face made me stop. Cold. He was looking at Piper so intently that my breath actually caught. I was positive no guy had ever looked at me that way before. A wistful feeling washed over me.

Or maybe it was something else?

I'd been totally off since my impromptu study session with Ty two days ago. He'd behaved totally weird and now - that's how I felt. It was like he'd stirred up something inside of me. And I couldn't figure out how to make it stop.

"Hey Liv," Dave greeted, appearing out of nowhere, scaring the crap out of me. "Sorry, didn't mean to startle you." A grin tugged at his lips as our eyes met. He nodded towards Gabe and Piper. "They've been talking for quite a while. Must be a fascinating conversation."

"Apparently," I choked out, realizing that I wasn't the only one who'd seen the way Gabe was looking at Piper.

Crap!

"She's pretty hey?" he asked before my brain could come up with something witty to say. Something that would distract him from the fact that my supposed boyfriend was looking at another woman like she was the best thing since Google.

"Definitely." I was forced to agree surveying Piper's tall, perfectly proportioned figure and delicate facial features. "I love her fuchsia colored hair. Wish I had the guts to do something that drastic."

I was boringly normal – average height and weight, no tattoos, outrageous piercings, pink hair or anything else of interest. The best word to describe me was non-descript. No wonder Gabe found Piper so fascinating.

Dave grinned. "With the way she looks, you'd think she was on the wild side, but it's not true. The opposite actually."

I looked at him in surprise. "Really? The nose ring and tattoos had me fooled."

Piper's left arm from wrist to shoulder blade was peppered with shadowy black birds, getting increasing larger as you neared the top of her arm. I had been fascinated by it this morning when we first met. The tattoo reminded me of freedom and, from the little I knew of Piper, seemed to fit her perfectly. She also had a guy's name inked across the inside of her right wrist. It said Garret in script writing. I suddenly wondered if he was Piper's boyfriend, or possibly more.

"So Piper and Gabe seem to have hit it off," Dave prodded. He paused for a moment studying my face intently, giving me a chance to respond, but I couldn't think of anything to say. I mean, what could I possibly say that wouldn't either make Gabe seem like a letch, or me seem pathetic? Instead, I just shrugged.

"Doesn't it bother you that Gabe is spending so much time with Piper today? I know that ALL of my exes would have been totally pissed at me," Dave pushed.

Still unsure of what to say, I glanced back at Gabe. The giant smile plastered across his face made my heart melt. It had been a long time since I'd seen him genuinely interested in a woman. With his ice blue eyes, perfect European features and hunky physic – not to mention the rock god thing he had going on – Gabe always had his pick of women, not that it ever really seemed to matter to him. Which made his obvious interest in Piper, so interesting. It also made it unfortunate right now.

"Liv?" Dave prompted. "So, it doesn't bother you?"

Drawing in a deep breath, I looked back at Dave.

Game face Liv.

I smiled big and bright, feeling like the Joker from Bat Man. Based on the weird look Dave shot me, it was obviously over kill. My nerves jacked up another notch.

"Not really," I finally answered, hoping that my voice sounded normal. "Piper seems nice and she and Gabe have obviously found a lot of things in common to talk about."

"But he's YOUR boyfriend," Dave said slowly, his eyebrows lifting in astonishment.

At my obvious stupidity. Yup, got it. Boyfriend's getting friendly with another woman - while I watch.

"I'm really not the jealous type," I tried, hoping that he'd buy this line of crap.

"Besides Gabe's never given me anything to worry about."

"Fair enough. That's a healthy way to look at things – especially with Gabe's profession and looks. So how long have you and Gabe been together? I mean you seem really comfortable around each other," Dave asked, clearly digging for information.

"I guess we really are comfortable around each other. We've known each other for five years," I shared, trying to seem relaxed. Hoping to hide the fact that all I wanted to do was run over and yell at Gabe to smarten the fuck up. "His younger sister Laina and I are best friends," I added, although wasn't quite sure why.

"That's interesting," Dave mused. "So you and Gabe have been together for five years?"

"No, no. Our... umm... relationship has just changed recently," I hedged not wanting to say too much. "So are you single?" I asked, attempting to redirect the conversation to something safe. Knowing me, if we stayed on this topic, I'd slip up and say something that would make Dave more suspicious than he apparently, already was.

"Yep," Dave confirmed nodding his head, "actually aside from Phil, we're all single."

"Seriously? I find that hard to believe. All of you are so great, well, except for maybe Ty," I added under my breath.

Dave chuckled. "Yeah you and Ty sort of got off on the wrong foot. You'll have to forgive him. He's just had a bad run with some off-the-wall women lately, not to mention a crazy ex-fiancé." A wry smirk pulled at Dave's lips. "There was one girl a few months back who managed to sneak into the storage compartment underneath our bus. She rode with us to three concert stops before our tour manager realized what was happening. After she got caught, the chick claimed that she and Ty were having a secret affair and to keep her safe from the press – and aliens - he told her to travel in the storage compartment."

Laughter filled the space between us, easing the tension.

"Seriously? That's absurd!" I exclaimed.

"That's not even one of the best stories," Dave shared, his bronzed face lit up with amusement. "A while back there was a girl who claimed that Ty was the father of her unborn baby. He's had that happen a few times obviously, but this girl was really smart about it. She had pictures of her and Ty from one of our meet and greets and somehow – we still haven't figured out how she pulled this part off – naked pics of her in our tour bus. She used those pictures to photo shop some racer pics of the two of them – if you know what I mean." Dave grimaced. "Anyhoo, she threatened to release the photos to the press if Ty didn't acknowledge that the baby she was carrying was his love child. And that's just one of the reasons he went ballistic when he found you in his bunk. That and he's kind of sworn off women. Which isn't necessarily a bad thing for Ty."

"Oh?" The realization of what Ty's life was like sunk in. I almost felt bad, and probably would have, if he wasn't such a dick.

Trust me, it wasn't easy avoiding someone when you were literally stuck together twenty-four seven. I'd spent more than one night holed up in my hotel room while the guys went out or played video games in another room.

Not that I was bitter. At all.

And then there was the coffee shop incident.

Let's hope that was a one timer. Spending another afternoon with Ty Benson was not on my list of favorite things to do.

"Yeah, he and his fiancé broke up almost two years ago. He sort of went wild after their split – if you get my drift. But he's back on track now. Hopefully he'll meet a decent woman, who appreciates him for him." Dave paused looking at me earnestly. "Believe it or not, Ty's a great guy."

I nodded in agreement, not because I actually agreed. But, because it seemed like the right thing to do.

"So, why did they break up?" Dave grinned at me. "Oh – sorry - I guess that's none of my business," I tried to recant, wishing that I could hit rewind. Not wanting Dave to think that I was actually interested in his majesty's personal life.

"Mindy, his ex, lied to him, cheated on him, and seriously used him to further her career – among other things. It was a really bad scene when Ty finally realized what she'd been doing, although we were always telling him what a complete bitch she was. Worse thing is that after they split, she kept coming back to Ty every time she needed money or whatever. She made it really hard for him to move on. Hence his overt bitterness towards women. Thank God he's finally done with her, poor guy," he shared. Dave paused for a moment obviously lost in thought. "I have no idea why I'm telling you all this? Ty would kill me. You mind keeping this conversation between us?" He looked at me hopefully.

I'd suffered through a few bad relationships myself, and even more bad dates, but at least no one had purposely used me. To be fair to Ty, that must have been rough. Too bad he let one rotten woman and a few bad experiences, make him act like a complete ass towards the rest of the female population.

"No worries Dave. That's pretty easy since I'm forbidden to speak to or be within fifty yards of Ty anyhow." I cracked a huge grin.

"True enough," he chuckled. "Good thing you and Gabe are together, sort of made everything easier." Dave studied my face for a second before glancing back at Gabe and Piper who were now laughing hysterically. "Something must be funny," he added. "Well, I should get back to work. Catch you later Liv."

Thank God.

"Sounds good," I agreed.

I waved to Dave then quickly headed towards Gabe and Piper, eager to interrupt their love fest before anyone else noticed.

· · · · ·

"So, Piper seems pretty interesting," I commented after she left to do her sound check.

A giant grin lit up Gabe's face and I couldn't help but smile too. "She's great. Did you know that she's into Shakespeare? Would you ever have guessed that? And that she can play four different musical instruments? And that she got the bird tattoo on her arm after her Dad passed away from cancer? She's amazing!" he enthused, staring off in the direction Piper had taken.

"She sounds amazing. You two really seemed to have hit it off, which makes me wonder." I paused, waiting for Gabe to look at me, his blue eyes brimming with happiness. "If you're interested in her? Gabe, that would be great if you are," I quickly added when a frown replaced the smile on his lips. "Seriously, you haven't been interested in anyone in forever. It'd be nice to see you happily attached – for a change. Although taking you off the market would devastate half of UBC's student body."

"Ha ha," Gabe returned wrapping me in a tight hug. "Very funny, Baby Doll. I'm immensely happy. I have amazing friends, a wonderful family, my career is taking off and," he added with a devilish grin, "I have the best girlfriend EVER!"

"Can't argue with that," I agreed with a chuckle, "but if you are interested in Piper then maybe it might be best to come clean about us. Tell her you're free and see what she has to say?"

"Seriously Liv," Gabe replied, "there's no way in hell I'm going to let Ty know that I lied to him. That's a career ender. You can't let the cat out of the bag on this one - no matter what," he warned. "Promise me."

"Fine. Then tell Piper I'm a complete bitch," I suggested with a wry grin, "and that we're splitting up. I'll happily go back to Vancouver if it means that you have shot with her." I studied Gabe's face, trying to ascertain what he was thinking. His mouth pressed into a thin line as he looked back at me.

"You'd give up traveling all summer for me? But you've been looking forward to this for months Baby Doll."

"Of course I would, I love you Gabe. After all, you ARE my brother from another mother." I stood on my tip toes to plant a kiss on Gabe's cheek. "And don't even say that you wouldn't do it for me."

Gabe grinned. "Baby Doll, you're too good to me. I really appreciate that but it doesn't matter, Piper already has a boyfriend. And, honestly, I'm not into her that way. Don't get me wrong," he added as I eyed him skeptically. "I find her interesting but only in a professional sort of way. We have a lot in common musically, that's all."

"Seriously?" I returned, making sure that cynicism dripped from that single word.

"Definitely. She's not my type at all. I prefer feisty little brunettes who insist on giving me a hard time and hogging the bed," Gabe countered ruffling my hair.

I raked my fingers through the disheveled mass on my head. "If you say so," I replied slowly, not believing a word Gabe had just uttered. "But, if we are going to keep on with this girlfriend-boyfriend charade, we need to be more careful. Dave saw you talking to Piper and asked if I was upset that you were fucking her with your eyes all day."

"Looks like someone woke up on the hilarious side of the bus today."

"Maybe my words, but definitely Dave's sentiment."

Gabe winced. "Ouch! Guess we'd better work on that. Maybe we should start right now. Come here and give your honey a little sugar!"

Gabe pulled me into a bear hug, tickling my sides until I was gasping for air. Managing to wiggle free, I took off running towards the concert hall.

"Get back here!" Gabe yelled as he sprinted after me. "I'm not finished with you yet."

I yanked open the back door of the concert hall and rushed in, smacking face first into someone's rock-hard-chest. Two arms wrapped around my waist, stopping me from hitting the floor as I rebounded backwards.

"Thanks," I huffed. Sucking in a huge breath, I looked up into Ty Benson's dark brown eyes. And froze.

Oh, crap, I'd ran into the devil himself.

"Ha, caught you!" Gabe cheered as he hurried into the building, stopping just short of creaming into me and Ty.

"Actually, I think I caught her," Ty countered his arms still wrapped around me, our bodies pressed together in a way that felt uncomfortably intimate. Like at the coffee shop.

Ty's masculine scent – like soap mixed with the outdoors - permeated my nose, tempting me to bury my face in the crook of his neck and inhale.

"Does this mean that I get to keep her?" A cocky smirk played across Ty's full lips for just a second as he glanced down at me. His eyes holding mine.

"Sorry man," Gabe returned, shooting me a look as I stood frozen in Ty's arms, like a deer caught in the headlights of an oncoming car. Ty studied my face for another moment before slowly dropping his arms from around my waist.

"Sorry," I muttered slinking over to Gabe, sucking my body against his.

Gabe wrapped his arms around me, pulling me even closer.

Ty nodded at me. "At least you didn't do any damage this time," he returned dryly, running a hand over his injured thigh. "I think they're looking for you," he said to Gabe, motioning towards the stage. Ty glanced at me one more time before stepping outside.

"OK, that was weird," Gabe said looking down at me as I peeled my body from his.

"Everything with Ty is weird," I replied, trying to calm my nerves. Hoping that the uncomfortable feeling I got whenever Ty was near, wouldn't last for the rest of the summer.

Chapter 4 ~ Liv

Two tour stops later I trudged into the local coffee shop toting my laptop and thesis notes. In order to make it to this venue on time we'd spent last night on the tour bus. And thanks to bed hog Gabe, I'd barely gotten any sleep. So was beyond bitchy now.

To top it off, Dr. Purdon had sent an e-mail demanding to see my progress by the end of the week. I'd put in a decent effort so far, but not nearly enough to satisfy him. And I knew it. I was going to have to crunch in some serious hours over the next few days if I wanted to appease Purdon and give myself some time to enjoy New York. One of our upcoming tour stops.

"Liv, hey Liv," a deep voice called over the noise of the bustling coffee shop slash bakery. "Liv Madison, over here."

I turned scanning the crowd, shocked to hear my name. A waving arm caught my attention. A waving arm attached to one seriously annoying Ty Benson. He was sitting alone at a table, motioning me over.

First Purdon. Now Ty. This day was going from bad to worse.

I plastered a fake smile on my lips as I moved through the maze of tables that separated us.

"Great place hey?" Ty enthused gesturing to the wooden chair across from him. "Have a seat."

I glanced at the mug of colored liquid and piece of cake on the table in front of that seat. Relief coursing through my body. He was already here with someone.

Thank God!

"Hey Ty," I greeted cordially. "I see you already have company," I added, nodding toward the food. "I'll just grab a seat somewhere else. Thanks though."

A grin spread across Ty's perfect lips. "Actually that's for you."

"For me?" I asked staring at him like an idiot. Waiting for hell's inferno to open up and swallow me whole.

"Yup." He motioned to the chair again.

But I just stood there. My feet rooted to the spot. My brain refusing to process the fact that Ty Benson was here. Waiting for me.

WTF?

"I guessed that you'd end up here so took the liberty of ordering for you. I hope you like carrot cake. The lady said it's their specialty. Got you a peppermint tea too." He grinned. "With honey of course."

He'd guessed that I'd be here. Seriously WTF?

Giant, awkward pause. Both of us staring at each other. Ty waiting for me to say something. My brain still malfunctioning.

Get it together Liv!

"That was super nice of you," I finally managed, plunking down in the chair, trying to compose myself.

Our last interaction had been uncomfortable, to say the least. And the idea of trying to make polite conversation with Ty for the next hour, or hours as it turned out last time, instead of working on my thesis - didn't thrill me. Grudgingly, I put my backpack on the floor then pulled my chair closer to the table. "So what are you doing here? Shouldn't you be setting up for tonight's concert?"

Oh, please say that you're not staying.

Ty shrugged. "Ah, the guys can handle it today. I had some, umm, business to take care of this morning so thought I'd just take a chance on meeting you here," he explained.

"I thought we could share a table. You can work on your thesis and I can work on some of my stuff." Ty tapped the laptop that was propped open on the table. "The coffee here is amazing. So is the carrot cake, I already ate my piece." He took a sip from the bright blue ceramic mug in front of him.

Apparently we were doing the study buddy thing.

Awesome.

"Sounds like a plan," I reluctantly agreed. Picking up my mug of tea, I took a small sip of the sweet liquid. "Thanks for this," I said motioning to the cake and tea. "I'll treat next time," I offered. Hoping that there would never be a next time.

Because I hated the way Ty made me feel. It was like a whirlwind of emotions when we were together. He could drive me from furious to astonished in mere seconds. And it was maddening. Probably because he was the opposite of Gabe. My semi-serious, even tempered, easy to be around - Gabe. He was the ideal guy. Ty, on the other hand, seemed to be as far away from ideal as you could get.

Ty's face lit up. "That's a deal. I happen to know of a great little dessert shop at our next stop. Remind me to give you directions in case we can't get away at the same time."

You've got to be kidding! I was just being polite. It was a fake invitation. Didn't this guy understand social convention, at all?

"Sounds good," I replied, doing my best to feign excitement.

"So how's the thesis coming along?"

"Don't ask," I groaned, before shoveling a piece of carrot cake into my mouth, savoring the taste as the icing melted on my tongue. "Oh my God!" I moaned, experiencing the best oral orgasm ever. "This is amazing!"

"I know," Ty agreed watching me closely as I shoved another sizable piece of cake into my mouth. "I think I inhaled mine in about a minute."

A weird expression crossed Ty's face as he stared at me. But I was too absorbed in the cake to really care.

"I can see why," I mumbled, using my hand to cover my cake filled mouth. Swallowing, I added, "I'll have to get a piece for Gabe on the way out. He loves carrot cake. Well, actually he loves anything with cream cheese icing, especially my chocolate cake."

"You cook?" Ty asked obviously surprised.

"Yeah," I answered with a grin. Surprising Ty was weirdly satisfying.

Being around him must be warping me.

"I love to cook, especially when I should be studying for a test or working on my thesis," I elaborated.

He nodded in understanding. "So you cook to avoid doing whatever you should be doing. I'm the same, except that I write music. In fact, I wrote most of our current album when I was supposed to be finishing my Master's thesis."

"No way!"

"Way!" Ty grinned. "I ended up defending it four months later than I was supposed to. Fortunately, it turned out pretty good so they let me slide. And, as a bonus, the album turned out pretty decent too."

"I'd love to read your thesis sometime," I said. And shockingly meant it.

He really must be warping me. That, or I needed to lay off the sugar.

Ty's smile widened. "Sure, give me your e-mail address and I'll send it to you. Let me know what you think. Actually, I should get your phone number. I'll give you mine too. In case of emergencies you know," he added, his cheeks turning slightly pink as I stared at him in astonishment.

This was just getting weirder and weirder. First Ty was waiting for me. Now he was giving me his phone number.

Seriously, WTF times a hundred?!

"Thanks. Sounds like a good idea." I jotted my e-mail address and phone number on a piece of paper then handed it to Ty.

"Great, I'll text you my info. You know, I would be happy to read over what you've got for your thesis so far. If you'd like. I mean our fields of study are related," he offered. "Although, Gabe probably does that for you already."

I chuckled. "Gabe's a fine arts guy. Psych is NOT his field."

Ty looked at me for a moment, his eyes slowly sweeping over my face. "You and Gabe seem very different. I guess that's why they say opposites attract."

"In our case that's true. Although Gabe and I are more alike than Laina and I. And we're best friends."

"Laina is Gabe's younger sister, right?"

"Yup." I nodded, wondering how Ty had figured out that connection. I was certain that I'd never even mentioned Laina to him.

"My sister would die if I went out with her best friend. Aren't you worried that it could get messy if you and Gabe broke up?" He stared at me expectantly.

"I hope not, since we all live together," I revealed, then instantly regretted sharing this piece of information. The less Ty knew about me and Gabe, the better. I looked down into my cup of tea feeling Ty's eyes on me. Feeling like a bug being dissected under a microscope.

"You live with Gabe? I didn't realize you two were that serious. Dave said that you and Gabe had just started seeing each other."

"Dave told you that?" My eyes flew up to meet Ty's again. And everything suddenly made sense. Dave obviously told Ty about seeing Gabe and Piper together. And now Ty was fishing for information.

Shit!

"Yeah, he just happened to mention it," Ty said in casual tone, although the expression on his face was anything but nonchalant.

"Oh," I muttered, bending down to pull the laptop out of my bag. Thankful to escape Ty's scrutiny for a moment.

"So," Ty continued as I untangled the computer cord. "ARE you and Gabe serious?"

I held in a sigh, concentrating on setting my computer up, so that I wouldn't have to look at him.

"Well, you live together, usually that means it's pretty serious," Ty continued before I even had a chance to form a response in my head. "But then again, you just started going out." He leaned forward, resting his chin on his hand as he studied me. "So what's the deal?"

Yup, I was definitely a bug under his microscope.

"Gabe and I have been friends for a long time," I answered noncommittally, hoping that Ty would let this go. "We should probably get some work done. Purdon wants to see my progress by the end of the week," I added, attempting to change the subject. Or better yet, curtail the whole getting-to-know-each-other portion of today's festivities.

"And that's a bad thing, I'm guessing?" Ty replied and my heart leapt in joy.

Safe topic. Yes!

"That's a very bad thing. I haven't been as diligent as I should have been over the past few weeks." I pressed the start button, booting up my computer as I arranged my notes on the table.

"Well then you'd better get to it. Let me know if I can help you at all."

"Thanks, Ty, I appreciate that." I flashed him a smile before staring down at my laptop, pretending to be interested in what my screen held.

Several agonizing minutes passed while I tried to immerse myself in my work – with zero luck. Ty's questions had totally rattled me. And to make matters worse, I could feel him watching me from across the table.

It was going to be a long afternoon.

"Hey Liv, sorry to bug you, but I just have one more question."

I forced my lips to curl into a smile before looking up. "No worries. What's your question?"

"I don't understand what being friends with Gabe for a long time has to do with your living together? Considering that you just started going out."

Apparently I hadn't escaped. Dread filled my body as I contemplated what to say. Nothing amazing came to mind so I decided to stick as close to the truth as possible.

"Well," I began slowly, "Gabe and I have been friends for almost five years now. He's one of my very best friends actually. And he, Laina and I have been living together for the last two years." Ty nodded, clearly interested in what I was saying. I shrugged apathetically. "I don't know. Our friendship has just evolved. For lack of a better word," I added trying to keep my explanation as ambiguous as possible. "That probably doesn't make sense, but it's the best way I can explain it."

Let it drop, I silently urged Ty from across the table. His eyes narrowed in consideration.

"So you and Gabe were already living together before you started seeing each other?"

I simply nodded before looking down at my lap top again.

"What if you and Gabe don't work out?" Ty pushed. "Aren't you worried about that?" He leaned in even closer, waiting for my answer. If things kept going this way, Ty would be sitting on my lap in another minute.

I searched Ty's face for a moment, wondering if he suspected Gabe had lied to him about our relationship?

God, I hoped not.

"Nope," I returned fighting the urge to hold my laptop up between us like a shield.

"Nope?" Ty parroted his thick, dark brows lifted in surprise or maybe disbelief.

"Nope," I confirmed. "No point in worrying about something before it happens." If only I believed that. I constantly worried about stuff that hadn't and hopefully never would happen. But being accident prone, that wasn't necessarily a bad thing. "Besides I can't imagine anything ever happening between Gabe and me that would be bad enough to ruin our friendship."

"Ruin your friendship? Don't you mean relationship?"

"Not exactly. I mean if Gabe and I don't work out romantically, we can just go back to being friends. No harm, no foul."

"No harm, no foul?" he repeated and I nodded. "You seriously think that you and Gabe can just be friends again – after being together romantically - sexually?"

Sexually? Oh my God! I wanted to run away screaming right now. I glanced at the door longingly.

"Yup," I said meeting Ty's gaze again. Hoping that I sounded confident.

I shot him a giant, toothy smile.

He grinned, shaking his head. "Liv Madison, you definitely are not like any other woman I've ever met."

"More then you know," I muttered under my breath.

Ty and I spent the remainder of the afternoon working and chatting – mostly amicably. He let up on the personal questions, although the way he looked at me every now and then still made my heart pound. It was another weird afternoon with Ty. I wondered how many more of these I had to look forward to over the next few months.

· · · · ·

"Oh my God, Gabe! Ty Benson sat at the coffee shop with me for like three hours while I worked on my thesis again," I complained as we relaxed on the bed in our hotel room that night.

"Guess that explains where he was while Raincheck set up for tonight's show. Again. Don't you think it's weird that he keeps showing up when you're studying? Alone." Gabe asked, searching my face after he clicked off Kismet's Facebook page.

"Stalking Piper again?" I teased. It had become Gabe's daily habit to check Kismet's Facebook and Instagram pages, not to mention creep Piper's personal pages. They'd also begun to exchange a Facebook comment here and there. A wry grin spread across my lips as Gabe grimaced.

"You make me sound mental. And just for the record, I'm not stalking her. I was only interested in a picture that she posted from the show we did together."

"Uh ha." I nodded. "The show you guys did a couple of weeks ago?" I couldn't resist teasing Gabe every chance that I got. It was painfully apparent that his interest in Piper went way beyond some picture on Facebook.

"And so, what did Ty do while you were working on your thesis?"

"Changing the subject, nice play Larson." I nudged him with my shoulder. "He was working on his laptop too." I rolled towards Gabe, propping my head up on my arm.

"Did you guys talk?"

"A little here and there. Although he seemed really interested in our relationship. Even more than last time." I watched concern, then something else, flicker across Gabe's face.

"Shit!"

"Yup. I honestly didn't think that he even noticed us, but he was asking a lot of questions about our relationship, us living together and whatnot," I shared, raising an eyebrow.

"I don't think he's interested in us so much, Baby Doll. I think it's more that he's interested in you. Did he know that you'd be at the coffee shop? I mean did you happen to mention that to him?"

"Of course not, Gabe. Except for the last time that I saw Ty at Starbucks, I've barely talked to the guy – as per my agreement. And, actually," I hesitated for a moment, not sure if I should share this part with Gabe. Considering the bus incident had already started things off on a bad note.

"Actually what?" Gabe asked, concern evident on his face.

I'd never kept anything from Gabe before and really this wasn't a huge deal. Right?

"Actually, Ty was already at the bakery. Waiting for me." I watched concern transform into anger on Gabe's face.

"How do you know that he was waiting for you?"

"Because he said so. He'd already ordered me a peppermint tea and cake. Had it waiting on the table for me," I explained. The anger on Gabe's face intensified, making me wish that I'd kept this to myself.

"Son of a bitch!" he yelled, jumping off the bed. "That bastard is trying to move in on my girlfriend. I heard he was a player, but never thought he'd have the balls to do something like this."

"Gabe, wait, please," I begged, grabbing his hand. "I think you're wrong. Ty's not interested in me the way that you think he is." Gabe looked down at me with doubt in his eyes.

"Oh really?"

"He's a psych major too. He's supposed to start his PhD soon," I rambled, desperate to stop Gabe from confronting Ty. Or doing something even worse. Ty was very influential in the music business and Gabe didn't need any bad blood between them. Plus, I seriously doubted that I was Ty's type anyhow. I could see him with a wafer thin, big boobed, blond model. And that was definitely not me. "His Master's thesis is actually close to mine. I think he enjoys talking shop with me. That's all."

Gabe's eyes narrowed and I knew that he was considering what I'd said.

"Seriously Gabe, think about it," I pushed, "why would Ty be interested in me? Let's face it, with his looks and career, he could have any super model he wanted."

Astonishment crossed Gabe's face. "You think that Ty's good looking?"

I shrugged my shoulders, surprised that Gabe would even care. "I guess, if you're into those perfect model types."

Objectively speaking, Ty was perfect. Cappuccino colored eyes framed with thick, dark lashes. Sculpted cheekbones. Square jaw with a cute little dimple in the middle. Full, pink, very kissable lips. Great body. Really great body.

Not that I'd really noticed. Much.

"Personally," I continued, pulling Gabe back onto the bed, "I'm more into blonds with ice blue eyes and a smile that could melt any woman's heart." He rolled onto his side, fitting my body against his, wrapping his arms around me.

"Baby Doll," Gabe said into my ear, his voice low and soft, "you melt my heart."

Chapter 5 ~ Ty

Two nights later, I spotted Liv standing alone on the side stage watching Diesel play. Her hips swayed to the music while her lips moved with the lyrics. She looked so happy that it was impossible not to watch her.

I was seriously tempted to go over and say hello, but we'd already spent the entire afternoon together at a coffee shop. So, it was probably best if I just left her alone. Before she started thinking that I was some weirdo stalker.

Although, the way she looked at me sometimes, made me wonder if the stalker idea had already crossed her mind.

So really, if that was the case, what did I have to lose? I should definitely say hi.

And, thinking about it, the time we'd spent together today was really good. Fun. We talked about her thesis, the tour, my upcoming PhD, family, and pretty much everything else under the sun. Except for Gabe. I didn't feel like talking about him and Liv seemed happy with that.

Apparently, taking Gabe out of the equation made all the difference for us.

"Your boyfriend is really talented," I said moving up next to Liv, raising my voice so that she could hear me over the music.

Complimenting the boyfriend of the woman you're infatuated with. Nice work Ty. I was such an idiot.

Liv turned her head towards me, nodding in agreement. "Definitely. I'm lucky to have him. He's an amazing man in so many ways."

I winced. Her words like a stake through my heart.

"You excited to get on stage?" she added, her focus bouncing between me and Gabe.

"Always am," I shared. "It's like another world once I step out onto the stage. I wish you could experience it." The thrill of being on stage was unforgettable. And I wanted to give that to Liv. Somehow.

She let out a loud barky laugh. "I'm not really a get-on-stage-in-front-of-millions-of-people, type of person."

"Don't knock it till you try it," I countered. "Want to meet before the show tomorrow? I have some ideas for your thesis."

Oh, my God! Why, did I just say that?

I had zero ideas, other than wanting to spend time with Liv. And make her laugh. I loved her laugh and the goofy smile she'd shoot me whenever I said something weird. Or stupid. Which happened more times than I cared to remember.

"Sounds good," Liv agreed, slowly. And I'd swear that she sounded almost reluctant. I studied her face, wondering for a second if she actually wanted to meet again. Admittedly, our first few afternoons had been a bit strained, but today things between Liv and I felt good.

"Don't forget it's your turn to treat this time," she added with a smile.

And my confidence returned. "I'd never forget something like that."

We stared at each other for a moment, both clearly appraising.

"Supper was good tonight," Liv offered.

"Yeah, my meal was tasty," I agreed. "How was the special? I almost went with that, but the ribs were calling my name."

Liv hesitated for a moment, obviously surprised that I knew what she ate. We'd sat at the exact opposite ends of the table and hadn't said a word to each other. Guess I happened to glance her way a time or two during the meal. Not a big deal, not stalker-ish at all, I was just observant. Came with the psych degree.

Yeah, right.

"The pasta was really good," she finally responded. The look on her face a mixture of wary and questioning.

"Something wrong?" I asked, looping my arm around her shoulder, pulling her into me. Surprisingly, her body felt rigid against mine. Not soft and yielding like it had this afternoon, when I'd leaned against her as we picked through research articles together.

"No, sorry, I'm just a little tired. I didn't sleep very well last night," she explained. "Guess it's finally caught up with me." Drawing in a deep breath, her shoulders relaxed a bit.

I nodded in understanding. "Yeah, sleeping on the bus isn't the greatest."

"At least you get a bunk to yourself."

"Hmm," I mumbled, suddenly feeling tense myself. "That's right, you sleep with Gabe."

"Yup, want to trade next time?"

Her hazel eyes gazed up at me.

"So you want to trade buses and sleep with me instead?" I asked teasingly. Shamelessly flirting with her like I'd done all afternoon.

Liv gave me that goofy grin and I couldn't help myself. Leaning closer, I slid my fingers lightly across her cheek, brushing the hair back. "I'd be OK with that," I breathed into her ear. Then breathed in her sweet scent, running my nose along the side of her face.

God, she smelled good.

An explosive shiver rippled through Liv's body and I couldn't stop the smile that pulled at my lips. She wasn't impervious to me. I affected her. And I wanted to get that same effect again. And again.

Preferably when we were alone. And naked.

Liv pulled back, staring into my eyes with her mouth hanging open for a second before offering me an awkward half smile. She looked back towards the stage, her body completely rigid.

Fuck. I went too far.

"Well, I'd better go and do my vocal warm ups. You watching me tonight too?" I asked, needing her to look at me again.

Her eyes slowly found mine. "Depends on Gabe. If the venue lets fans or press back stage, he likes me to stick close. He's not really comfortable chit chatting," she explained.

Gabe. Fuck.

I straightened up, pulling my arm from around her shoulder.

"Hmm, he seemed fine talking to Piper the other day. In fact, they spent most of the day together - chit chatting - didn't they?"

Shit! Why did I say that?

Liv gritted her teeth together, clearly annoyed. "That's different, Piper's not a fan or press, she's a fellow artist," she returned defensively.

"Sure, sure. Well I hope Gabe LETS you see our show sometime."

Shit! I did it again.

Liv's eyes narrowed as she stared daggers at me.

"Gotta go," I mumbled, stepping backwards, needing to get away from her before I said something else that was beyond stupid.

· · · · ·

I hurried into the dressing room, desperate for a few minutes alone to get my mind back on track. Liv was really fucking with my thoughts lately. As I turned to shut the door, I came face to face with one angry Dave.

"What the fuck are you doing man?" he raged, stepping in and shoving the door closed.

"What are you talking about?" I returned even though I knew exactly where this was going. We'd been friends for too long, not to know.

Liv.

"Don't use that bull shit on me. You know exactly what or, in this case, who I'm talking about." Dave eyed me, his face riddled with judgment.

"You're out to lunch," I denied, flopping down on the ancient couch. Leaning my head back, I closed my eyes. Wishing he'd disappear. First, I'd acted like a complete idiot with Liv, now this. Could the day get any worse?

"You've been watching her. You've been meeting her. Alone. And just now you were touching her with Diesel twenty feet away. Not OK Ty! She's going out with Gabe for fuck sake! Are you trying to tank this tour on purpose?"

"Fuck you," I spat, not bothering to open my eyes. Dave was right, except for the tanking this tour part. I'd never do that. The tour, the band, and the fans were too important to me. To all of us.

"Ty, open your goddam eyes up and look at me!" Dave ordered.

I could feel him standing over me. Waiting.

Slowly, I forced my eye lids open, meeting Dave's angry stare. "What?"

"Exactly. What are you doing Ty?" He plopped down beside me. "Things have been going so good lately. You've laid off the booze and women and Mindy isn't calling you anymore. Is she?" he added tentatively.

I shook my head no.

Dave hated Mindy, my ex-fiance, probably more than I did and for a good reason. She literally shredded me when she started fucking around with another man. A man who'd been close to me. It'd taken months and months of wallowing before I'd managed to climb out of the hell hole that

I'd been living in. And Dave was right there waiting for me. I still owed him for that.

But that was then and this is now. And Liv was nothing like Mindy. Or at least I didn't think she was. Not that it even mattered. She was taken and I wasn't actually interested in her. I just found her interesting, that's all.

That's right, keep telling yourself that Ty.

"What's the Liv thing about?" he asked again.

I turned my head, meeting Dave's eyes. "I honestly don't know."

"Are you, are you attracted to her?"

"Don't know," I replied with a shrug. "Maybe."

"Fuck man! Be honest here. Liv is definitely hot, so I wouldn't exactly blame you."

"Sure Liv's hot, but so is every other woman who offers to blow me."

A grin crept across Dave's face. "Fair enough. If it's not the way she looks, then what is it?"

"God, I wish I knew." I scrubbed a hand over my face. "I don't know, it's just that she doesn't react to me like other women do. I mean she doesn't gawk after me or follow me around or," pause, "even seem to want to be around me most of the time. I mean, she outright ignores me. And it's completely hot. She's driving me crazy."

Dave let out a howl, almost keeling over with laughter. "Seriously, that's what this is about? You're upset because Liv isn't panting after you?" He got up, striding toward the door. "Grow the fuck up man. She's not interested in you because she's in love with Gabe. Her boyfriend. The guy she lives with. The guy who's opening for us for the next three months. A pretty great guy in my opinion. Who you don't want to hurt by screwing around with his girlfriend."

"I know," I admitted, shame bubbling up in my throat. Choking me. "There's nothing to worry about anyhow. I act like a complete idiot every time I'm around her. And usually end up pissing her off." Liv's angry face flashed before my eyes.

Oh why did I have to mention Piper? Or touch her like that? Fuck!

"You're the smoothest guy I know. I mean, you're like honey with women. Makes me sick to watch sometimes." I shot Dave a look of disbelief. "And sometimes it leaves me in awe," he amended.

"Well, not with Liv. I'm a raving lunatic around her."

Laughing like I'd just said the funniest thing in the history of mankind, Dave yanked the door open and walked out. Leaving me alone, trying to convince myself to stay away from Liv.

Chapter 6 ~ Liv

We arrived in New York City early this morning and I was primed for three wonderful days of shopping, sight-seeing, eating, and more shopping.

After a lot of promising that I wouldn't get lost or mugged or anything else, Gabe had agreed to let me go shopping on my own while he and the guys did some sight-seeing. It was a hard sell, but Gabe absolutely hated shopping. And I intended to shop until I had to crawl back to the hotel.

. . . . .

I slowly strolled down the busy Manhattan street, trying to take everything in. Building after building, fit tightly together. People and more people. Some hurrying up and down the sidewalk, obviously in a rush to get somewhere. Others, like me, taking their time and taking in the sights. And then there was the smell. It was like a combination of car exhaust, french fries and asphalt. Hot, melting asphalt. Because Lord, it was hot. Not that I minded the heat or the smell. I was in New York City, with all of the wonderful things it had to offer, and that was all that really mattered.

A funky looking shoe store down the block caught my eye and I could almost hear my wallet groan. Fortunately, my family had been especially generous with birthday money this year. And I intended to put every cent of that cash to good use.

"So, is Liv short for something? Olivia maybe? No Olive. Yep, that's it, you definitely look like an Olive," Ty joked, pulling the brightly colored shopping bags from my fingers.

I leapt back, my heart pounding like it wanted out of my body. "Oh my God! Where'd you come from?!" I shrieked.

Laughter shook Ty's entire body as I clutched my chest. "I was in there," he gasped, pointing to a music store half a block up. "Saw you walk past." He waggled my shopping bags back and forth still grinning like crazy. "Looks like someone's been busy. Anything I'd be interested in seeing?" he asked suggestively.

"Not yet, but I know how much you like looking through my personal things. Buying new underwear - so that I can burn the ones you molested - is definitely on my list of to do's today. Especially the leopard print thong," I returned sarcastically, pissed that he'd scared the crap out of me. Beyond shocked to run into him in a city filled with millions of people.

Seriously, what was the chance?

"Hmm I don't think I've ever been accused of molesting a girl's underwear before," he said thoughtfully, peering up into the sky. "Why don't I go to the lingerie store with you and molest the underwear while you're trying it on? That sounds way more fun." A slow smile spread across his lips as he eyed me. "You wouldn't happen to be wearing the leopard print thong right now, would you?"

Oh my God! Did this guy ever stop?

"You think you're funny and cute – don't you?" I returned, eyeing him.

"You don't think that I'm funny and cute?" he asked, turning his expression from sultry to innocent in the blink of an eye.

I rolled my eyes then began heading down the street again, instinctively knowing he would follow. But not exactly happy about that. Because I never knew what to expect with Ty. He could be incredibly sweet and thoughtful. But he could also be over the top annoying and just plain weird. And after our last encounter, for lack of a better word, the thought of spending time alone with him was even less appealing than usual.

"I'm going to take that as a yes," Ty stated, keeping pace with me. "So you never answered my question about your name. Or should I just decide for myself?"

I turned into the shoe store with Ty stuck to my butt. "It's just Liv," I responded, surveying the shoes that lined shelf after shelf.

"Liv," Ty mused, rolling the L off of his tongue. "I like just Liv. It suits you somehow."

"My mom thanks you." I shot Ty a wry grin before handing two pairs of shoes to the saleslady. "Can I get these in a seven please?"

She merely nodded, all but ignoring me while she gawked at Ty. After living with Gabe for the past two years, her behavior didn't faze me at all. I had gotten used to women crawling over me to get to him. The funny thing was that it never worked. Gabe couldn't be bothered to give those women the time of day. Just another thing that I loved about him.

"Can I show you anything?" she asked Ty suggestively, a wide smile plastered on her bright red lips.

Interestingly, if she wasn't wearing a ton of makeup, she'd be quite pretty. Ty shot her a cursory smile, shaking his head no before turning his attention back to me.

"Wait," I said, spying a pair of grey low-cut boots on the opposite shelf. They had an almost vintage look to them that I instantly liked. If Ty didn't buy them, I might have to drag Gabe in later. "He'll try those on," I added pointing at the boots. I peered down at Ty's Converse clad feet for a moment before adding, "in a size twelve." I looked up at Ty for confirmation. He nodded, a look of astonishment on his face. "I used to work in a shoe store," I explained as the lady sashayed toward the backroom.

"So why aren't you with Gabe and the others?"

"Because Gabe hates shopping and I love shopping. And what could be better than shopping in the fashion mecca of North America!?" I bubbled.

"I'm a bit surprised that Gabe let you loose in New York."

"Believe me, it took a lot of convincing," I shared, plopping down in a chair then kicking my sandals off. Ty sat down beside me, slipping his shoes off, stretching out his long legs.

"Yeah, Gabe seems very protective of you."

"I guess." I shrugged, eager to talk about anything other than Gabe. "So why didn't you go sight-seeing with everyone?"

Ty grinned at me. "I was going to, but ended up changing my mind. When you spend twenty-four-seven with the same people, it's nice to have a break sometimes." I nodded in agreement, happy to have some time away from my guys too. "And there was someone I wanted to visit this morning."

"Someone you wanted to visit? Do you have friends here?"

It was Ty's turn to shrug. "I guess you could say that she's a special friend."

"SHE'S a special friend?" I reiterated.

Ty merely nodded before glancing out the large front window. I was positive that Dave had said Ty was single. I was also positive that Ty didn't want to discuss his 'special friend.' Which made me even more curious. I seriously wanted to push the subject, like he'd done with the personal questions about me and Gabe. But the melancholy expression on his face made me hold back. Instead, I moved on to the first thing that popped into my head.

"I've barely seen you for days. Something up or are you just avoiding me again?" I joked, although I actually wanted to know. Maybe our study buddy sessions were officially over and I could stop worrying about where he'd show up next.

"No, I'm not avoiding you," he said with a half grin and not very convincingly. "I've just had some stuff to take care off. I'm surprised you even noticed that I wasn't around."

"Well, it is your turn to buy," I reminded him, flashing a giant toothy smile.

"Dessert. That explains it." Ty returned my smile, although it never reached his eyes. "I've never met a woman who enjoys food as much as you do."

"Ha ha, Benson," I quipped. "That's because you've never met a woman like me before – remember?"

A genuine smile lit up Ty's face. "Nope, you are one of a kind Liv Madison."

The lady appeared with our shoes in hand, and I wasted no time slipping my feet into one of the pairs.

"Can I help you with the boots?" she asked Ty hopefully.

"No, I'm fine thanks. Liv, you need anything?" Ty asked.

"Yes, a seven-and-a-half in these shoes, please," I requested, pulling the black leather Mary Jane's off. The saleslady rolled her eyes at me before heading towards the back room again. I slipped my feet into the pair of sandals. "What do you think of these?" I stared in the mirror at the light brown Gladiators.

"They're nice. So, do you always date older guys?" Ty asked casually.

"I don't think I've ever really dated an older guy," I answered, walking up and down the aisle. Both of my ex-boyfriends had been my age. "These are pretty comfortable and totally cute. Think I'll get them."

"Isn't Gabe older than you?"

Oh shit! Gabe.

"Yeah, I guess he is," I covered, trying to seem nonchalant. "It's only a couple of years though so I never really think of him as older."

"Mmm," Ty mused, slipping on the grey boots. "Exactly how many years older?"

"Um, Gabe's three years older, although he seems like three years younger a lot of the time," I said, trying to joke about it.

"Guess that makes me five years older than you."

The saleslady appeared again, creating a welcome diversion from wherever this conversation was heading.

· · · · ·

"Told you those boots would look great." I nudged Ty with my elbow as we continued down the busy street. My latest purchase, the Gladiator sandals, dangled from Ty's hand along with his new boots and my other bags.

"You have a great eye for fashion, Liv. How about I treat you to supper in exchange for helping me do a little shopping? There's a store I really like in Soho. What do you say? We'll hop on the train, then grab a bite at a little Italian restaurant I know of. Best fettuccini carbonara you've ever had!"

Willingly spend my day in New York City with Ty? Not happening.

I looked up at Ty, searching for a polite way to say no. Hanging out for a few hours at a coffee shop was one thing but shopping and having supper together would be another.

As if sensing my reluctance, he pleaded, "Come on, it'll be fun. Please Liv. I promise I'll be on my best behavior."

For some stupid reason, the pitifully hopeful look in Ty's eyes killed my ability to say no. "Buy me a glass of wine to go with the pasta and you've got yourself a deal, Benson," I agreed. Reluctantly. Very reluctantly.

OK, worst case scenario, I fake a headache and head back to the hotel. Right?

"Ah, perfect!" Ty enthused, pointing to a train station across the road. "We're going to have a great time, Liv. I promise."

He grabbed my hand, pulling me across the street before the light changed color.

"You don't look like a guy who needs help picking out clothes," I commented as we walked toward a set of stairs that disappeared beneath the sidewalk. My hand still tucked in his.

Which didn't feel that weird or awkward. Which was completely weird.

"Thanks, my ex used to shop with me," he explained as we headed down into the train station. "I like shopping, I just don't have a great eye for what looks good on me. Stick close Liv, it's going to be busy down here."

Ty swiped a card in the turn style and we headed further into the station. Wide eyed, I watched everyone move through the immense underground cavern. It felt like a mini city in itself with all of the stores, walkways, buskers and people. Lots of people. I think I'd seen more people today than I saw in an entire week back home.

Someone bumped my side, sending me crashing against Ty. Shooting me a grin, he threaded our fingers together, and we headed towards a set of train tracks. "We're hitting a busy time of day. It won't be this hectic when we come back."

"Oh, that makes sense," I said, pressing in closer to Ty when we stopped. I sort of felt like Alice in Wonderland, and he was the only thing keeping me from getting sucked down the rabbit hole. Ty squeezed my hand reassuringly, as if he sensed my wonder and apprehension.

"I'm guessing you've never been to New York before?" Ty's grin was huge as he stared down at me.

"That obvious hey?" I answered, returning his smile. "This is slightly larger than the Skytrain in Van. How many times have you been here?"

"Lots. I love New York. There's so much to do and see in this city, it's amazing. Oh, I should see if there's a late show we can catch. If nothing else, we have to go to Times Square when it's dark. Just standing there with all of the people and lights is an experience in itself. And, there's a great little piano bar that we've gotta stop by."

I could feel a smile stretch across my lips.

Maybe today wouldn't be so bad.

· · · · ·

Ty

"Find your key yet?" I asked in a hushed voice as Liv continued to fish through her oversized purse. We'd been standing outside of her Manhattan hotel room for several minutes already. Not that I minded. Right now, I would have stood in the sewer as long as I was with her. "So what exactly do you have in there?" I inquired, looking down into the abyss that held everything known to man.

"Just stuff. Crap, where did I put that key?" she muttered shifting through random items. "I think I need to clean my purse out."

"You think?" I teased, grinning at her.

Pulling the plastic rectangle from her purse, Liv returned my grin. "Eureka!" she exclaimed.

"Shhh," I warned, putting my forefinger against her soft lips. Wishing that I could replace my finger with my lips. "You're gonna wake everyone up," I quietly reprimanded. "It's late."

Liv smiled up at me and I couldn't help but inch closer.

"Thanks again for supper. I have to admit that was the best fettuccini carbonara I've ever had. It was fun tonight."

She reached over taking her shopping bags from my hands, a warm sensation shooting through my body as our fingers brushed. It had been like this all night. The way Liv looked at me and the feeling I had every time we accidentally - or, maybe, not so accidentally - touched was electric.

And absolutely maddening.

"You sound surprised that we had fun?"

"Well, you can be kind of a jerk some times," Liv teased and I wondered if the alcohol was fueling her words or if she was always this way. With guys who didn't constantly act like idiots. Or maybe even with guys she liked. Who she was attracted to.

That's right Ty, keep hoping. Real healthy.

I looked at Liv, my eyes slowly sweeping over her beautiful face. "Guess I owe you an apology."

"For what exactly?" she pushed, making me fall a little bit more.

I never had a woman call me out for being a jerk before. And, fuck me, I liked it.

"For being such an ass the first day we met – and pretty much ever since," I continued, my eyes devouring her. But I couldn't help it.

She swallowed hard under the weight of my stare. And I thought about how amazing it would feel to run my lips up her smooth neck.

Easy man. I'd managed to keep my thoughts in check – mostly – so far. Just a few more minutes and we'd have had the perfect day together. And I need that. I needed Liv to see how great we were together.

"Oh," Liv replied, her eyebrows raised in amazement. "No worries, water under the bridge. Does this mean that I'm not ordered to avoid you at all costs anymore?"

The corners of my mouth turned upwards. "Yeah," I chuckled. "Sorry about that too. It's nice to have a girl to hang out with for a change. You're pretty fun – for a girl," I teased. I loved teasing her. Making her smile. Being with her.

Get out of your head man! Hold it together.

"Thanks – I think. You sure know how to make a GIRL feel special," she returned, sarcasm laced through every word.

I shook my head, feeling my smile stretch even wider. "So now that I've lifted the restraining order, you seem pretty comfortable giving me a hard time."

"Just who I am, better get used to it," Liv returned, her voice becoming lower and breathier with each word.

And that was it. I started to come undone. Stretching my forearm up, I leaned against the wall, angling my body closer to hers. The smell of her floral perfume wafted into my nose, making me feel dangerously intoxicated.

God, I wanted to touch her.

And the feeling was getting more intense by the second. "Yeah, you're definitely not like other girls. You know, the girls who are nice to me," I flat out flirted.

"Nice is overrated," she countered, her eyes fixed on mine, her tongue slipping out to wet her lips.

She wanted me to kiss her. I could feel it.

I bit the inside of my lip, warring inside, knowing this was wrong. Knowing that I should walk away before things went too far.

But how could I, when she was standing there. So close. Looking at me like that. Lips wet and ready. Waiting for me to touch her. Waiting for me to make her feel good. I took a step forward, closing the remaining distance between us.

A look of surprise crossed Liv's face but she didn't move away. We stood toe to toe, not quite touching, just staring at each other. And suddenly, it felt like this was the end of our first date with the infamous good night kiss looming between us. Should I just lean in? Will she meet me half way?

I thought Liv would. I hoped Liv would. Because I wanted to kiss her.

God, did I want to kiss her. And touch her. And hear her moan my name as I made her come.

But it would be wrong. So wrong.

Me. Liv. Gabe. Not good.

As if she somehow sensed my inner turmoil, or more likely thought that I'd completely lost it, Liv stepped back. Creating space between us again.

"See you tomorrow rock star," she muttered, shoving the keycard into the slot then pushing the hotel room door open. Without looking back, she moved into the room letting the door close behind her.

• • • • •

"Fuck!" I seethed, still staring at the door that Liv had just walked through. "What the fuck am I doing? This is insane. The woman's making me insane."

I strode down the hallway, stopping when I reached Dave's room. My fist banged against the wood. About to explode, I banged again, making the entire door rattle this time.

"What?!" Dave yelled as he ripped the door open.

"I need to get laid or drunk or something," I returned gruffly. "Get dressed."

Dave sighed, turning back into his room. I followed him, kicking the bed when he flopped down on it. "You've been with Liv all day haven't you?"

"I need to go out!" I demanded, kicking the bed again. "Get up."

Dave sat up, staring at me. "Answer the question Ty."

"Why? You already seem to know the answer." I plunked down on the edge of the bed, rubbing my face roughly. "I'm not in the mood for a lecture."

"Fine, then how about a little information instead? Gabe, Liv's boyfriend, has been going out of his freaking mind. He's been pacing the halls, going room to room, asking if anyone has heard from Liv. It's." Dave paused, glancing at the clock on his bedside table. "Fuck Ty, it's four thirty in the morning! And you just left her, didn't you?"

Shame filled my gut. "I need a drink and some female distraction Dave. Come with me or I'll go alone." I stood, staring down into my friend's wary eyes.

"Sit back down!" Dave ordered. The pissy look on his face overruled my need and I plopped back down. "What happened today?"

"I followed her. Well, actually I found her."

"Fuck Ty, you promised me. You promised that you'd stay away from Liv. This morning, you said that you were going to visit the hospital then come back to the hotel to rest."

I shrugged. "I guessed she'd be down 5ᵗʰ ave. And she was. We spent the day shopping. No big deal."

"Really, if it wasn't a big deal then why do you need a drink? And why didn't Liv call Gabe? Or better yet, answer his million phone calls? What the fuck were you two doing?"

"Not what you're thinking. Or I wouldn't need to get laid, now would I?" I fell back onto the bed. "I'm completely fucked, aren't I?"

"If you go near her again, you are."

Chapter 7 ~ Liv

Laina would be flying in from Vancouver this afternoon to spend the week with us. To my extreme happiness. Things between Gabe and I had been tense ever since New York and I was hoping that having Laina around would even us out again.

Although it had almost been a week, I could still remember every single moment from our argument that night. Gabe had literally exploded as soon as I stepped into the hotel room.

And Gabe rarely got angry.

In the five years I'd known him, I'd only seen Gabe really mad three times. Once when a friend - now ex-friend - of his, had sex with Laina when she was completely wasted. The second when Jake, my former boyfriend, had skipped out on meeting my parents to go to the bar - and I'd made an excuse for him. And the third was on the first day of the tour, when he thought that Ty had attacked me. Other that those times, Gabe was the most even tempered person I knew. Sure he'd get irritated once in a while, but never mad. Not like that night in New York.

But I couldn't really blame him, I'd created the problem or, in this case, series of problems. Problem number one: I'd spent the entire day with Ty. And it was no secret how Gabe felt about him. Problem number two: I'd only sent Gabe one text in the afternoon, letting him know who I was with and not to worry.

Yeah right. That was stupidity at it's finest.

Problem number three: I was having so much fun that I never checked my phone. If I had, I would have noticed the twenty some texts and even more missed calls from Gabe.

All of which, lead to problem number four: An angry Gabe. Still.

I guess it was fortunate that I'd barely seen Ty this week. There had been no coffee shop meetings, no backstage talks, no hanging out with everyone at night. Nothing. And for some reason, it kind of bothered me. We'd had a great time in New York and now it was like I didn't exist again.

The guy could drive me completely insane. It was probably better if we stayed away from each other. Or so I was telling myself.

• • • • •

A country tune blared through the speakers, regaling a tale of lost love and heartache as Laina and I made our way through a crowded bar later that night. I watched heads turn as Laina swept her long blond hair over one shoulder, readjusting the black cowboy hat she'd just charmed off some random guy.

"Hey ladies," Dave greeted as we slid in next to him at a long, wooden table filled with members from both bands and crew. "Nice hat, Laina."

"Thanks. When in Rome," she said, gesturing towards the hay bales and other country paraphernalia scattered around the bar. "I think you still owe me a drink and a dance," Laina purred, smiling at Dave.

"You bet, just name your poison and your song," he agreed, shooting me a token smile before focusing on Laina again.

I shook my head in amusement. Used to being Laina's sidekick, I'd already watched this very scene twenty million times or so.

The squeal of high-pitched laughter suddenly drowned out the music, drawing our attention to the far end of the table.

"Looks like Ty's getting lucky tonight." Dave chuckled, nodding towards where Ty sat surrounded by five women. All competing for his attention.

A sickening feeling welled up in the pit of my stomach as I watched a gorgeous blond run her fingers down Ty's chest.

"Is it always like that?" Laina asked, surveying Ty's little harem.

"Yup," Dave answered taking a swig from his beer bottle.

"Doesn't he get tired of it?"

"More than you know," Dave shared, looking thoughtfully at Laina. "Ty went through a period after he broke up with his fiancé where he was with a different girl all of the time. He said that he was just enjoying," - Dave stuck his fingers in the air to make quotes - "being on the market again. But I think he was trying to forget. You know, lose himself in the booze and women. It was really hard to watch him go through that and to hear what people were saying about him. Fortunately, he pulled it together again." Dave hesitated for a moment, making eye contact with me. "I just hope that he can hold it together." With a sigh, he turned, watching Ty for a moment. "I think he's almost had his fill. I should probably be a decent friend and go save him."

"How do you know that he wants to be saved?" Laina prodded, lightly running her fingers over a skull shaped tattoo on Dave's upper arm, a devilish smile on her lips. "I mean, maybe he's enjoying himself." She bit her lower lip suggestively. "What'd you think, Liv?"

Ty's eyes found mine. 'Help me,' he mouthed, wide eyed, and I couldn't help but grin. 'Please,' he mouthed, putting his hands together under his chin as if he were praying.

I rolled my eyes before nodding, hoping that Ty's groupies wouldn't go ballistic on me for stealing their reason to live. And feeling oddly overjoyed at the thought of getting him as far away from that blonde as possible. "Guess I'LL help Ty. Back in a minute," I shouted over the music. Although the way Laina and Dave were looking at each other made me wonder if either heard, or cared, what I'd just said.

Slowly, I strolled towards the end of the table. Ty watching my every step with anticipation. The song changed just as I reached his horde, giving me the perfect excuse to intervene.

"Excuse me," I hollered, quickly pushing in between the blond and Ty.

"Hey!" the woman objected grabbing my arm, anger distorting her perfect features. "This spot is taken! Get in line sister."

"Whoa, simmer down ladies," Ty cautioned standing up, wrapping his arms around me from behind. "She's with me."

I wove my fingers in between Ty's, a smug smile on my lips. I had done this hundreds of times for Gabe – intervening when women hit on him - but this felt different. It was nothing less than pure satisfaction, making those women think that Ty was mine. That he'd be sharing my bed tonight.

A giddy feeling bubbled up at that thought.

Ty – in my bed. Naked. Hmmm.

"They're playing our song baby," I cooed, pulling Ty's arms even tighter around my waist.

He bent down planting slow, sultry kisses from my collarbone to jaw line. Making my mouth go dry and stomach tighten. Making me acutely aware of why these women were chasing him.

"Excuse us ladies," Ty said with a nod. He held my hand tightly, leading me through the crowd toward the center of the dance floor. My smile widened as he twirled me into his arms. "You look like the cat that just swallowed the canary."

"Well, I can't go to the bathroom alone for the rest of the night, but that was too fun!" I gushed, remembering the feel of Ty's lips on my skin and the murderous look in the blonde's eyes. "If I hadn't already promised to be Gabe's wing-woman, I'd totally be yours. Did you see the look on blondie's face when you said that I'm with you?" I was grinning so much that my cheeks hurt. But I couldn't stop. Ty smiled back at me, his dark eyes filled with amusement.

"Priceless," he agreed. "I've never seen you so," he paused looking for the right word, "animated."

"Blame it on Laina. We can get a little crazy sometimes."

That's right, Laina was the reason my legs felt like jello right now. Sure Liv.

"I've already realized that. You two are insane on the dance floor." Ty gaze swept over my face as we swayed to the music, our bodies woven together. "What did you mean by you're Gabe's wing-woman?"

I shrugged, "just an expression."

"Hmm, I've never heard that expression used quite in that way before. Especially by a guy's girlfriend." Ty's eyes searched mine.

Not in the mood to talk about Gabe, I laid my head against Ty's chest, snuggling in to him. His arms tightened around me and I relaxed, enjoying in the way that Ty felt. The way that he smelled. Clean and so very masculine.

As we moved in time, our bodies pressed together, the first song bled into the next, then the next, and the next. Until Ty suddenly stopped moving. I looked up at him, hoping that we weren't finished dancing yet. Because I could easily spend the rest of the night in his arms.

Breaking our embrace, Ty nodded behind me. And the blonde immediately popped into my head.

That bitch was probably trying to cut in!

With fire in my eyes, I swung around, ready to tell the prom queen to back off.

"What the fuck?" Gabe said looking from me to Ty then back again. I could feel my fury die and heart start to thump as Gabe's lips tightened into a thin, angry line.

Oh, shit! I'd been so wrapped up in Ty that I'd completely forgot about Gabe. Crap!

"Gabe, I," I started to explain until Ty curled a hand around each of my upper arms, shifting me to his side, out of the line of fire.

He stepped closer to Gabe and I held my breath. Waiting to see what was going to happen. "You have the nicest girlfriend," he began – and I inhaled. Gabe's eyes narrowed as he stared at Ty, his right hand curling into a ready fist. "She saved me from the mob." Ty jerked his head to the left, indicating the small group of women still waiting for their chance to swoop in. "On the downside, she can't go to the bathroom alone again." He cracked a grin, his eyes finding mine for a just a moment.

Gabe shook his head, his body relaxing - slightly. "She pulled the girlfriend routine, did she?" Ty nodded. "That was really nice of you, Liv," Gabe said dryly as he reached over taking my hand, pulling me next to him. "It's time to call it a night Baby Doll. Night Ty."

Gabe pulled me through the bar like we were on a mission.

"Laina, we're leaving," he ordered when we finally found her at the shooter bar with Dave.

She turned around, a smile on her bright pink lips. "I'm having fun."

"I said, we're leaving," Gabe reiterated. "Let's go. Now!"

"Why, because Liv was dancing with Ty?" She looked from me to Gabe then laughed. "Seriously, back up the jealousy bus, Gus. They were just dancing. Liv dances with other guys all the time at home and you don't freak out. Overreact much?" Laina snickered and I could see Gabe's jaw clench tighter.

Not only could Laina calm Gabe down. She could also rev him up. And I was stuck in the middle with an already pissed off Gabe.

Perfect.

Knowing that I needed to do something to diffuse the situation. Fast. I turned to Gabe, placing my hand on the side of his face. Softly, I ran my thumb across his stubbled cheek. With a deep sigh, he looked down at me, the fire in his eyes slowly dying as our eyes locked. "Laina's having fun. Dave will make sure she gets back to the hotel. Right Dave?" I asked, glancing at him for confirmation. "Come on sugar dumpling, let's go."

Avoiding Laina's surprised stare, I took Gabe's hand leading him towards the exit.

· · · · ·

When Laina stumbled into the hotel room hours later, Gabe was fast asleep, his arms and legs curled around mine. We hadn't spoken much on the way back to our hotel room or even as we got ready for bed but I could tell by the way that Gabe looked at me, there was something on his mind. I just hoped it didn't involve beating Ty to a pulp.

I pressed my eyes shut, not in the mood to discuss what was on Laina's mind. There would be plenty of time for her to grill me tomorrow.

· · · · ·

"So now that Gabe's gone to the concert hall, are you going to tell me what the fuck is happening?" Laina demanded the next morning, crawling from her bed to mine. When I ignored her, she reached over, pushing the cover of my laptop down. "Liv!"

"Happening with what?" I asked, feigning ignorance. Not that it would do any good. Laina was like a pit bull, once she got her teeth into something, she just wouldn't let go.

"How 'bout we start with Ty, then move on to Gabe." She stared at me expectantly. "And don't even THINK about saying that you don't know what I mean, because I saw you with Ty last night. Dirty dancing. Looking at each other with hearts in your eyes. Or maybe that was lust." Laina paused studying my face for a moment. "Thought he was a giant dick?"

"He was a giant dick. And we weren't dirty dancing."

Were we?

"So you're into giant dicks now?" A sly grin tugged at Laina's lips. "I knew that you were my best friend for a reason." She wiggled under the covers, letting her eyes drift shut. "Fuck, I feel like shit."

"That's because you drank half the bar."

"Ha ha," Laina said dryly. "Remind me not to drink tonight. Please," she added massaging her temples. "My eyes may be closed but my ears are still open. So when did Mr. Hottie stop being a complete asshole?"

"In New York. We spent the day together. Had a great time." I shrugged even though Laina couldn't see me. "I got to know him better."

"In the biblical sense?" Laina asked, peering at me through one eye. "I feel like you've been holding out on me."

"Very funny. And for clarification, no, not in the biblical sense. We shopped, ate, saw a show. But I've already told you all about New York," I hissed, feeling exasperated for no good reason.

"You spend a few hours together in the big apple and all of a sudden Ty's Mr. Wonderful?"

Good point.

"Fine, I know what you're getting at - but there's not much else to say. He just stopped being weird. Stopped pissing me off."

"And now you two are best buddies?" Laina asked skeptically, opening the other eye.

"I have lots of guy friends. It's not that weird. Stop looking at me like that!" I demanded, itching to wipe the smug grin off Laina's face.

"Friends. Sure. But just to clarify, all that you're interested in is Ty's friendship. Right?"

"Ahhh!" I howled crawling off the bed, moving over to the mirror. "Probably."

I stared at my reflection for a minute. Laina may have felt like shit, but I looked like shit. Dark circles had dug their way underneath my eyes and my olive skin looked pale. Barely sleeping for the past few nights had definitely taken its toll on me.

It was stupid. I'd just lay in bed with weird things, like a conversation with Ty or a look on Gabe's face, flicking through my brain. Making it impossible to fall asleep.

"Probably?" Laina parroted.

"I mean Ty's crazy gorgeous and he's sweet and talented and really smart," I continued. "I told you that he's going to do his PhD, right?" Pivoting on my heel, I looked at Laina.

"Once or twice. Although you didn't mention the gorgeous and sweet part." One perfectly sculpted eyebrow lifted.

I bit my lower lip. "I didn't think he was gorgeous or sweet until lately."

"Until New York?"

"More or less. Something seemed to change between us there. Like we found our footing or something."

"So does that mean you're interested in him?" With visible effort, Laina sat up. Eyeing me.

I shook my head. "I don't think so. We're too different. He can make me completely nuts."

"Nuts can be delicious," Laina said wiggling her eyebrows. "I bet Ty's nuts are huge. And tasty."

"You're disgusting."

"That's why you love me. So, no to Ty?"

I pressed my lips together, contemplating. It was hard to deny that I found Ty attractive, but he could push my buttons like no one else. We were getting along now, however, I wouldn't bet my favorite pair of shoes that it would last.

Although I wanted it to. Probably. Maybe?

"No Ty," I finally said.

"So how are you going to deal with him then?" Laina asked.

I shook my head, not understanding. "Same as always."

"You know that the guy's crazy about you?"

Really? No.

"Are we still talking about Ty?"

"You mean that tall hottie, who watches every move you make? Who practically drools when you're within twenty feet of him? Who moved you to the side when Gabe went ape shit at the bar last night? You know, Ty was ready to go a couple of rounds with Gabe to protect you."

No! No? Had I missed something?

"Liv, I saw exactly what Ty did," Laina continued. "I'm pretty sure that he'd jump on a live grenade for you."

"I think you're reading more into this than there really is," I disagreed, although the idea made my stomach twist. In a good way. Could Ty actually be interested in me?

It just didn't make sense. Ty was a hot rock star who could have any woman on the face of the planet. And I was with Gabe. Or at least Ty thought that I was. And he'd clearly been avoiding me after New York. Or, maybe, he wasn't. Fuck! This was confusing.

"I don't think I'm wrong, but maybe." Laina shrugged her shoulders. "I'm definitely not wrong about Gabe though. Something's changed between you two."

"Yeah, he's my faux boyfriend now." I chuckled although it sounded forced, even to me.

"Well, your faux boyfriend is sure acting the part. Gabe's always been protective of you, but now it's over the top. He was ready to rip Ty's head off last night, Liv. That's not Gabe. My brother rarely gets that mad."

"I know. I think maybe it's the stress of the tour."

"Stress of the tour. That's what you're going with? Really?" Sarcasm dripped from Laina's voice, although her face remained expressionless. Probably because it hurt to move any part of her head.

"And maybe me. The thing with Ty is getting to him," I admitted.

"That, I agree with. Is there something else you want to share? Maybe something related to why you and Gabe are constantly pawing each other? It's sort of sickening to watch." Laina pressed her lips together to stop from grinning.

"Ba ha ha, Laina. We're supposed to be going out. Just acting the part," I justified.

Laina was so off base on this one. Nothing had changed between me and Gabe. That I knew for sure.

"And were you acting last night in bed? I couldn't get a sheet of paper between the two of you if my life depended on it," she accused.

"We were sleeping. Sleeping doesn't count."

"Gabe was sleeping. You were faking," Laina countered.

I hated that she knew me so well.

Chapter 8 ~ Liv

I settled back into the padded leather chair, inhaling the mouth-watering scent that filled the steak house. Doing my best to not look across the table at Ty. Ever since my conversation with Laina three days ago, I had a hard time even meeting his eyes without my face heating up. I wished that Laina never mentioned her theory about Ty liking me. Because now I felt self-conscious. And confused. And was behaving like a complete idiot.

I didn't miss the irony in that either.

"Mr. Bedroom eyes is watching you again," Laina half whispered, interrupting my thoughts.

"Laina," I cautioned, glancing around the table to see if anyone else had heard.

"Seriously, I'm one hundred percent positive that Mr. Gorgeous has a thing for you. The way he watches you is absolutely primitive. Makes me horny," she added, biting her bottom lip suggestively.

"You're seeing things. So what are you going to order?" I asked casually, keeping my eyes glued to the menu. Hoping she'd let this drop. Now was not the time to discuss Ty. Actually, if we never discussed Ty again - that would be great. Because I didn't need Laina jumping to the wrong conclusion.

Not that I was even sure what the right conclusion was.

"He hasn't taken his eyes off you since we sat down." Pause. "Yup, he's still watching you."

"Laina," I warned, fighting the overwhelming urge to glance at Ty. "This isn't the time or place." I looked at her, silently pleading to let it go before someone overheard.

Gabe turned towards me, planting a soft kiss on my cheek.

"Want to share an appetizer Baby Doll?" he asked. "Laina?"

"Sure," I answered with a smile. "Pick whatever you'd like."

"Not me," Laina said. "My stomach still isn't feeling good from last night."

"Shouldn't have done those last FOUR shots," Gabe teased. "Good thing you didn't sign up to tour with me this summer. I'd be worried you'd crash and burn a month in."

Gabe's mood had markedly improved over the past few days. Ever since I started acting like a maniac around Ty.

Go figure.

Brian put his arm around Laina, hugging her. "Leave her alone, she's just getting her tour legs. Right Babe? We'll show Gabe who can hold their liquor tonight." He smiled brightly at Laina, adoration filling his eyes.

"Whose hotel room is it tonight?" Laina asked, glancing at me with a devious smile.

Since the tour started, we'd usually have one or two hotel rooms designated each night as a hang out for the bands and crew. Until Ty and I had mended fences, or whatever you'd call it, I'd skipped the nightly get-togethers. Lately, Ty had been skipping them.

Making me wonder why. Making me crazy.

"Winner, winner, chicken dinner – pick me!" Dave hooted from three chairs down, sending Laina a suggestive smile.

Poor Brian, I thought, noting the pained expression on his face. He removed his arm from Laina's shoulder, staring blankly at the menu while Laina turned her full attention to Dave.

"What are we doing?" she hollered back over the din of the busy restaurant, raking her fingers through her golden hair.

"Well, now that we have a few more ladies in our midst, I vote for strip poker." Dave's eyes were bright with anticipation as he took in Laina's voluptuous figure.

"Strip poker, hey?" Laina repeated, eyeing Dave. Liam chuckled.

"She's a shark man, don't do it," Liam warned, a grin stretching from ear to ear.

Laina reached across Brian to pinch Liam's arm.

"Ouch," he protested rubbing the red mark on his skin. "She's mean too."

"Then it'll feel even better when I win!" Dave shouted.

Gabe's hand gripped my arm. I looked over and it wasn't hard to tell that he wasn't crazy about this suggestion. His mouth had disappeared into a fine line and his eyebrows were almost knit together. "I don't think that strip poker is a good idea," he said in a low voice.

"Take a chill pill bro," Laina sang. "It's not like I ever lose." Watching Gabe's eyes fall back on me, she added, "don't worry, I won't let your gf lose either."

"Then you're both playing," Dave confirmed glancing at me before focusing on Laina again.

"Of course we are!" Laina returned. "My best girl wouldn't leave me hanging. Sorry bro, but I'm stealing your girlfriend for the night. You're gonna have to make other plans."

"No doubt. The thought of seeing my sister naked gives me nightmares," Gabe said flipping Laina the finger. A weird look crossed his face for just a moment as he stared at me. "But, I wouldn't mind seeing you naked," he added. "Maybe the two of us should play strip poker in our room instead." Gabe leaned in, tenderly working his mouth against mine.

"Get a room," someone yelled from down the table.

"We have one," Gabe fired back, "but my little sister is cramping my style. And ruining my sex life."

"Ha ha," Laina quipped, sticking her tongue out at her brother. "As if I'm the only reason you're not getting laid."

I glanced across the table to see Ty watching us. A pained expression on his face.

Chapter 9 ~ Ty

'You're not going tonight,' I repeated into the mirror as I redid my hair - for the fifth time. I'd already showered, shaved and put on clean clothes. All while trying to talk myself out of dropping in on Dave's poker game. The strip poker game that Liv would be at. Right now. Without Gabe.

Although the chance to see her naked was enticing, I was even more interested in spending time with her. Talking with her. It'd been days since we'd had a chance to talk. To laugh.

I wasn't sure if she was avoiding me, but it definitely felt that way. And, if that was the case, it was probably for the best. Because that night at the bar had been intense. For a moment there, I was positive that Gabe and I were going to go a round or two.

Although I was taller and packed a few more pounds than Gabe, the fire in his eyes made me worry that he might actually get the best of me. But as long as Liv was safe - I didn't care. I would have happily taken the brunt of Gabe's anger.

I wished that I could have taken all of Gabe's anger.

Because the thought of leaving Liv to deal with Gabe alone had been eating at me. It wasn't something I normally would have done. But staying with her didn't seem like a viable option. So, I'd watched her walk away with him. And been regretting it ever since.

Another drink, that's what I needed.

The two I already had, hadn't done a thing to calm my nerves or stop me from wanting to see Liv. What was that saying? Third time's the charm?

"Here's hoping," I said, pouring another generous glass of vodka. With three large gulps it disappeared along with my resolve to stay away from Liv.

• • • • •

'I'll just play a hand or two,' I assured myself, turning the handle to Dave's room and stepping inside.

"See, I told you that it'd be fun tonight," Laina's voice rang out. I watched her hug Liv and an intense longing overwhelmed me.

So, Laina was a hugger when she drank. Lucky for Dave. Because I knew that Dave was more than a little interested in Laina. And I envied him. The woman he was interested in was single. I'd give up our last three Grammys if it meant even a chance to be with Liv. If it meant that she was single. Right here. Right now.

My eyes swept over the back of Liv's head, taking in her long dark hair and bare shoulders. I could only see the straps of her black bra, which meant that she was shirtless. My cock twitched.

'Down boy!' I commanded. Going over to the table with a raging hard-on wouldn't the best way to start the evening.

"You're just saying that because you two are kicking our asses!" Dave complained. He leaned his elbows on the small wooden table while his eyes roamed over Laina's face then down the deep valley exposed by her snug fitting tank top. "I'm down to just my boxers. You've only taken your sandals off and Liv still has her jeans and underwear left."

"Stop whining Davy wavy," Laina soothed, giving him a big hug. "Another round and it'll all be over for you." Dave leaned in planting a huge, wet kiss on her lips and my envy sky rocketed.

"Save it for later, Davy wavy," I mocked, moving up behind Liv. "Looks like you guys could use some help. Mind if I join the game?"

My heart pounded as I waited for Liv to turn around. But she didn't. Instead, she seemed to stop moving altogether.

"You can have my seat," Will offered from his place beside Liv.

Yes! I almost broke into a happy dance.

"I'm up next to play Gabe on the Xbox anyhow." Will vacated his seat, stopping to kiss both Liv and Laina on the cheek before collecting his discarded clothing. "I'll be next door if you need anything, ladies. Good luck Ty. Watch this one," he added patting Laina's shoulder.

Feeling almost giddy, I took the seat next to Liv. "I can see that," I mused looking around the table, stopping when my eyes met Liv's.

She didn't look happy to see me. No. That definitely was not joy on her face. It was mortification.

What the fuck? I thought things were good between us again. The way she clung to me while we danced, made me hope that we were on the same page. For once.

Liv stared down at the beat-up table, running her fingers along the faux wood grain.

"Interesting how the guys are almost naked but you two seem to be mostly clothed," I continued, wondering what was up with her. She'd been acting completely weird over the past couple of days. I'd assumed that had more to do with Gabe than me. But Gabe wasn't here. "Hope I can even out the odds a little."

"Well, I think you should start right now," Laina purred nudging Liv with her elbow, a giant grin on her glossy lips.

At least she was happy I was here.

"It's not fair that you're still fully clothed while the rest of us are almost naked," Laina said to me.

"Almost naked?" I mocked, surveying Laina's fully clothed body. Quick as lightening, she worked her lips into a pout. "Fair enough," I acquiesced, yanking my favorite vintage Motley Crew t-shirt off.

"Keep going, rock star," Laina encouraged, staring at me expectantly.

I glanced at Liv, surprised to find her eyes glued to my chest.

Maybe I'd read her wrong before? Lord knows, I'd done that a time or twenty.

My confidence amped up. Shooting Liv a grin, I pulled my shoes and socks off.

"Lose the watch and you're in," Laina demanded, smiling triumphantly as I undid the clasp. "Ok, let's play. Losers get to choose between drinking a shot of tequila or taking off one article of clothing."

"Thought you were staying in tonight Ty?" Dave asked with a smirk, throwing Liv a not so subtle glance.

Bastard!

"Book wasn't as good as I thought it would be. By the way, I picked up a magazine that you might be interested in Liv."

Slowly. Very slowly. Liv's eyes met mine.

Was I missing something here?

"I'll grab it for you after I'm done winning," I said. And then I couldn't help myself. My gaze slowly swept down her face to her breasts. They looked perky and just the right size to palm.

A warm sensation filled my entire body and I didn't know if it was caused by my proximity to a half naked Liv or because the alcohol had kicked in.

"Nice bra – it's one of my favs," I added, my gaze wavering between her perfect boobs and beautiful eyes.

I watched Liv's face heat up and suddenly it felt like the first few times that we were alone at a coffee shop. When I'd antagonize her until she'd either blush or blow a fuse. Apparently, pushing Liv's buttons came easier than playing nice with her. Although the things I wanted to do to Liv right now were anything but nice. My cock hardened, but this time I didn't care.

"You win!?" Laina hooted. "Not in this lifetime. Ty, your turn to start."

"Thanks Ty, you didn't have to do that," Liv half mumbled, staring at her cards as if her life depended on those five little pieces of cardboard.

"No trouble, I wanted to read a couple of the articles anyhow," I replied laying down my first card, deliberately shifting so that my bare arm rested against Liv's. Wanting to see if she'd pull away.

She didn't. If anything it felt like she'd shifted closer to me.

God damn, this woman was driving me crazy!

"Come on, Liv, we don't have all night," Dave said impatiently. "Besides it doesn't matter which card you play, Ty's gonna win anyhow."

I've already won, I thought to myself as I pulled an ace from my hand. If I win, Liv takes off more of her clothing and if she wins, I take more off. Either way, I was with Liv. And at least one of us was going to be naked.

. . . . .

An hour later, the game was down to Liv, Laina and me. All of us with just our underwear left. The other guys had all migrated to Liam's room soon after they lost, leaving just the four of us now. To my overwhelming happiness.

Dave and Laina. Liv and me. Something about that felt right.

True to her word, Laina had done her best to keep her best friend clothed by throwing a few hands Liv's way. And sacrificing most of her own clothing in the process. But, even with her help - Liv was done. And we all knew it. She'd drunk three consecutive shots and, from the look on her face, wouldn't be able to stomach another one. Which meant the bra was coming off! My heart began to race at the thought of actually seeing Liv's boobs.

I know it was childish, but I was miserable and horny. And, if nothing else, a good look at Liv's tits would fuel several nights' fantasies.

"Woo hoo!" Dave cheered dancing around the room in his boxers.

The rule, well Liv's imposed rule since she still had to live with us morons for the rest of the summer, was that after you lost – and got naked – you had to put your underwear back on. Personally, I wasn't interested in having any of the other guys' junk on display, so thought that rule was genius. The girls, if I had my way however, would stay just as mother nature intended them to be. Naked.

"My man Ty wins again!" Dave slapped my bare back in congratulations. "Guess we forgot to tell you ladies that Ty's something of a card shark himself. Tops or bottoms – take your pick cause it's all good from where I'm standing."

Laina rolled her eyes at Dave before looking over at Liv suggestively. "Liv, hun, would you mind?" she asked turning so that Liv could unhook her bra. Dave's mouth dropped open as Laina slowly slid her bra off and I had to grin. It was like he'd never seen a pair of tits before. "They're real by the way," she confirmed, eyeing Dave suggestively. Then she gave Liv this devilish look that even made my heart skip a beat. "Ty, hun, would you mind helping Liv?" she asked.

Fuck! I couldn't believe she just did that! Someone up there must like me. A lot.

"I'm, uh," Liv started to object. Meeting my eyes as I slid my palm across her warm back, expertly undoing the clasp of her bra with a flick of my fingers.

I could definitely get used to doing this. Over and over again.

"Let me help you with that," I offered slipping the straps over Liv's shoulders. Her breath caught and her eyes locked with mine as my hands slowly slid down her arms, taking the bra with them. "Do or die round," I breathed, my face only inches away from hers.

I wanted to kiss her. Hard. And long. Not caring that Dave and Laina were only a few feet away. Until my eyes caught site of her nipples. They were perfectly pink, perfectly round, and pointed at my chest like two little rockets, ready to take off.

Liv was aroused. By me. Fuck, yes!

My eyes flew up to hers, expecting to see the same pure, unadulterated desire that I was feeling. Instead, I saw mortification. It was all over her face.

And I was a complete asshole for not realizing how uncomfortable Liv was feeling.

I glanced at Dave, who was almost vibrating with excitement, then at Laina. "OR we could call it even and leave Dave frustrated. Trust me, he's used to it anyway. Your call ladies?"

A look of relief passed over Liv's face as she eyed Laina.

"OK fine," Laina grumbled, "you two are killjoys. It was just getting interesting."

A hiss of air escaped from Liv's lips and I felt relieved. For her. I wasn't sure that relief was even in the realm of what I was feeling right now.

"Maybe Ty and Liv should go back to Ty's room and, uh, read and we should continue the party here?" Dave suggested, staring at Laina hopefully. And I swear he was almost salivating.

"You got a key Laina?" Liv confirmed. "Not that you'll need it," she mumbled as she glanced under the table.

"This what you're looking for?" I asked holding out her lacey bra. Although I tried not to look at her boobs again, my eyes seemed to have a mind of their own.

Or maybe they were sharing one with my cock.

An evil pang came over me and I couldn't resist teasing her.

"So are your boobs real too? Maybe I should have a feel just to make sure," I offered.

"Seriously?" Liv huffed pulling a shirt over her head before shoving the bra into the pocket of her jeans. I could almost feel the heat radiating from her cheeks as she glared at me.

"What?! I can't give you a compliment?" A coy smirk played across my lips as we stared at each other.

"Offering to feel me up isn't what I'd call a compliment!"

"Don't act like such a princess Liv, you have nice boobs. I should know, I've seen a pair or two in my day. So, I'm guessing that's a no to feeling your tits then?"

Liv blew out a huge puff of air while her hands clenched into tight fists at her sides.

"Can you guys finish fighting in your room, Ty?" Dave interrupted, opening the hotel room door. Liv started to turn towards Laina and I took the opportunity to scoop her up, holding her firmly against my chest.

Holding Liv was another thing I could get used to. This night was turning out better than I ever imagined.

"Much obliged," Dave said as I carried Liv out of his room. The door slamming shut behind us.

I stepped into the hallway, glancing down at Liv. The expression, 'if looks could kill' popped into my head, because angry did not even come close to describing the look on her face.

"Put me down!" she demanded, wriggling in my arms. Seriously turning me on.

I either needed to set her down and put some distance between us. Or push her up against the wall and let her feel exactly what she was doing to me.

"I'm not a piece of meat, you know," Liv hissed and my decision was made. I set her down gently. "Or one of those chicks who follow you around just hoping you'll give them the time of day!" she continued. Taking a giant step backward as soon as I let her go.

My expression hardened and dick went soft. "I know Liv, that's why I suggested ending the game," I explained in a hushed voice. Her mouth dropped open in surprise, and her eyes penetrated mine. "Did I do something to piss you off tonight? Because I didn't mean to." I motioned towards Dave's room. "I was just having a little fun in there. I know I can act like a jerk sometimes, but I,"

"I thought you weren't going out tonight!" Liv cut in, her voice wavering.

"You didn't want me to hang out with you guys?" I asked, feeling like my guts had just been yanked out.

"No, it's not that." A giant sigh escaped Liv's lips as we stared at each other. "Never mind, I'm going to bed before I say something I'll regret," she muttered stepping around me, heading towards her hotel room.

No way was I going to let her run away from me - again!

I reached out, grabbing her forearm before she could escape. Slowly, Liv turned back towards me, our eyes locking.

"What's up, Liv?" I demanded. "I said that I was sorry for teasing you."

"Can you just let this go? Please? I'm tired and I've had too much to drink," she pleaded, looking down at my fingers still wrapped around her arm.

"Not until you tell me what's eating you?"

"Fine," she huffed, "it just feels weird for you to...to...I don't know, see me naked. Kind of awkward."

"But it's OK if the other guys see you naked?" I blurted, feeling both anger and hurt well up in my gut.

"No, I'm not really good with that either. Laina never lets us lose, but then you come along and – I'm naked and you're looking at me like, like that. And it feels, oh I don't know," Liv blabbered looking down at the beige carpet. Looking like she'd rather be anywhere than here. With me.

My heart twisted.

I inched closer to her. So close that our bodies almost touched. For a brief moment, I considered closing those few remaining inches but worried that she might run.

"I'm really sorry Liv, but I couldn't help it. You're obviously attractive and we have this amazing connection and..." I sighed, sliding my hand down Liv's wrist to weave through her fingers, my words faltering. She glanced up meeting my eyes and I knew that I had to go on. This was my chance to tell her how I felt. "I know that you've heard the rumors about how I am with women. Probably that I've been with a lot of women," I said quietly, wishing that I could take back the last two years. Make that three years of my life. Because if I could, I would have waited for her. "But I want you to know that I'm not like that anymore. And I think that you're amazing."

"You, you think I'm amazing?" Liv asked, her voice filled with surprise.

It was like she didn't know how I felt about her.

Didn't she know how I felt about her? Was that even possible?

"Of course I think you're amazing. You're the most amazing, smart and beautiful woman I've ever met." I drew in a breath. "I can't get you out of my head, Liv."

Her eyes widened with surprise, then something else. Happiness. Desire. Maybe?

Hopefully.

She leaned in. Then I leaned in, my heart pumping double time. My eyes wavering between her lips and her eyes.

"Baby Doll? Ty?" Gabe exclaimed, making us both jump as he pulled the door to Liam's room closed. I watched his eyes lock on our interwoven hands.

Oh, fuck!

Dropping Liv's hand, I took a giant step backward. Although that didn't help to break the tension between us. I wondered if Gabe could sense it or if it was only something that Liv and I could feel.

"Gabe," I replied, but couldn't tear my eyes away from Liv. She didn't look particularly upset that Gabe had caught us together. Holding hands. About to kiss. No, she looked pissed.

What?

"Night Ty," Liv directed, turning to face Gabe. I stood there for a moment, unsure what to do.

"Night?" I returned.

Had I just been dismissed?

"Goodnight Ty," Liv confirmed while Gabe eyed me.

"Night," I mumbled before heading to my room.

I needed another drink. And to get my head examined. This entire thing was beyond fucked up.

I shoved the key card into the slot and pushed my door open.

"What was that about?" I could hear Gabe fume as I stepped into the room.

"What was what about?" Liv returned, sounding equally pissed off. And I let the door shut. Almost.

I knew that I shouldn't listen, but Gabe was furious. And it was my fault. Again. I'd just listen for a bit to make sure that Liv was OK.

Yup, just listen for a bit. Right.

I cracked the door open enough to see out. Gabe's expression looked murderous and my adrenaline spiked, readying me to rush back out.

"Seriously, Liv?" Gabe thundered. "I'm not a complete idiot. You were standing in the middle of the hallway holding hands. I'd have to be completely blind to NOT notice the way that Ty was looking at you. The way that he always looks at you."

Fuck! Apparently Liv was the only one who didn't know how I felt about her.

"Oh my God, Gabe! I'm not doing this again with you," she huffed, sounding completely enraged. "Why does it even matter?"

Why did it matter to Gabe? Her boyfriend. OK, that was a weird question.

Liv turned away, taking two strides before Gabe's arm snaked around her waist. I could see her eyes flash just before he twirled her back around.

Shit! Should I go out there?

I pulled the door open a bit more. Ready to pounce.

"You're right. It doesn't matter if Ty is interested in you, unless," pause, "you're interested in him?" Gabe asked. And I froze.

I strained to hear Liv's answer.

"We're not having this discussion again Gabe," Liv said as she tried to push away, but he held onto her. "Gabe! Let me go!" she demanded, her voice pure acid.

Fuck! Should I go out there? Should I wait? Gabe clearly wasn't hurting her. If anything, it sounded like he was the one who should be afraid.

"Tell me if you want to be with Ty," Gabe returned, his voice low and unsteady.

He was losing it. Hell, I'd lose it if Liv was mine and I thought I was losing her.

"Just let it go Gabe," she commanded. "I'm not going to blow your secret if that's what you're worried about."

Secret?

"Fuck the secret."

Gabe's hands curled into Liv's hair and his mouth crashed against hers. Even from my limited view point, I could tell that the kiss was deep and demanding. He was kissing her like he was claiming her. Like he was making Liv his.

My gut twisted and I wanted to turn away. But it was like a car wreck where you don't really want to look at the carnage, but find it impossible not to.

Watching Gabe almost devour Liv was agony. And just when I thought that I wouldn't be able to stomach another second, it was over. Gabe stepped back and Liv turned her head just enough for me to make out her expression. Absolute astonishment shone on her face.

"For someone so smart Liv, you can be totally dense," Gabe uttered before heading down the hallway, leaving her standing there.

I eased the door shut, not wanting Liv to realize that I'd been watching. Trying to sort out what I'd just seen. Wondering what Gabe's secret was and what the fuck was going on between those two.

And between me and Liv.

• • • • •

It took everything that I had to knock on Liv's hotel room the next morning. But I needed her. And there was no way around it. I just prayed that Gabe would let her come with me.

I still hadn't sorted out what exactly happened last night. Between me and Liv or her and Gabe. None of it made sense. I was sure that Liv wanted me to kiss her and I was equally sure that she was surprised when Gabe HAD kissed her.

And then there was the secret.

Just as I raised my hand to knock again, the door pulled open and Liv stood there. Looking like a wreck. Looking like she hadn't slept at all last night.

Probably because Gabe had kept her up, finishing that kiss.

My guts wretched but I didn't have time for this right now. I forced my emotions back.

"Liv, I'm so sorry to wake you up but I need a giant favor," I began, reigning in my hesitation. Time was running out. "I need you to come somewhere with me, right now." I glanced at her wild hair and loose fitting, grandma-ish nightgown and couldn't help but grimace. "OK maybe in ten minutes from now. I wouldn't ask if this wasn't important. Will you come with me? Please, Liv," I pleaded.

"Go where? What's this about?" she asked, wrapping her arms around her mid-section. Her cheeks flushing pink.

The poker game and her perky breasts popped into my head. Based on her reaction, I guessed that she was thinking the same thing. That I'd seen her almost naked last night. It was obvious that Liv would change that if she could, but I sure wouldn't. Her body was even better than I'd imagined.

Stop it Ty!

Drawing in a deep breath, I tried to focus again. "I'll explain everything on the way. You just need to get ready – right now - really fast. It would mean a lot to me. OK? And just you, Gabe can't come," I clarified. I had enough to deal with, without Gabe watching over us.

"That won't be a problem since I don't know where Gabe is."

"What do you mean, you don't know where Gabe is?" I asked in complete surprise.

She shook her head. "We had a fight last night and he didn't come back to the hotel room."

Apparently Liv and Gabe hadn't made up.

Yes! OK, that was petty. But still, yes!

"What were you fighting about?"

It felt weird to ask, since I knew very well what the fight was about. But I wanted to hear what she'd say.

Liv hesitated, looking up at me with those beautiful eyes.

"Liv, you can tell me," I cajoled. "Maybe I can help."

"I doubt that," she said with a humorless laugh. "We were fighting about you. Gabe thinks you have a thing for me."

"Oh," I said quietly, shocked at her honesty. "I think we need to talk about that. Maybe we can do it on the way. Can you please come with me? You know that I wouldn't ask if it wasn't important."

"Come where?" Liv asked reluctantly and I realized what an awkward position I had put her in. She and Gabe were already fighting, because of me. Now I was standing here, almost begging her to go somewhere – alone - with me.

"It's really important. I'll explain everything on the way."

"OK," she half-heartedly agreed. "Give me fifteen minutes to get ready."

"Can you make it ten? I'll wait in the lobby for you."

"Ten," Liv agreed before closing the door.

I made my way down to the lobby praying that Gabe wouldn't show up and stop her from coming with me. It was a shitty thing to hope for, but I couldn't help it. I absolutely needed Liv to come and the thought of spending the morning with her had me almost vibrating with excitement.

God, I was so fucked.

•　•　•　•　•

"Liv," I called as she ran into the lobby. "Perfect, the car's here for us." I took her hand, leading her toward a blue SUV.

"All set Mr. Benson?" our driver asked as he held the back door open.

"All set," I replied, squeezing Liv's hand, overjoyed to be alone with her. She crawled into the back and I followed, glancing at the dark partitioning glass that separated us from the driver. "Thanks again, Liv, I really appreciate this." I slumped back into the seat, feeling the tension ease from my body.

"So what exactly are you thanking me for?" she asked, angling her body towards mine.

A huge sigh escaped my lips as we looked at each other. "I'm thanking you for coming to the hospital with me."

Liv's mouth dropped open and she shifted closer to me, pressing our thighs tightly together. Her fingers wrapped around my forearm. "Oh my God, Ty! You're not sick are you?" Panic contorted her features.

Her concern - true and heartfelt - touched me. And I hoped that, maybe, she felt something more than just friendship, and annoyance, for me.

"No, I'm not sick. We're going to visit someone."

"Someone?" The relief on Liv's face was instantaneous, jacking my hope up a little more.

"This isn't something that I like to tell people, for people to know about. So I'd appreciate if you keep it as quiet as possible." Liv nodded, her eyes trained on me. "When we tour, I usually visit the local hospital in the morning. You know go sign some autographs, take some pictures, sing a few songs."

"And why don't you want anyone to know? I mean I've seen other musicians post on Facebook when they do things like this or get the local media to come out and what not. It's good publicity."

"Because I'm not doing this for publicity, I'm doing this for my fans. I don't want to exploit them for a bit of good PR. All I want is to help them forget that they're sick for a few minutes. I know that I wouldn't want people in my face taking my picture if I felt like crap. Would you?"

"No," Liv replied quietly. "Is it just you who goes or does your entire band go?"

"Sometimes the guys will come, but usually it's just me. I find it's less obtrusive that way. And it gives me a chance to really connect with the people I visit."

She nodded her head, obviously processing what I'd just told her. "OK, so if you usually go alone, then why am I here?"

"Good question. And this part has to stay completely between us." I waited for Liv to nod before continuing. "Today one of the people that I'm visiting is a young girl." I paused, drawing in a deep breath. "She's been severely abused by her step-father and step-brother over the past two years. In every possible way. Liv, they had her chained her up in the basement at times."

The therapist's account of May's horrific ordeal echoed in my mind. Dr. Vegan had shared a lot of May's story with me so that I'd be able to react to her properly. So that I'd understand how and why she'd react to me. I'd had several days to process everything, but was still filled with rage and sympathy for this little girl. Based on my experiences with other patients, I knew that these feelings would lessen over time, but never truly go away. Carrying those emotions around was hard, especially when I was feeling low. But knowing that I was able to help, even a little, made it worth it.

"Her therapist," I continued, "said that this little girl, that May, heard my song, 'Broken into Pieces of Me', on one of the first days that she was in the hospital. And for whatever reason, it resonated with her. Now she listens to my music – to me – at night before she falls asleep because it makes her feel safe. My music, my voice, makes her feel safe Liv. Can you imagine that?" I paused for a moment, drawing in another breath, trying to collect my thoughts. Liv tucked her hand into mine, weaving our fingers together, giving me the strength to continue.

"When my manager called the hospital to arrange the visits, they told him a bit about May and what she's been through and asked if I would visit her. I called to speak to May's therapist myself and Dr. Vegen told me some of May's story. God, I just can't stop thinking about what that poor girl went through." Liv nodded, her eyes wide and misty. "Because of what May went through, she's fearful of men – obviously – so Dr. Vegen asked if I could bring a woman along. She felt it would be better, more beneficial, to have someone who isn't staff. Who isn't involved with May's treatment or the hospital, come with me for the visit. Allison was supposed to come but she's sick today and we can't risk exposing any of the patients to the flu or whatever she has. So - here we are." I sat still, watching Liv. Waiting for her to process everything.

"Where is her mom?" she finally asked, her voice shaky.

"She passed away. That's when things went sideways for May."

"How, how did May, umm, get away?" Liv pressed closer into me. I wrapped my arm around her, drawing her even tighter.

"Her teacher was suspicious. She'd been May's teacher a few years before and saw a huge difference in the little girl. Apparently, she was like another child altogether. The step-father blamed it on her mother's death but May's teacher just knew that there was more to it. She eventually got May to tell her what was happening and then they went to the police together.

Everything from the chains in the basement to the, uh, signs of physical abuse that May had been suffering supported what she said. She's still in the hospital recovering. They did a lot of damage Liv. She's only ten." My eyes started to tear up, but I didn't care. I felt safe sharing my emotions with Liv. Somehow I knew that she'd never judge me for it or think less of me because of it.

"The step dad and brother?" Liv asked, her voice barely above a whisper.

"Are in jail waiting to be tried. Just makes me sick to know what May has gone through. And that there are other kids right now, going through something similar."

Liv laid her head against my shoulder, cuddling so close that I didn't know where her body ended and mine began. And I was good with that.

"Want to talk about Gabe and me?" I asked after a few moments had passed.

"Can we leave that for the ride back? My mind's filled with other things right now."

"Sure," I agreed kissing the top of Liv's head. Enjoying the way that she smelled. The way that she felt pressed against me.

We rode the rest of the way in silence. Each of us wrapped in our own thoughts.

• • • • •

Three-and-a-half hours later, Liv and I crawled back into the blue SUV and huddled together again. Emotionally spent. Like all of my other visits, it had been an amazing experience meeting all of those wonderful people. Meeting May, however, had been the highlight of the morning for me. And, if I had to guess, for Liv as well.

May was absolutely unforgettable. Despite all that she'd been through, including losing her mom at a young age, the little girl was still filled with such optimism and life. She was my new hero. I'd sung her favorite song 'Broken into Pieces of Me' three times, plus one of my new songs. I'd also promised that the next time Raincheck played here, May and a friend would have front row seats and back stage passes. The smile she gave me, made my day. And I'd hoped that I helped to make hers.

As we started back towards the hotel, Liv ran her fingers along my forearm, tracing the lines in one of my tattoos. It was an intricate piece filled with koi fish, bamboo and Chinese characters.

"What does this say?" she asked.

"For the love of music." I placed my hand on Liv's thigh, enjoying the feel of her fingers running over my skin. She snuggled closer, although there was almost no space left between us already.

I could definitely get used to this.

"So what are you thinking about, Darlin'?" I asked, feeling exhaustion take over. These visits always did me in emotionally.

"I'm thinking, that I don't know how you do that all of the time. I feel beyond tired. I mean it's exhilarating – if that's even the right word – when you're meeting everyone, but afterwards it just saps you."

"That's why I visit in the morning and try to grab a nap in the afternoon. Except for the days when I meet you instead."

Liv smiled at me. "You still come and meet me, spend the entire afternoon with me, even when you feel like this?"

I shrugged. "Spending time with you isn't exactly a hardship."

Her cell phone buzzed.

"That's probably Gabe again," I said, moving my hand off Liv's thigh and onto my own. He'd been blowing up her phone all morning.

Gabe. That guy had the best timing. And the best girlfriend. A twinge of jealousy ate at my insides.

"It's Gabe," Liv said with a sigh as she stared down at her cell. "Guess I probably should have called or at least texted him where I was."

"He doesn't know that you went to the hospital with me?"

"No," she admitted with a grimace. "He'd have a cow. I thought it'd be easier to just deal with him when we got back."

I couldn't hold it in any longer. We needed to talk about what was happening between us.

"He'd have a cow." Pause.

Just spit it out man. This is your chance.

"Because Gabe thinks that I'm in love with you," I finished.

"He's never used the words 'in love with' exactly. More like he thinks that you want to get in my pants." Liv rolled her eyes, obviously trying to make light of the situation.

But I wasn't going to let her. Because I needed her to know that what I wanted from her went way beyond sex.

"Do you think that I just want to have sex with you?" I asked. My heart lodged in my throat, painfully thumping.

Please say no. Please say no.

Liv inhaled sharply, her eyes roaming over my face. "No."

Relief flooded my body.

I ran my fingers lightly across Liv's cheek and down her throat before sliding them behind her neck. Our eyes locked and I wanted to kiss her more than anything in the world. And the way Liv was looking at me right now, made me think that she would let me. But that wasn't good enough. I didn't just want Liv to 'let me' kiss her. I wanted her, no I needed her, to want me as much as I wanted her.

"Things don't seem right between you and Gabe," I pushed, watching her closely. The fight I witnessed last night, fresh in my mind. "I mean you obviously care about each other, love each other. You just don't seem to be in love with each other. Or, at least, you don't seem to be in love with him. Tell me that I'm wrong," I begged.

I needed to know how she felt. Because if she was in love with Gabe, then I'd do whatever I had to – like castrate myself – to stay away from her. But if she wasn't in love with him, then I'd hope. And I'd wait for her to realize that we belonged together.

"Ty," Liv whispered, her expression filled with as much pain as I felt. "This is really complicated."

"I know Darlin', but we can work through anything. Together."

Even breaking your boyfriend's heart. Cause I'm a giant prick who would do anything to have a chance with you.

Slowly, she moved her face closer to mine, inch by agonizing inch, until I could feel her warm breath against my skin. I held perfectly still, my eyes locked with hers. Waiting.

Finally, her sweet lips pressed against mine. And I knew what it was like to be in heaven and hell at the same time.

Her lips were slow and gentle, softly brushing against mine. Again and again. Teasing. Tasting. Kissing me like we had all the time in the world. Driving me absolutely crazy with want.

After fantasizing about having Liv's mouth on mine for months already, I craved so much more from her. I desperately wanted to push her back against the seat and deepen our kiss, pushing my tongue into her mouth. Ravaging. Taking. While my hands roamed over every inch of her sumptuous body.

But I didn't. I held back. Barely. Letting Liv control the kiss. Trying to revel in everything that she was giving me. And not ask for more.

Although I wanted more. So much more.

A painful ache began to build deep in my chest. And the need to touch her became almost unbearable.

Slowly, maddeningly, Liv ran her hand up my abdomen. Stopping when she reached my nipple. Her fingers flicked back and forth over the hardened nub, before pinching it. I gasped with pleasure while my cock twitched like it had just been given CPR. Liv lifted her head, finding my eyes, a coy smile on her lips. She pinched my nipple again then bit her bottom lip, watching my self-control unwind.

"You like that?" she whispered, playing with my nipple.

"I think I'd like anything that you do to me," I returned, my voice already hoarse with desire.

I'd been with lots of women but couldn't remember any of them affecting me so deeply. So quickly. But then, none of them had been Liv.

Liv brought her mouth back to mine, sliding her tongue along the bottom of my lip as her fingers slipped beneath my t-shirt to find my nipple again. I moaned against her lips as she finally deepened the kiss, pushing her tongue into my mouth.

I dug my hands into the bottom of her shirt, willing myself to hold back. Trying to savor every touch, every kiss. Worried that at any moment, she'd pull back and it would be over.

Liv lifted her leg over mine, straddling my lap. Snapping the tenuous control that I'd been clinging to. A groan, so loud that I was sure the driver could hear us through the partitioning glass, ripped from my throat as Liv ground her pelvis against my hard cock. I could feel the smile on her lips as she tilted her head to deepen our kiss even more, her tongue sliding against mine.

My hands clawed their way under her t-shirt and up to her bra, pulling it down beneath her perfect tits. I took each nipple in between my thumb and index finger, tugging at them. Teasing like she'd been doing to me.

"Oh Ty," Liv moaned, running her tongue down my neck while she dry-humped my cock.

I pinched her nipples. Hard. And she bit down on my shoulder.

"Fuck, do that again," she hissed, pushing her tits into my hands.

So my girl liked it rough. I might just come in my pants.

I pinched her nipples, pulling them, then pinching again as she brought her mouth back to mine. Her hand snaked between us, finding my throbbing cock. With steady pressure she explored my dick through the fabric. Rubbing her fingers up and down along my length. Again and again, taking me close to climax.

Needing more of her, I shifted Liv up. Pulling her t-shirt down to expose her breasts.

"I love your tits," I mumbled against her heated flesh.

My tongue circled her nipple, licking at it like a lollipop, before sucking one deliciously hardened nipple into my mouth with a popping sound.

"Yes," she hissed, unzipping my jeans, freeing my cock from the restricting fabric. "Fuck, Ty, your dick is huge."

A sound somewhere between a whimper and a moan escaped my lips as Liv closed both hands around my cock, working it. Up and down she ran her hands. Brushing my balls with each stroke. Taking me closer to ecstasy then I'd ever been before.

I wanted to do nothing more than sit here and revel in the feel of her soft hands fondling my dick while I sucked on her tits. But, the need to touch her – everywhere – was too overpowering. I wanted to make her feel as good as she was making me feel.

Slowly, I ran my hand up the inside of her thigh and underneath her shorts. Sliding my fingers against the crotch of her panties. They were completely soaked through.

She wanted me. Really wanted me. Fuck, yes!

I worked two fingers underneath the saturated fabric, gliding my fingers back and forth between the lips of her slick pussy. "Darlin', you're so wet," I mumbled around her nipple.

"You make me wet," she moaned as I pushed those fingers inside of her. "Yes, fuck me with your fingers Ty," Liv commanded as she worked my cock like it owed her something.

I thrust my fingers in and out of her wet pussy, pushing in as deep as I could, while rubbing my thumb against her clit.

"Suck my tit. Hard," she directed pushing her nipple further into my mouth.

Fuck, being with this woman was even hotter than I imagined. She knew what she wanted and wasn't shy about asking for it. I loved that. I also loved what she was doing to my cock. I was sooo close.

"Liv," I pleaded, "Darlin', I'm close. I want to come inside you."

"No," she mumbled, tightening her hand around my cock, squeezing until I almost burst.

"Oh, Liv, Darlin'," I moaned, jutting my cock up and down, unable to hold back any longer. Fucking her hands. I pushed harder against Liv's clit while I worked a third finger into her pussy, stretching the wet, tight skin. Driving my fingers deeper and deeper inside of her with each stroke.

"Fuck," she whispered as her pussy tightened and she began to tremble. "Ty," Liv mumbled against my forehead as she came on my fingers. And I couldn't hold back any longer. I came in her hand.

Liv let out a long sigh. And I waited to see what was going to happen. Would she freak out or would she cry?

Pressing a lingering kiss against my mouth, she reached over pulling tissues from the box in the door. Without looking me in the eye, she began to wipe off her hands then my dick. Tucking it back into my pants once the wetness was gone.

"Um Ty," she murmured, finally meeting my eyes. "I um, need to clean up."

And then I realized that my fingers were still inside of her. Warmth spread up my neck and face.

"Oh," was all I could manage to get out. I pulled my fingers out of her underwear and she handed me a tissue. A giant grin lighting up her entire face.

She was so unpredictable. And I loved it. I loved her.

That realization hit me hard. And I had to force myself not to say those words. Because I didn't think that she would welcome them.

A lump formed in my throat.

Shifting off my lap, Liv pulled her shorts down and began wiping the wetness from between her legs. And I couldn't look away if my life depended on it.

"You're, you're shaved," I muttered reaching out, running my fingers over the smooth, fleshy mound on each side of her inflamed clit. I was pretty sure that I could spend hours just looking at her pussy. It was soft and smooth and absolutely beautiful.

"I thought you would have already figured that out. Considering that you just had your hands in my underwear." A wicked smile played over Liv's lips as I dipped one finger inside her again.

God she was beautiful and bad. I wanted to fuck her. Right now. I wanted to make her come while my cock was inside of her this time.

I leaned in, pressing my lips to hers. "I was too busy to notice right then."

"You're so good at this," she moaned, thrusting her hips against my hand, wetness beginning to drip down my finger.

"Lay back and spread your legs," I commanded, pulling her shorts lower. "I want to look at your sweet pussy."

"How do you know that it's sweet?" Liv asked in a low voice as she pulled one leg out of her shorts and spread open for me.

My fingers were greedy, touching, plunging again into her wet tunnel.

"Make me sore Ty, I want to know that you've touched me," she said, her fingers finding her nipples and tugging.

"Fuck, you're the hottest woman I've ever met," I hissed, watching the pleasure grow on her face as I plunged three fingers in her again and again while she played with her nipples.

Needing to taste her skin, her wetness, I bent down, running my tongue along the inside of her breast and down her stomach. I could hear Liv's breath hitch as I reached the top of her pubic bone, stopping to blow on her swollen clit. Glancing up, I could see her watching as I ran my tongue down one side of her pussy and then the other. Withdrawing my fingers, I used them to spread her open even wider, exposing the small nub that I planned to tease and suck until we'd both had our fill.

Slowly, again and again, I licked Liv's clit, reveling in the guttural sounds coming from her throat. Her hands wove into my hair and her hips began to move as I ran my tongue up and down.

"That feels so good," she moaned, her head falling back against the truck door. "Please, don't stop."

With one quick motion, I sucked her entire clit into my mouth.

"Fuck Ty," she whispered thrusting her pussy up against my mouth.

And I sucked. Hard. Working my fingers deep into her pussy again.

"Is that too much?" I mumbled against her wet skin.

"No," she almost hissed, "I want it. I want to feel you inside of me for the rest of the day."

I smiled against her pussy then began to fuck her with my fingers and my mouth. Rough and greedy. Making sure that when she closed her legs she'd know that I had been there, inside of her. I licked and sucked and plunged my fingers in and out as she squirmed beneath me. Slowly coming undone. Moaning my name as she came all over my tongue and my fingers.

Slowly, Liv's hands loosed in my hair and using my shirt, she pulled me back up to her meet her mouth.

"You taste like me," she whispered running her tongue over my bottom lip.

"I love tasting like you," I returned, pushing my wet fingers between our mouths and into her mouth. She sucked them, swiveling her tongue in between my fingers. And I needed my cock inside of her. Now. I work my pants down my hips, then grabbed my dick, sliding against her wet entrance.

"My mouth," Liv says. "I want to taste you. Suck on you."

Fuck, I really loved this woman.

"OK, but I want to come inside of you this time."

Liv looked up at me with a grin as she grabbed my ass, directing my dick into her open mouth. And I was in heaven.

"Fuck," I groaned as her lips closed around my shaft. "Yes, Darlin', suck me," I begged already thrusting my hips, pushing my cock in and out of her mouth.

And she did. She sucked my cock hard while her fingers roamed over my balls. In and out I pushed, so deep that I touched the back of her throat. Until I couldn't take it anymore. Pulling back, I slipped my dick out of her mouth ready to make love to her.

"Not yet," Liv commanded, wrapping one hand around my ass, holding me captive, while her other hand grabbed my cock. With a wry laugh, she ran her tongue down the underside of my shaft until she reached my balls.

"Oh my God," I muttered as she sucked both of my balls into her mouth. "Darlin', I'm not going to last if you do that. Please, I want to make love to you."

Liv continued to suck on my balls and pump my cock with her hand, ignoring my plea until I couldn't take it any longer.

"Liv," I hissed, "I'm gonna come."

"Come in my mouth," Liv commanded before taking my cock deep in her mouth.

And I did. It was like a volcanic eruption as I exploded in her mouth. And, as soon as it was over, I wanted to do it again.

I found Liv's mouth with mine again, brushing sweet kisses against her lips.

"Now you taste like me," I muttered in between kisses and could feel Liv smile.

The SUV slowed as we neared the hotel and we both sighed. "Great timing," Liv complained, smoothing her t-shirt down then wiping the wetness from between her legs, while I yanked up my pants.

"Liv, Darlin', I," I started, staring into her eyes, trying to find the right words. Wanting to tell her much she meant to me. How much being with her meant to me.

"Mr. Benson," our driver greeted as he pulled the door open, breaking into our moment.

Liv glanced at the open door and I watched her face cloud over. We crawled out of the SUV and back into reality. And I prayed that she didn't regret what had just happened between us.

• • • • •

Liv

My mind was reeling as I climbed out of the SUV.

Oh my God! What had I just done with Ty? When he looked at me like I was the only woman in the entire world, then called me Darlin' – I just came undone. And then he made me come. Twice.

My stomach tightened as I thought about the feel of Ty's fingers pushing inside of me. And the look on his face as he stared at my half naked body.

And now I was wet again. Perfect.

Turning, I watched Ty chat with our driver. A casual smile on his face. His body relaxed.

Undeniably beautiful. That was Ty. His face, his hair, his body, his smile. I wouldn't change a thing. And he was funny. And sweet and amazing. I'd witnessed just how amazing today. Ty was a lot of things. A lot of things that I really liked.

But he could also be an ass and annoy the crap out of me. Although with Ty, I knew that I gave as good as I got. And I would rather have a guy who'd mess with me a bit than one I could walk all over.

And we just. Fuck! Fuuuuck! I was supposed to be Gabe's girlfriend.

Panic started to set in as I thought about Gabe. About what he'd do if he ever found out what had happened between me and Ty. He'd kill us both. And then never speak to me again.

After a handshake, the driver headed towards the SUV while Ty strode towards me. The laid back expression on his face changing with each step. By the time Ty reached me, he looked absolutely stricken.

"Liv, you OK?"

"Sure," I muttered, glancing anywhere but at him.

Liar. I was moving into full freak out mode. Wondering if there was a way to go back in time and not do what we just did.

The soreness between my legs, however, reminded me that was utterly impossible.

"You're sure?" he asked and I could only nod. Not trusting myself to speak. "Ready to go in?" I nodded again and Ty put his arm around my shoulder, guiding me into the hotel.

I glanced around the lobby nervously, half expecting Gabe to be waiting for me. But there was no one from our group around.

Thank, God.

An awkward silence settled between us as Ty and I made our way down the long hallway towards my room. His fingers tightening around my shoulder a little more with each step, making me feel trapped. Making me want to run away. Because I knew that we'd have to talk. Have to say something to each other and, considering what we'd just done, even a simple goodbye felt like too much right now.

I was supposed to be with Gabe. Be in love with Gabe. And I was fooling around with Ty. There had to be a special place in hell for me.

By the time we stopped in front of my room, I was on the verge of crying. That feeling intensified when Ty's eyes found mine. And I watched his face crumple. In slow motion.

It was sheer torture.

"Thanks for coming with me, Liv," Ty said in a low voice, his eyes searching mine.

"Thanks for taking me." I returned quietly, looking away. Struggling to hold it together. I took a step toward my room door, longing to get inside. Desperate to be alone. "You should go and get some rest before tonight."

A half smile formed on Ty's lips. "Yeah, I probably should. What are you going to do?"

"Same thing. Sleep." He moved closer, eliminating the gap between us. Bending down to kiss my forehead, Ty whispered against my skin, "I'm so sorry Liv. I hope that I haven't created a problem for you - and Gabe."

Ty's eyes met mine again and he looked absolutely miserable.

Because he obviously regretted what we did and didn't want me expecting anything more from him. Got it.

"It's fine," I lied, knowing that things between Gabe and I were anything but fine. This morning had probably put him over the edge. If he wasn't already there after last night. What I'd just done with Ty would be the nail in his coffin. If he ever found out.

And I prayed that he never would.

"You better go and get some rest," I murmured.

Ty nodded then continued down the hallway. Worn out and on the verge of crying, I opened the hotel room door, a loud crash and male cheers greeting me.

Perfect.

Sucking in a huge breath, I worked to pull myself together. The last thing I needed was for the guys to see me upset. "Hello," I called as cheerfully as I could manage.

"Hey Liv," a chorus of voices called back. I rounded the corner to see Laina and Dave cuddled up on one bed, while Liam and Will stretched out on the other. An explosion rocked the TV screen.

"What are you watching?" I asked looking at the fiery scene.

"Speed! Woman, don't you recognize a classic when you see it?" Liam chastised. "Either get your ass over here and shut up," he patted the space in between him and Will, "or get the hell out. This is the best part."

I crawled up the middle of the bed, settling in between the two guys. Liam shifted my body over, tucking my head into the crook of his arm. I settled into him with a sigh, my eyes feeling heavier by the second.

"Where's Gabe and Brian?" I whispered to Laina.

"They went to find a gym. Needed to work off some stress or something," she replied, raising an eyebrow.

We exchanged knowing glances. Seeing Laina and Dave together, I knew exactly why Brian had wanted to leave. I also had a good idea why Gabe had wanted to join him.

"I forgot to call Gabe," I shared. "Is he pissed?"

"Ladies please!" Liam beseeched.

"Chill Li, just one more second," Laina shot back.

"Dave told him that you went with Ty to the hospital to visit sick kids." Dave held up his hand, giving me the thumbs up sign.

"Seriously?" I confirmed.

"It's all good," Dave said. "Gabe was fine with it." He planted a kiss on Laina's mouth before looking back at the TV.

"Apparently our Ty is quite the do-gooder," Laina shared receiving a chorus of shushes from the guys. Ignoring them, she continued. "He also volunteers for Habitat for Humanity, a few kids' music programs and with the Boys and Girls Club in Vancouver. Impressive." Her eyes held mine, a coy smile playing across her shiny, pink lips.

Liam rolled me toward him, wrapping his arms tightly around my torso so that I couldn't turn back towards Laina. "Conversation time is over ladies." With a sigh, I snuggled into Liam's chest letting my eyes drift shut. I just wanted to go to sleep then wake up at home, in my own bed, with this tour being nothing more than a nightmare.

. . . . .

When I woke up from my nap, everyone was gone – except for Gabe. As soon as my eyes opened, they met his baby blues. And a fresh wave of guilt washed over me.

"Hey," I whispered.

Gabe set down the book that he was reading then ran his fingers through my hair, fanning it out on the pillow. "Hey," he whispered back, a slight smile on his lips. "How was the hospital?"

"Sad and amazing all at the same time. Sorry I didn't let you know where I was."

"I'm sorry too," Gabe said shifting closer to me, fitting our bodies together. "For calling you dense. For - everything. I was completely out of line."

I wrapped my leg over Gabe's thigh, unable to stop from snuggling closer to him. Wanting the comfort that always came with being near him. "Does this mean that you're done being mad at me?"

Gabe's eyes narrowed for just a second. "Do I have anything to be concerned about?"

My mixed up feelings for Ty. What I'd done with Ty. Ty – in general.

"I don't think so."

Liar! BIG FUCKING LIAR!

Gabe searched my face, clearly not buying it. But then he knew me too well.

A surge of guilt overwhelmed me, closing off my throat. I couldn't do this. I couldn't flat out lie to Gabe. Even though, in reality, I was free to be with whoever I wanted, this whole Ty situation was wrong. And it was going to end up killing my friendship with Gabe.

"I think that we should talk about last night. About Ty. About everything," I said, feeling the lump in my throat grow.

"I agree. But I'd prefer to wait until after Laina leaves. Having her here, complicates things. Especially now that she's hooked up with Dave." A grimace pulled at Gabe's mouth. "If that's alright with you?"

I wasn't sure if it was relief, at being given a reprieve from having this conversation. Or anxiety, knowing that we were only delaying the inevitable, that I felt more.

"Dave's a good guy. Knowing Laina, we should probably be more worried about him." Amusement filled Gabe's eyes, lifting a bit of the tightness in my chest. "As long as we're OK, I guess it can wait," I reluctantly agreed. "Laina's only here for a few more days anyway."

"We're fine. Baby Doll," Gabe said softly. "I love you."

"I love you too, Gabe."

Gabe pressed his lips against mine, softly, sweetly. And everything felt wrong.

Chapter 10 ~ Liv

Two very long days later, Laina held my hand in a vise grip as she dragged me through the concert crowd towards our seats. Dave had somehow managed to snag us two front row tickets for tonight's show. Which meant that I could stare at Ty for the next hour without it being weird. Without anyone noticing.

I hadn't been able to look at him since our trip to the hospital. Since we did what we did, and then he looked like he'd never regretted anything more in his entire life. Saying that just being in the same room with Ty now was awkward, would be a gross understatement.

"What the fuck happened between you and Ty?" Laina practically yelled as she plunked down in her seat, looking absolutely pissed.

Awesome. Here it comes. I'd been hoping that Laina wouldn't realize something was wrong.

I sat down in the seat beside her, feeling instantly defensive. "What are you talking about?"

"Well, Ty looks absolutely miserable and Dave said that he's been this way ever since you two got back from the hospital. Two days ago! And you're not much better. You've been a complete space cadet. What happened, Liv?"

"I don't know exactly. Maybe Ty's upset because of the patients we visited? There was one little girl who really touched his heart."

And there was one stupid woman who touched his dick.

"No, it's more than that. He couldn't keep his eyes off you before. But now, something's changed. It's horribly obvious that you're avoiding each other. What did you say to him?"

"Nothing. Nothing!" I confirmed.

Pretty sure he wasn't avoiding me for anything that I said.

Laina eyed me. "You're fucking lying. Spill it Madison."

Tears welled up in my eyes and I couldn't keep it in any longer. Everything that had happened from the time that Ty and I left the poker game until I woke up with Gabe the next afternoon spewed from my mouth.

"Holy fuck Liv! Why do things like this always happen to you?" she asked, her blue eyes wide as saucers.

"Things like this never happen to me! Complicated guy things only happen to you."

"Fair enough," Laina agreed. "So let me get this straight. You and Ty basically fucked in the back of a truck? With the driver sitting only a few feet away?"

God, that sounded bad.

"First of all, there was a dark partitioning glass. I'm sure the driver never saw anything."

Heard, maybe.

"Second," I continued, "Ty and I never actually had sex."

"Did you come? Twice?" I reluctantly nodded, knowing exactly where Laina was going with this. "Did Ty come? Twice?" I nodded again, waiting for her impending judgment. "Then you pretty much had sex. Penetration of any part of his body into any part of your body, plus orgasms, equals sex. Deny it all you want, but it still counts."

"I know," I mumbled, covering my face with both hands.

"Was it good?" Laina asked, pulling my hands down.

"Soooo good. He definitely knows what he's doing," I answered, thankful that the room was dark because my face was on fire.

"So what's the problem? Besides Gabe," she added as I opened my mouth.

"Ty regrets it."

"How do you know that?"

"It was written all over his face when we came into the hotel. And you said it, he can't even stand to be in the same room with me anymore."

"Oh shit, Liv. You OK?" Laina patted my back sympathetically.

"Yeah, I'm fine."

Liar. But I couldn't stand to admit how hurt I was. And, besides, my feelings for Ty weren't that serious anyway. Right?

"You're sure about that? You don't usually fuck around with random guys." Laina's eyes narrowed as she studied me.

"Ty's not some random guy," I shot back.

"So, you're admitting that you like him?"

"No. I mean I like Ty, obviously, but not. Oh. Things just got a little out of control, that's all," I muttered. "And it's not like we actually had sex. Real sex. With his cock in my vag," I justified.

"Because then it would be serious," Laina returned with a smirk. "That would mean you actually liked him."

"Screw off."

Laina chuckled. "Sorry Liv, you just have a warped sense of sex. I don't see the biggy about having actual intercourse. Especially considering you let him touch your girl parts. With his tongue."

I was pretty sure that my face just burst into flames.

"It's totally different!" I squeaked. "Oral sex can't get you pregnant. And, I know it's weird, but it's just not as intimate as feeling a guy inside you. Come inside you. Have the possibility of making a baby together."

My best friend in high school had gotten pregnant when we were in grade twelve. Of course, the jack ass ditched her as soon as he found out. Leaving her to face her parents and deal with the consequences. Alone. After watching Connie go through that, I vowed I'd never have sex with a guy unless we were serious. Unless we were making love. So far, I'd been in love with two guys. And neither relationship had turned out that great. So needless to say, I wasn't in a hurry to add another heartbreak to the list.

"Fine," Laina acquiesced. "If you and Ty are no big deal, then why are you both acting like the world's ending?"

"That's so not true. I'm just worried about Gabe finding out. He already thinks that Ty's a womanizing ass. This would send him over the edge. And they still have another month of touring to get through."

Laina shook her head. "Gabe's a whole other story. I think there's more going on there than just his sketchy opinion of Ty. Anything else you haven't told me Madison?"

She eyed me and I felt like shit for keeping so much from her. Laina was my best friend after all, and best friends were supposed to share – everything.

"No! I swear. Really. You know everything now."

"What about all of the kissing and cuddling?" Laina asked, and it wasn't hard to hear the skepticism in her voice. Not that I blamed her for that.

"I don't know," I replied with a shrug. "It's just part of the act."

"Kissing and cuddling with Gabe, even when you're in bed – alone - is just part of the act?"

"I already told you that sleeping doesn't count. We always cuddle on the couch at home when we're watching movies. And it's not like Gabe's never kissed me before."

"On your birthday or New Year's Eve." Laina's eyebrows lifted as she stared at me like I was a complete idiot.

OK, maybe I was a complete idiot. Maybe I hadn't wanted to see what was happening between me and Gabe. But now, there it was. Blaring like a neon sign right in my face.

"I'm screwed, aren't I?"

"Only if you don't feel the same way. Do you?" Laina asked slowly, her eyes glued to my face. "I mean it'd be kind of cool if you were my sister-in-law."

"Gabe's like a brother to me," I denied.

"A brother that you kiss and sleep with?" she pushed.

"Why do you have to make everything dirty?"

"It's a gift." A wicked grin played across Laina's lips.

"What am I going to do? I can't hurt Gabe."

"So then you hurt Ty."

"Ty? I thought we established that he couldn't care less," I returned, feeling my heart squeeze.

· · · · ·

Ty

"Do you regret what happened between you and Liv?" Laina demanded, cornering me as we packed up equipment after the show.

I glanced around to see if anyone else was within ear shot before meeting her eyes. They narrowed as she waited for me to answer.

"Well?" Laina asked again, placing her hands on her hips.

"I have no idea what you're talking about."

Had Liv told her about us?

"Cut the bull shit, Ty. Liv told me everything. Back of the SUV. You and her. Fucking around," Laina added as I just stood there. Staring at her.

Guess that'd be a yes.

"Laina, I, I," I stuttered, not sure what to say. Liv was going out with her brother for Christ sake. She was probably about to crucify me.

"You totally ignoring her afterwards. That's just shitty Ty. Liv isn't the type of person to fuck around with just anyone. Actually, she's fucked around with barely anyone."

My mouth dropped open as I tried to process her words.

Was she saying that Liv thought I regretted being with her? Clearly, she regretted being with me. Right?

"Of course," Laina huffed, shaking her head when I continued to stare at her with my mouth hanging open. "Neither one of you will admit how you feel for fuck sake. You're both totally infuriating. And, obviously perfect for each other. Look," Laina said, stepping so close that my gut reaction was to move back. Or cover my balls. Or, based on the look on Laina's face, possibly both. "If you like Liv half as much as I think that you do, then talk to her. Tell her how you feel."

What?! Gabe's sister is telling me to go after his girlfriend. This was beyond fucked up.

Laina eyed me for a second before turning around.

"Laina," I called, "what about Gabe?"

She swung around with a smug smile on her lips.

"Things aren't exactly what they appear to be with Liv and Gabe. Talk to her. Get her to open up."

What the fuck does that mean?

"She's out back by the bus, talking on the phone. Alone," she added before heading towards the stage.

I didn't need to hear anything else. Glancing over to where Gabe was taking apart the lighting rod, I strode towards the back door. Stepping into the parking lot, I spotted Liv perched on the bumper of the last bus. My bus. Our eyes locked and I closed the distance between us in record time.

"We need to talk," I said quietly, pointing toward the bus door.

Liv stood, mouthing, 'I'm on the phone.'

"Get off," I directed, impatient to get her alone before someone wondered out. Without waiting for her to say goodbye, I grabbed Liv's free hand pulling her up into the bus.

Her eyes widened as she watched me shut – and lock – the door.

"Look Mom, I've got to go," Liv said as she moved away from me. "I know, I know, I'll try to call you first thing tomorrow."

I followed her to the lounge at the back of the bus, doing my best to keep my hands to myself. God, I wanted to touch her. I wanted to run my hands through her silky hair then down to her ass.

Liv turned, catching me staring at her ass and I watched anger transform her features.

"OK, I love you too Mom. Bye for now." She pressed end, pocketing her cell. Her eyes never leaving mine. "What do you think you're doing?" she demanded. "Everyone is loading the buses. They're going to wonder what we're doing in here – alone – with the door locked!"

With a shake of her head, Liv brushed past me heading into the hallway. And I grabbed her, pushing her up against the wall. Pushing my body against hers as I held her hands captive in mine.

"What the fuck, Ty. Let me go!" she said through gritted teeth, hazel eyes flashing.

God, she was beautiful. Especially when she was mad. Slowly, I lowered my face to hers, putting my lips to her ear.

"Kiss me. Then I'll let you go," I whispered, coming unraveled from just touching her.

Just one kiss, then I'd let her go. Definitely.

"No," she muttered but I could feel her body lean into mine. And that's all the invitation I needed.

My lips skimmed across her cheek, searching for her lips. I wanted to kiss her soft and slow, like she'd done to me at first. But the second our lips touched, an overwhelming need hit me. Fisting my hand into the back of Liv's hair, I tilted her head while my lips pillaged hers. The kiss was rough and demanding. But I couldn't help it. I needed to taste her. I needed to show her how desperate she made me feel.

My hand pushed underneath her t-shirt finding a taut nipple. I played with it, pinching and pulling like I knew she liked while her hand found my cock. Fondling it, making me harder than I thought was humanly possible. Touching me. Just like I liked.

"God, I want you. I can't stop wanting you and it's killing me," I breathed then crushed our lips together again.

Without uttering a word, Liv unzipped my pants, pushing them and my boxers down. She tore her mouth away from mine, our eyes meeting for only a second before she dropped to her knees. The instant my cock entered her mouth, I knew that this was it. She was it. I had never wanted another woman as much as I wanted her. As much as I needed her.

"Oh, Liv," I moaned, reveling in the way she was alternating between sucking my cock then licking it. It was like she was inside of my head. And I wanted to be inside of her.

"Darlin', I want to be inside of you," I said in a ragged voice, echoing the thought in my head. "Let me make love you," I pleaded.

Instead of stopping, Liv sucked harder, taking my cock even deeper into her mouth. And I was powerless to do anything other than stand there, letting her pleasure me. I twisted my hands into her long hair, watching her suck my shaft into her mouth over and over again. Until I couldn't last any longer. I started coming in her mouth, reveling in the feeling, as she swallowed around me.

After the last spasm ripped through my body, Liv looked up, giving my cock one last – hard – suck before standing. I pressed my mouth against hers, pushing my hand down the front of her shorts, gliding two fingers into her wet pussy.

"Fuck, you're so wet," I murmured against her lips as I fucked her with my fingers. "Spread your legs a bit more, I want to push in deeper."

"Yes," Liv hissed, already working her hips against my hand. "Make me come Ty. Please."

My tongue slid into her mouth, probing, tasting, while my thumb rubbed against her clit. She grabbed my other hand, moving it from her ass up to her tit. Pressing my fingers into her nipple. And I knew exactly what she wanted. And how she wanted it. Hard, I pulled and played with her nipple. Hard, I thrust my fingers in and out of her pussy. Until a guttural moan ripped through her throat and she came all over my fingers.

Liv's head fell against my chest as I continued to caress her swollen clit and gently rub her nipple.

"You make me feel so good," she finally said, bringing her lips up to meet mine again. We kissed, slow and deep while she ran her hands over my shoulders and I kept one hand in her pants and the other up her shirt.

There was no way that I was going to stop touching her. Until she made me.

"Ty, I need to go," she muttered against my mouth.

"No."

Liv moved her head back, glancing up at me. A wicked smile on her lips. Still not removing my hands from her body.

"I have to go."

"No," I returned with a slow shake of my head. "I'm not done with you yet."

Liv laughed, finally pushing me away. "I have a feeling that if you had your way, you'd never be done with me."

If she only knew just how true that was.

"What are we doing?" I asked, watching Liv smooth her clothing back into place. Pulling my own pants up.

"Getting dressed."

"That's not what I meant and you know it, Liv. What's happening between us?" I could see the apprehension build in her face as we looked at each other.

"Ty," she finally said with a sigh.

"I know that it's so wrong, but I can't help the way I feel about you. Trust me, I've tried." I paused, giving Liv a chance to say something. Anything. But she just stood there, staring at me. "Laina said that things aren't what they seem between you and Gabe. What does she mean?" I demanded, needing answers.

Shock wiped the apprehension from Liv's face. "Laina said that?"

"She also told me to tell you how I felt."

"Fuck! I'm going to kill her." Liv took a step towards the hallway, but that's as far as she got. My hand closed around her arm.

I was going to get an explanation. Now.

"Why would Gabe's sister tell me to go after you?" I demanded, becoming more irritated by the second. I'd basically poured my heart out to Liv. Again. And she seemed more concerned about what Laina had said. I watched the shutters start to come down as I stared at her. "Don't do this Liv. Talk to me, Darlin'. Please," I begged.

Guilt, over wanting another man's girlfriend. A decent, good man's girlfriend. Anger, that I was laying my heart on the line and being offered nothing in return. And longing, for the woman in front of me and the life that I knew we could build together. A life that I was more than ready for. All mixed together as I waited for the woman I was helplessly falling in love with, to throw me a bone. To say something, that would make this better.

Or even worse. Because right now, I didn't care. I'd take anything from her.

Liv's face softened and she reached up, wrapping her arms around my neck. Hugging me tight. "I'm sorry Ty, but I don't know what to say. Things with Gabe are really complicated right now."

"I get that," I muttered into her hair. "Just tell me what's happening. I'd never do anything to hurt you, Liv. Just trust me."

"Please. I just need a little time."

And that was it. I snapped. Pushing her away, I seethed, "Time? How much time Liv? A week? A month? A year? While we sneak behind Gabe's back, fooling around. I can't keep doing this anymore. It's so wrong. It's killing me."

"Ty, please, I just need a few days to talk to Gabe. To sort everything out. I love him and I won't hurt him. For anyone."

She loved him. She wouldn't hurt him. But was fine with tearing my heart out.

Rage grew in my stomach while my heart bled. No wonder she wouldn't let me make love to her. She didn't love me. She loved Gabe. Twisted as their love was – he was what mattered most to her.

"You're already hurting him," I fired. "And you're torturing me. But maybe this is just what you do. That's why Gabe is so crazy when it comes to you. Isn't it? Because he knows what you're like. You're a fucking cock tease and a cheat!" The words spewed from my mouth like lava from a volcano. Hot and burning.

"Fuck you," Liv said quietly, then turned, leaving me standing there. Feeling utterly alone.

· · · · ·

Liv

Tears welled up in my eyes then began to roll down my cheeks, warm and wet, as I jumped into the bunk that Gabe and I shared. With a tug, I yanked the curtain shut behind me. Wanting to hide from the world.

"Liv." I heard Laina call, but didn't have the energy to deal with her. I prayed that she'd leave me alone for once. She'd already done enough damage for one day.

"Liv, are you in here?" she called again.

A second later the curtain flew back and Laina stood staring down at me.

"Oh my God sweetie, what happened?" she asked, moving in beside me.

"You tell me," I replied, wiping the tears from my face.

"Ty."

"How could you have told him to come and find me? To tell me how he feels? Fuck Laina, you've just made everything so much worse," I fumed, sitting up. "I just needed a few more days to work everything out."

Confusion contorted Laina's face. "OK. I just don't understand how having a hot guy - who you're crazy about - tell you that he's crazy about you, can possibly make things worse?"

"He told me that he thinks I'm a cock teasing cheat."

Saying those words out loud made everything seem completely real. And horrible.

Because, for all intents and purposes, I was exactly what he said. And the truth always hurts more than lies.

· · · · ·

Ty

"Shit," I mumbled as Laina strode towards my bus, a look of death on her face. She'd obviously talked to Liv.

"Ty Benson, where the fuck do you get off talking to my best friend like that? Calling her a lying cheat?" Laina demanded as she climbed aboard.

Actually, I called her a cock teasing cheat.

"That's not exactly what happened, I –"

"Liv's the last person you should be calling a lying cheat, you prick," Laina cut in. "She's had sex with exactly two guys. Both who she loved and was in a relationship with. Liv does not just sleep around and she never just fucks around. Except with guys that she cares about."

"Like Gabe," I spat, Liv's words replaying in my head.

A hysterical laugh left Laina's lips. "You're such a dick. Liv's never had sex with Gabe. He's never even touched her. Because - they're – not – going – out," she said slowly, annunciating each word as if she was talking to a child.

My mouth dropped open and I was almost certain that my jaw was now lying on the floor.

"Wha, what?" I sputtered.

"Fuck Sherlock, they've been pretending to be a couple because you threatened to kick Liv off the tour."

The secret. Everything suddenly made sense. I was such an idiot!

"Why wouldn't she just tell me that?"

"Because she wanted to talk to Gabe first. Tell him that she was falling for you. That she wanted to be with you. But you fucked that right up," Laina ranted stalking back and forth in the kitchenette. "And now she's pissed at me too. I could just kill you."

"Laina, I'm so-"

"Sorry?" she cut in again. "You should be. Because I went to bat for you. I'm pretty sure that Gabe wants to be more than just friends with Liv and now you've just pushed her into his arms. Fuck wad!" she hissed then headed toward the stairs.

"Laina!" I shrieked, the most unmanly voice ever coming from my throat. "Why don't you want Gabe and Liv to be together?"

She glared at me. "It's not that I don't want them to be together. Before you came along, I would have been the first one in line to make that happen. But," she paused, drawing in a breath, "I see the way that you and Liv look at each other. You two have chemistry. Undeniable chemistry. That she and Gabe don't have. Don't get me wrong, they love each other, but Liv is in love with you. That's why I pushed her to give you a chance."

Fuuuccckkk, what had I done. Liv's in love with me and I was beyond horrible to her.

"I'll apologize. I'll do anything that I have to, to make it up to her," I groveled, moving over to the stairs. "I can make this right."

"It's too late. You blew it Ty. She doesn't want to talk to you. Ever again." A wry grin spread over Laina's lips. "Gabe should thank you though. He's in there, right now, consoling her. Picking up the pieces, convincing her that they should really be together. And I think it's going to work."

Laina climbed out of the bus, while I stood there, unsure of what to do. Unsure of everything except that I was the world's biggest prick.

• • • • •

"Whoa man, you're not planning on trying to talk to Liv, are you?" Dave asked, stepping in front of me as I headed towards Diesel's bus a few minutes later.

"You know I am," I said in a flat voice, moving to step around him. I was going to apologize even if it meant that Gabe and his entire band would beat the shit out of me.

"I just saw Laina. Liv doesn't want to talk to you," Dave said gently, putting his hands around my biceps.

"Well, she's going to." I tried to shake him off, but Dave tightened his grip. "Let me go!"

"You're making a giant mistake Ty. No one is going to let you near her. You're only going to make it worse. Give her a few days to calm down, then talk to her. Apologize for being a giant dick."

"A few days is too long. Gabe's moving in on her – right now!" I hissed.

"Probably. Can you blame him?" Dave said with a shoulder shrug. "I love you man, but you made your bed. Now you're going to have to lie in it."

I ripped my arms out of Dave's hands, sidestepping around him. Heading towards Liv again.

"Don't do it Ty. I mean it. You're going to make things even worse."

Defeat suddenly seeped through my body, sapping me. I turned back around, meeting Dave's eyes.

"Sorry man," he said quietly. "Now, where are you going?" Dave demanded, trying to keep up with me as I headed between the buses, down the darkened alley.

I stopped, but didn't bother to turn around and look at him. "Are you going to let me talk to her?"

I desperately wanted to go back. I needed to apologize. I needed to beg Liv for forgiveness.

"You're not going to talk to Liv. Laina will kill you and if she doesn't, I'm pretty sure that Gabe will gladly do the job," Dave warned.

"That's what I thought. Then I'm going there." I pointed across the street to the building front with a neon sign flashing BAR.

"Shit Ty, the concert's only been out for an hour. That bar will be filled with fans. We'll get mobbed." Dave looked around. "Just wait." He led me the rest of the way to the street, waving for a cab. "Get in," he directed when one pulled over. "Take us to an out of the way pub please. Apparently my friend needs to get good and wasted," he told the cab driver.

As the cabbie drove, Dave watched me come undone.

"I'm in love with her. Totally, fuckin' painfully, in love with her," I admitted.

A sigh escaped Dave's lips. "Oh buddy."

"She's not in love with Gabe, you know," I added, sounding desperate even to myself.

. . . . .

I woke up the next morning to the smell of spilled rye and cheap perfume. There was a petite brunette lying face down beside me and, although she didn't smell like Liv, I desperately wanted her to be.

"Liv," I muttered hopefully, rubbing my hand down her bare back. I couldn't remember how we'd gotten here, to my hotel room, or at least it looked like my hotel room. But I didn't care. "Liv, Darlin', I'm so sorry for everything."

She turned to face me. "Sweetie, I don't care if you call me Liv, as long as you actually finish what you start this time."

"Holy fuck! You're not Liv." I yelled, jumping out of bed. "Who, who are you?" I asked, pulling the sheet off the bed to wrap around my naked torso.

The chick grinned. "I can be anyone you want me to be. Just come back to bed rock star."

Oh, fuck!

Sheer panic raged through my body. I hadn't done a one night stand in forever. I stared at the woman sitting naked in my bed. Thick, black eyeliner smudged across her cheeks, a trace of bright red lipstick still on her lips.

And I wanted to throw up.

"Did we, um," I started to ask.

"Fuck?" she finished. I nodded. "No, you passed out before we could. But there's no time like the present." She smiled and I took off for the hallway.

"Dave," I hollered, pounding on his door. "Dave!"

The door pulled open and Laina stood on the other side, staring at me.

Shit! I'd forgotten about Laina.

The expression on her face was surprise mixed with amusement as she took in the sheet that I had bunched around my midsection.

"Dave's still passed out from your little escapade last night. But don't worry, I don't think the toga party has started yet," she said dryly.

At that very moment, I heard a door open and watched Laina's eyes become as wide as saucers, then narrow into tiny slits.

"Oh fuck," I said, glancing over my shoulder. Standing in my doorway was that nameless woman, wearing nothing but a towel.

She looked at me, then Laina. "Don't tell me this is Liv? You can do a lot better than her. Come back to bed and I'll show you what a real woman can do."

"Bitch!" Laina hissed and I had to physically stop her from lunging at the woman.

"Get back in the room," I commanded. "I'll be right there."

Laina glared at me. "You're a real piece of work Ty Benson. Stay the fuck away from my best friend." She slammed the door in my face but I still couldn't move.

My entire life was falling apart. And I was to blame for all of it.

Chapter 11 – Liv

Laina went back to Vancouver and I desperately wanted to go too. The only thing that kept me here, living in hell, was Gabe. He'd pretty much begged me to stay. Not understanding why I'd want to cut our summer short.

And what could I possibly say?

He had no idea about what happened between me and Ty. And, since nothing more was going to happen, I didn't see the point in telling him. Anything. The exposure Diesel was getting on this tour was too good to give up. They needed, and Gabe needed, to finish it – on decent terms with Ty. Because in the music industry, Ty was force to be reckoned with.

Which is the reason that I'd stayed. Gabe would do anything for me and I'd do anything, including having to endure being around Lucifer himself, for Gabe. For his future.

So now my poorly thought out, last ditch plan was to: 1. stay away from Ty for the next month, 2. convince myself that Ty means absolutely nothing to me, and 3. possibly join an out-of-the-way nunnery deep in the mountains of Lithuania.

No problem. Right?

If only it was that simple.

The following week turned out to be absolutely agonizing. Trying to avoid Ty wasn't as easy as I'd anticipated, because he was doing anything other than avoiding me. He seemed to be everywhere that I was. Hanging out in the lobby of every hotel, backstage when Diesel was doing sound check, in the guys' rooms playing video games – even on our bus.

It was beyond horrible.

So I was forced to glue myself to Gabe twenty-four-seven. Which made Gabe obviously happy, and made me worry that he was interpreting my new found need-to-be-near-him–all-of-the-time behavior, as something more. Something that it definitely was not.

. . . . .

It was after midnight when we finally pulled into our latest hotel. The guys had played five cities over the past seven days and were completely exhausted. Something that I hoped would work in my favor tonight. The way Gabe had been looking at me lately, gave me the impression that something was on his mind. And, right now, I preferred to keep it there.

I finally crept out of the bathroom, praying that Gabe would be asleep.

But I wasn't that lucky. Big surprise.

He was just lying in bed staring at the ceiling. A weird expression on his face. And, deep in the pit of my now acid filled stomach, I knew that tonight was the night.

I thought about bolting out of the room and hiding somewhere. But with the way things were going, I'd probably run into Ty. So, I had to choose between two evils. Stay in the frying pan and risk getting burned or jump and hope that I missed the fire.

Tough choice. Guess I was staying.

As I dragged my body towards the bed, I forced out a giant yawn. "I'm beat," I shared, yawning again, hoping that Gabe would get the hint. Crawling into bed, I turned my back towards him, squeezing my eyes shut. Anxiously waiting to see if my ploy was going to work.

A second later, the bed creaked under Gabe's weight as he rolled towards me.

Just great.

I held in the sigh that wanted to escape my body. Just like I wanted to escape this room.

Sliding an arm around my waist, Gabe pulled me against his body. Placing a single kiss on my bare shoulder. "Baby Doll, we need to talk," he whispered into my ear. "Liv, can you look at me please?" Gabe asked, his voice unusually tentative.

This was it. Our day of reckoning. Shit!

Reluctantly. Very reluctantly. I rolled over, meeting Gabe's liquid blue eyes. He studied my face in silence for a moment, while the butterflies in my stomach tried to beat their way out.

I definitely wasn't ready for this. But I didn't know how to waylay what was coming. So I just laid there - waiting.

"You know, Liv, I was thinking that we're the perfect couple," he began, his voice slow and meaningful.

Oh, fuuucccckkkk!

"I mean, we like each other's families. Well actually, I'm pretty sure that my family loves you more than they love me. And, of course, your parents already think of me as the son they never had." Gabe's lips curled up at the corners but I could see trepidation in his eyes instead of humor.

And it made me feel horrible. Gabe was the most wonderful guy in the entire world. He shouldn't feel anxious about telling any woman that he wanted to be with her. They should be – I should be - overjoyed that such a great guy was asking for more than friendship.

But joy wasn't even close to what I was feeling right now.

The fact that Gabe was absolutely right about our families, only made me feel that much worse. He and Laina had been coming home with me for a weekend here and there over the past four years. Laina and I would hang out with my Mom and three sisters while Gabe did guy stuff with my Dad. It was no exaggeration to say that every one of them would be over-the-moon happy if we got together.

Not that my Mom hadn't mentioned that a time, or several hundred, all ready.

And, it was fair to say that I loved his family. Since his parents lived on the outskirts of Vancouver, the three of us had been going over for supper on a regular basis since my first year in University. They had adopted me into their family. Making being away from my family so much easier.

Gabe was right. He and I fit perfectly into each other's families. Into each other's lives.

"OK fine, I'll give you that," I joked, trying to lighten the mood. Although I felt like the world was about to crash down around me.

Gabe slowly ran his fingers up and down my arm before continuing. "We have all the same friends. We know that we can live together. I mean after living REALLY CLOSELY together this summer and not ending up hating each other. It's a pretty good sign." He paused, drawing in a deep breath. "Guess what I'm trying to say, Baby Doll, is that maybe we make sense. Maybe this whole thing with you having to pretend to be my girlfriend happened for a reason."

"For a reason," I repeated desperately trying to come up with the right words to dissuade Gabe from going any further. But there were no right words. There were no words that wouldn't sound horrible when your best friend was laying his heart on the line. And you weren't sure whether you felt terrified or thrilled.

I definitely didn't deserve him.

"I'm going to kiss you," he began, this time his voice was filled with conviction instead of doubt. "And I want you to kiss me. I mean really kiss me Liv. I think we owe it to ourselves, to each other, to see if there's more between us than just friendship."

"Gabe," I hedged. "I don't know if this is a good idea. I don't want to ruin our friendship. You know how terrible I am with relationships."

So, unfortunately, true.

"Have you ever thought that maybe you just haven't been with the right guy yet?"

He might have a point. But - was Gabe that guy?

"A kiss isn't going to ruin anything, Liv," Gabe continued. "Please just try and see." His eyes pleaded with me to say yes.

What could I do? I was screwed either way and Gabe was right, it was just a kiss. Right?

"OK," I agreed.

Gabe stared into my eyes for another second before his lips met mine. I let my eyes drift shut, trying to do what he asked. Trying to see if there was more to our relationship than either of us thought there ever could be. Being with Gabe would be so easy. It would make sense for both of us.

His lips worked against mine, cajoling me to respond. And I did. I got lost in the moment. In the feel of Gabe's lips moving against mine and his hands gently caressing my body. The kiss was good. Really good. But freakishly it made me think of Ty.

OK, I was a horribly, rotten person.

As Gabe kissed me, I couldn't help but compare his kiss with Ty's. Kissing Gabe was sunshine and comfort – and stability. Kissing Ty was heat and desire – and uncertainty.

The kiss slowed and Gabe puffed out a breath of air as he inched back, his eyes meeting mine. Searching. We looked at each other for a few moments and I wondered what was going through his mind.

"Well?" Gabe asked slowly.

"Well," I responded, unsure of what to say because I was unsure of everything right now. My stomach flip flopped in time with my changing emotions.

Gabe brushed his fingers across my cheek. "What do you think, Baby Doll?"

"I didn't know that you were such a good kisser," I joked hoping to break the intensity of the moment.

"Just one of the fringe benefits of going out with me," he kidded, his entire face relaxing.

Going out with him! Holy crap! I was definitely not ready for this conversation.

"I don't know, Gabe," I hedged again, trying to be as gentle as possible. "It's just weird. I mean I've never thought of you in this way before. You're Gabe, my best friend, my brother from another mother," I explained hoping that he would understand where I was coming from.

He nodded slowly, his eyes never leaving mine. "I get it, Liv. This is new for both of us, but that doesn't mean we aren't right for each other. Don't they say that the best relationships start from friendships? You're one of my best friends, we know each other inside and out. How much better can it get?"

"True," I agreed, "but there's more to a relationship than just knowing each other Gabe. There needs to be chemistry and desire."

"You don't think that we have any chemistry?" Disappointment and pain distorted Gabe's beautiful face.

God, I was a horrible person.

Guilt chewed at my insides.

"That's not what I'm saying." I slid my fingertips over Gabe's forehead smoothing out the lines before pressing my lips lightly against his. It was impossible to deny that there was something wonderful between us.

"Then what are you saying, Liv?" he asked, his voice just above a whisper. His eyes desperately searching mine.

"I'm just saying that this is a huge shift in our relationship."

"So you ARE attracted to me?"

"Gabe, I'd have to be dead to NOT find you attractive."

Objectively speaking, Gabe was hot. With his broad shoulders, tight abs, and perfect features – he was like a Nordic God. Unfortunately, most of the 'looks' thing was lost on me. To me Gabe was perfect. Not because of the way he looked, but because he was the best person I knew. He was pure goodness and he was my best friend.

And, maybe, that's all I needed.

"Whew, you made me sweat a little, Baby Doll."

Relief and happiness washed over Gabe's face. And another wave of guilt washed through me. How could I let him think that I felt the same way he did? How couldn't I let him think that? The problem was that I had no idea how I truly felt. I was in hell right now and dragging the sweetest man in the world down with me.

"So I was thinking that we should give US a try for the rest of the tour. Everyone thinks that we're together so let's really be together Liv. I'm not saying that we have to have sex right away. Unless you want to," he added with a sheepish grin. "I mean being the wonderful, giving guy that I am, I wouldn't say no if you really wanted to. You know seal the deal."

"Oh Gabe," I rolled my eyes. "You're such a guy. Let's table the sex talk for the time being." I paused for a moment before continuing, trying to push my unfortunate feelings for Ty out of the way. "This is a really big decision," I began. "I don't want us to make a mistake that would ruin our friendship. Maybe we should think about it for a while." The smile disappeared from Gabe's lips. And my heart sank.

"So you don't think that we make sense?" he pushed. "You don't love me?"

"We make perfect sense," I conceded. "And you know that I love you, but..."

"Then let's try this. We only have three weeks left on tour. That's not a lot of time but I think it'll be enough to see if we have what it takes to move our relationship forward. If not, then we'll go back home status quo. Just like nothing ever happened."

This sounded familiar. Wasn't that exactly what I'd said to Ty about my relationship with Gabe? That if we didn't work out, we could just go back to being friends?

But could we? Really?

I stared at Gabe, contemplating what to say for what seemed like forever.

"If you're worried about the sex thing – don't," Gabe continued, obviously thinking that was what had me hung-up.

If only.

Sex to me was definitely a biggy, but there was so much more than that. As much as I tried to deny it, Ty was right there – wedged in between us. And I hadn't figured how to extract him. Yet.

"You can decide when or even if that happens between us. I just want to spend time with you – as my girlfriend. I want to be able to hold your hand and kiss you because I want to. Not because we're playing some role. Three weeks Baby Doll, that's all I'm asking," Gabe pleaded.

"Three weeks," I repeated.

Gabe reached over, turning the light off before folding me into his arms. He placed a kiss on my forehead. "You won't regret this Baby Doll, I promise," he whispered into the dark, obviously thinking that my last words had meant yes. "I'm going to prove that we're meant to be together."

'Please let that be true,' I wished over and over again as Gabe lay wrapped around me, sleeping.

. . . . .

Ty

Desperate, was how I felt. I'd been trying for the past week to talk to Liv. To apologize. To beg her to give me another chance. I'd even gone so far as to ride on Diesel's bus. Not that I expected to have a chance to talk to her then. I just needed to be near her. Not that it worked. She'd hid out in the bunk with Gabe. Laughing and talking. Making it the longest, hardest, three hours I'd ever spent.

It seemed that no matter how hard I tried to catch Liv alone, she was perma-fixed to Gabe. Driving me crazy. Making me more desperate with each passing day.

. . . . .

The elevator doors in our latest hotel opened and a miracle happened. There stood Liv. Completely alone. If I thought there was time, I would have gotten down on my knees and thanked God or the deities or whoever gave me this beautiful gift.

"Fuck," Liv muttered as our eyes met.

She tried to rush out of the elevator before I could get in, but that wasn't happening. This might be the only chance that I had. And I was going to make it count.

"We need to talk," I said stepping into the elevator. Shifting from side to side so that Liv couldn't slip past me.

"No way," she hissed, looking past me into the hallway. Hoping, I'm sure, that Gabe would magically appear to save her. "You've already said everything there was to say last time. Let me out!" Liv squeaked as I pushed the button to close the elevator door. She stalked from one side of the mirrored elevator to the other and back again. Reminding me of a caged animal.

"Not until you let me apologize." I reached over pushing the stop button, watching panic take over Liv's face. Hating that I was the cause of it.

"Go to hell!" Liv said, turning her back on me.

"Darlin', I'm already there," I returned, wondering if she knew just how true that was. I'd sent too many texts and left too many voice messages for her not to. But then again, I was pretty sure that she'd ignored all of them. "Liv, I'm so sorry. I didn't mean what I said. Please turn around and look at me." I reached out, touching her shoulder.

"Don't touch me!" she hissed, placing a hand over each ear. "Talk all you want, but I'm not listening."

I couldn't help it, a deep, roaring laugh ripped from my throat. "Liv, please, we're not eight years old. You and I both know that ear muffs don't really work."

"Yes, they do!"

"If they work, then how do you know what I just said?" Another chuckle escaped.

Even when I was fighting with this woman, it was fun. Well, sort of.

With a huge sigh, Liv's hands returned to her sides and she turned to face me. It took every bit of will power that I had to not touch her. To not wrap her in my arms and never let her go again.

"Say whatever you think you need to," she said quietly. "Then let me out of here."

"I love you," I returned simply. "I'm so in love with you."

A bitter laugh tore from Liv's lips. "Really?" she asked, sarcasm dripping from each syllable. "How can you possibly be in love with a, oh, just wait, I want to make sure that I get the wording right. A cock teasing cheat. That's it right? That's what you think I am?"

I could feel my face fall along with my determination. "I was wrong. Totally and completely wrong." Liv's eyebrows raised, and it wasn't hard to tell that she didn't believe me.

"Why are you so sorry all of a sudden Ty? Haven't been able to find another whore to suck you off?"

Fuck! I deserved that. But it still hurt.

"Please Darlin'," I implored dropping to my knees, placing my hands in a praying position in front of my face. "I'm literally begging you for another chance."

I'd never done this before. Begged a woman – for anything. But to have another chance with Liv, I'd do anything. And apparently was.

"I made a horrible mistake," I continued while Liv eyed me warily, as if I were an alien explaining my plan to disembowel her. "I was just so torn up when you said that you wouldn't hurt Gabe. For anyone. But, I didn't realize that you two weren't actually together. And that you just wanted to tell him how you felt about me. That you were in love with me."

Liv's eyes widened. "Laina."

"Don't blame Laina. Please. She tore a strip out of me for the way that I treated you."

She also told me to stay away from Liv. But I was banking - everything - that she hadn't told Liv about the hotel incident. And the woman.

I knew that I'd have to deal with THAT. Tell Liv about HER. Eventually. But right now, I had bigger things to worry about. Like just getting Liv to talk to me.

"She told you that Gabe and I weren't together?" Liv demanded, inching closer to me.

"Yes. She said. W, wait," I stammered, "weren't, as in past tense? Are you and Gabe together now?"

Please say no. Oh God, please say no.

Liv's face dropped for just a second before she pulled it together again. But I saw it. I saw the regret in her eyes.

Laina had said that Gabe was trying to convince Liv that they belonged together. I just never thought – or wanted – to believe that it would actually happen. Liv belonged with me. Period.

"Have you slept together?" I asked, forcing those vial words from my mouth. Feeling my world slowly come apart.

This gut retching feeling was the exact reason why I hadn't even contemplated getting into a relationship since my ex-fiance and I broke up. It had been two gloriously uncomplicated, heart-break free years.

So, what the fuck was I doing now?

"That's none of your business," Liv said fiercely, taking a step back.

I stood up, inching closer to her. Trying to hold my temper, and hurt, in check. "It's only none of my business if you really don't love me." I crept a bit closer as we stared at each other. "I love you with all of my heart, Liv. If I could take back what I said, you know that I would. I never meant to hurt you. Please believe me."

Liv's bottom lip began to quiver and I couldn't help myself. I leaned in, softly pressing my lips against hers.

Turning her head to the side, Liv sighed. "I can't do this with you. I'm with Gabe now. And despite what you may or may not think – I don't cheat."

My arms circled her waist, pulling her against me. "I know. I know," I murmured into her hair.

Sucking in a deep breath, I gathered the strength to ask what I dreaded most. It wasn't that I actually wanted to know. Because I didn't. Living in blissful ignorance, with the choice to believe what I wanted, was so much better. But deep inside, I knew that it wouldn't be enough. I needed to know.

Laina had told me that Liv only slept with guys that she was serious about. That she was in love with. So maybe, I still had a chance. Liv's answer would either give me hope or completely crush me.

"Have you had sex with Gabe yet?" I asked, pushing the words out of my mouth.

Liv's body went stiff in my arms. "Ty," she warned, "that's none of your business." Shoving me away, she moved towards the elevator doors.

Having the gift of long legs on my side, I stepped in front of her, blocking the way. "We're not going anywhere until you answer my question."

"Why does it matter Ty?" Liv asked, her shoulders slumping, her face filled with exasperation. "Even if I haven't had sex with Gabe, that could change at any moment."

"So you haven't had sex with Gabe!" I cheered, actually jumping up in the air. My heart pounding with excitement. Disneyland had nothing on this rollercoaster, drop of doom, house of mirrors relationship that Liv and I had.

"I didn't say that."

"You, more or less, just did."

Her tone and the way that she phrased her answer, told me everything I needed to know. I'd bet my waterfront loft that nothing had happened between her and Gabe.

And I intended to keep it that way.

"Have you fooled around with Gabe? Like you did with me?" I pushed, betting my entire emotional well-being that Liv hadn't. That she couldn't.

"Get out of my way," she ordered, although there was no fire in her eyes. She just looked sad.

"That'd be a no!" I exclaimed, on top of the world right now.

"Hold up psych boy. Just because you're going to start your PhD, doesn't make you a mind reader."

"You're right," I agreed, unable to keep a smile from my lips. "But I can read you. You may have told Gabe that you'll give it a try with him, but it's not going to work. We both know that. Because." I paused, an even bigger smile on my face now, "you're in love with me."

"You're," Liv started, but I pressed my fingers against her lips before she could say another word.

"Just know that I'll be waiting for you. So whenever you're ready to admit that we belong together, I'll be here." I pressed my lips against hers. Firmly. Possessively. Before pushing the button to restart the elevator.

The doors slid open and I strolled out, filled with hope. Knowing that, somehow, I'd get Liv back.

Chapter 12 ~ Liv

"Baby Doll, you've been so quiet today. You feeling alright?" Gabe asked as we lay cuddled up in bed together.

I ran my fingers along his jaw, feeling the prickle from his five o'clock shadow. Ever since Ty ambushed me in the elevator this morning, my thoughts and emotions felt as though they'd been switched to overload. Before I was just angry and hurt. Now I was both of those, plus confused. About the way that I felt. About what I should do.

"Gabe, we can do this, right? We can make this work, right?"

I needed Gabe to convince me that we were meant to be together. That we really did make sense. Because, right now, my heart wasn't so sure.

Gabe kissed me, soft and sweet. "Of course we can Baby Doll. It's just you and me against the world." He grinned, then kissed me again. And I tried to shove Ty out of my head.

I could do this. I could definitely do this. I loved Gabe and we were together now.

We belonged together.

I brushed my tongue along Gabe's bottom lip, pulling my body closer to his. Pushing my pelvis suggestively into his cock.

I could do this. It didn't feel weird at all. Right?

Crap Liv, get out of your head. Don't over think it. Just do it.

Gabe's tongue pushed into my mouth as his hand slid down, cupping my ass, moving me up and down against his now hard cock.

That felt good, right? Gabe's mouth on mine. My clit rubbing against his shaft.

Without taking his mouth from mine, Gabe pushed me back on the bed, rolling on top of me. Grabbing my knees, he hitched my legs up around his waist then began to work his cock up and down against my clit again. Slowly, his hand roamed down my thigh to the edge of my pajama top, pushing underneath the fabric.

Still OK, I could do this.

Then Gabe's fingers grazed the underside of my boob and my breath caught.

Gabe was touching my boob! Weird! Maybe I couldn't do this.

"Liv," Gabe breathed, planting kisses along my jaw and down my neck. "You feel so good."

Fuucckkk! This was it. I was going to do it –for Gabe and for me.

Sucking in a deep breath, I pushed my hand between our bodies and into Gabe's underwear.

Oh my God, I was touching my best friend's cock! I was actually doing this.

My heart thumped so hard that I could hear it in my ears.

"I want to make you feel good," I muttered as my fingers closed around his shaft.

"Yes," he whispered, pushing his cock into my hand, again and again. His breath becoming more ragged as each second passed. Gabe tugged at my underwear, working them down enough so that he could push his fingers along my clit, towards my entrance. "You're not very wet. Do you want me to suck on your pussy?" he mumbled against my neck.

"No," I said too quickly and too loudly. Gabe's head popped up, his eyes finding mine. "It's um, not a good time of month for that," I sputtered, feeling my cheeks heat up.

Gabe's eyebrows pulled down. "But you're not supposed to have your period for a while yet."

Oh shit!

I forgot that Gabe knew my schedule better than I did. I guess living with Laina and I had made that a necessity. Whenever it was 'that' time of the month, Gabe would magically show up with ice cream, chocolate and chick flicks.

God I loved him. I just wasn't ready to have sex with him. Or really fool around with him. Yet.

"You're right, I don't start my period yet. But at certain times of the month, I just, um just, have a hard time getting wet." My face was definitely on fire now.

I just lied to Gabe! About sex! I was officially the shittiest person in the universe. Make that the history of the universe.

"Oh, Baby Doll, don't be embarrassed. We don't have to do anything tonight." Gabe smiled at me reassuringly. "I'm just happy knowing that you want to."

Fuuucccckkkk! Again!

Guilt crawled through my body like a snake, chewing at my insides as it went. Even if I couldn't come, I could make sure that Gabe did. It was the least I could do for him.

I tightened my fingers around Gabe's cock, pumping up and down again. "I meant it when I said that I want to make you feel good. And just being with you this way, touching your cock, having it rub between my legs, feels so good."

I was definitely going to hell.

One of Gabe's hands found my boob again, while the other took his cock from my fingers, pushing it between my legs. We kissed, slow and deep while he moved his shaft up and down between my legs, pushing against my clit, harder and harder.

"Are you getting wet?" Gabe mumbled against my lips.

"I think so, this feels so good, please don't stop," I begged, fearing that if he did I wouldn't be able to start again.

"I'm so close Baby Doll, can I push inside you?" Gabe rasped as I drove my hips up further, meeting each of his thrusts.

"Don't stop Gabe, please, make me come. Just like this," I pleaded, knowing that I couldn't give, couldn't do, anything more.

At least not yet.

Gabe pushed his hand between us, using his thumb and forefinger to squeeze my clit. And that was it. Tension began to build between my legs until I wanted nothing more than to come. And I did. And then Gabe came. All over me.

"That was amazing," I said with a sigh. Relieved that I'd made Gabe come. Amazed that I'd actually managed to come.

It definitely wasn't one of the best orgasms I'd ever had. All of those explosive – animalistic – orgasms belonged to Ty. But right now, any orgasm with Gabe, was a good orgasm. And they would only get better.

Right?

A grin lit up Gabe's entire face as he looked down at me. "You're amazing Baby Doll. I'm so glad that I waited for you."

"I'm glad that you waited for me to come too," I returned with a grin. Feeling a hundred times better now. And not because I'd just had an orgasm.

"That's not exactly what I meant. I was talking about waiting for us to get together. You've never noticed that I haven't had a serious girlfriend for the past three years?"

"Yes," I said slowly, dread filling my body.

I was pretty sure that I didn't want to hear this.

"That's because I was in love with you. I am in love with you. No woman has ever compared." He pressed his lips to mine. "I tried a few times."

"Monica and Audrey?" I asked quietly.

Gabe nodded before continuing. "But it just never felt right being with someone else. That's when I decided that I wait for you. Wait until you were ready to be with me."

My heart sank and I knew that there was something seriously wrong with me. Instead of wanting to celebrate that the world's greatest guy was in love with me. Has been in love with me for the past three years. I wanted to cry.

"It was hell watching you with Jake. Actually, Eric was no picnic either."

An image of Gabe and Piper laughing together jumped into my head.

"What about Piper?"

"I didn't know that you and Piper were ever together. I'd be OK with that. Or even participating in that," Gabe added wiggling his eyebrows.

"Very funny Gabe," I replied. "I mean, it seemed like you were genuinely interested in Piper. I've never seen you even look at a woman that way."

OK, Gabe and I had just fooled around. For the first time. And now I was trying to convince him that he wanted another woman.

I was seriously warped.

"Then, I guess you've never seen the way that I look at you."

"Smooth Larson, but I'm being serious."

Why was I pushing this? Warped may not even cover how sick I actually was.

"Fine," Gabe huffed, rolling off me and onto his back, staring up at the ceiling. "Maybe if Piper didn't have a boyfriend, I might – stress, might – have been interested in her. Possibly." He looked at me again. "Why does this even matter anymore?"

"It doesn't. I guess I can just understand how watching me with Jake and

Eric felt. That's all."

Not exactly the truth. But not exactly a lie either.

The corners of Gabe's mouth turned up. "That's sweet Baby Doll. I'm feeling a little sticky. Want to take a shower together?"

Sweet? If Gabe only knew. I was anything but sweet.

"No, you go first. I just want to lay here for a bit. I kind of like feeling sticky from being with you."

Another lie. I was on a roll lately. I hated feeling sticky, but there was no way that I could shower. Naked. With Gabe.

Gabe pressed his lips against mine and I could feel him smile. "If you change your mind, you know where I'll be," he invited, getting up and heading for the bathroom.

Being with Gabe was so easy. And, my complete awkwardness aside, it was hard to deny that Gabe knew what he was doing - sexually. If he could make a, not-so-in-to-it, woman have an orgasm, then I could only imagine what else he could do. And I was in the position to take advantage of all those wonderful skills.

I just needed to stop feeling like I was cheating on Ty.

Warped. Yup. That was me.

Chapter 13 – Liv

Over the past three days Ty hadn't said a word to me and vice versa. Although I noticed him watching me again. A lot. And it made me sort of paranoid. Like waiting for the other shoe to drop.

He'd said that he'd wait for me to be free. But everything I knew about Ty, told me that he wasn't used to waiting. If he wanted something, he went after it. With both hands.

· · · · ·

"Hey everyone," Allison greeted as she climbed into Diesel's bus. "Here's the updated tour schedule." She passed by Liam, handing the piece of paper directly to Gabe.

"Thanks, Al," he returned studying the list of venue dates. A giant smile creeping across his face.

"Ah, I was wondering if you'd catch that," Allison commented, returning his grin. "Looks like we'll be seeing our friends Kismet at the next venue. They're a last minute addition."

My eyes met Allison's and it was obvious that she was watching for my reaction to this 'good' news. Apparently, Gabe's interest in Piper and vice versa hadn't escaped anyone the last time around.

"Nice," Gabe said, still grinning like a maniac. "It'll be good to see the girls again. They're amazing performers."

I looked at Gabe knowing exactly who he was stoked to see. And it wasn't all of the girls.

A weird sensation hit me as I watched Gabe look at the paper again. Was it jealousy?

Please let it be jealousy. That would be awesome.

Oh God, I was so screwed.

"A last minute addition?" I questioned, still trying to figure out what I was feeling.

"Yeah, I just got the update. Guess they had some extra money in the budget or something. Anyway, you guys will go on at nine pm instead of seven-thirty like usual. Kismet is planning to be there tomorrow afternoon. Which gives us some time to unwind together then set up for the concert the following evening."

"So the girls will be around for almost two days then?" Gabe asked, clearly interested.

"Actually we've tacked on an extra day after the concert. So looks like we'll be together for three days. That way we can tear down and rest a bit before hitting the road again," Allison shared.

"I thought we had an extra day at the next venue?" I asked, wondering why the schedule had shifted so suddenly. This hadn't happened even once in the past three months.

Very odd.

Allison shrugged. "I'm not too sure. I was just told to update the hotel and transportation arrangements."

"So, are the girls staying at our hotel?" Gabe jumped in, his grin widening by the second.

"That's next on my to-do list," Allison shared. "I have to book a couple of rooms for them. Hopefully they have something available near our rooms."

"That'd be great," Gabe enthused. "I just mean because we'll end up hanging out and it's easier if everyone is close together," he explained looking from Allison to me.

"Well, I'd better get going so we can hit the road. There's still a long drive ahead of us," Allison said. "See you guys at the next rest stop."

Gabe glanced at me, a sheepish look on his face, before peering down at the venue dates again.

· · · · ·

The next night, everyone had supper together at a funky restaurant that transformed into a nightclub in the evening. The food was delicious. The nightclub was jamming. But the evening as a whole, left something to be desired.

Gabe and Piper spent the entire time talking. Only to each other. And I had to spend my time pretending that I didn't notice everyone, especially Ty, watch me as Gabe and Piper acted like they were on their first date. Eyes trained on each other. Constant laughing. Subtle touching. Sexual chemistry so overt that it made everyone within a fifty-mile radius horny.

Except for me. I just wanted to be somewhere else. Anywhere else. Away from Ty. Which was the real problem.

Two and a half painful hours later, I couldn't do any more pretending, so faked a headache. Instead of coming with me, Gabe made up some bogus excuse about wanting to hear the next band. And right then, I could have cared less that he wanted to stay. I just needed to leave. So with a quick good-night to everyone, I trudged back to the hotel.

Alone and feeling absolutely pissy.

•   •   •   •   •

"Baby Doll," Gabe breathed into my ear as his hand pushed underneath my tank top. "You asleep?" He caressed my boob and it reminded me of the time when my friend's ex-boyfriend felt me up in high school. That incident left me feeling slightly dirty and, for some weird reason, so did this.

I feigned sleep. Not in the mood to deal with, or do anything with, Gabe.

"Liv," he tried again, planting wet, beer scented kisses down my neck. His hand trailing from my boob down into my sleep shorts.

Pretending to be asleep apparently wasn't going to cut it.

"Gabe!" I huffed, pulling his hand out of my shorts. Rolling to face him, I tried to make out his features in the darkened room. "Seriously, I was sleeping and have a huge headache."

"Oh, I forgot. Sorry, Baby Doll. Can I get you anything?" he asked brushing the hair back from my face.

"No - thank you."

"Go back to sleep," Gabe said quietly, planting a kiss on my forehead before climbing out of bed.

"Where are you going?" I demanded, suddenly on edge.

"I'm not really tired yet. Think I'll go and hang out with everyone," he answered, his voice getting fainter as he moved towards the door.

"Hang out with everyone? Or hang out with Piper?" I pushed, itching for a fight. For no real reason. I wasn't truly angry about Gabe hanging out with Piper instead of me. I was just angry – in general.

"Fuck Liv, it's not like I'm going over to, to, fuck her!" he snapped. "I told you before that I'm not interested in Piper. We just have a lot in common. That's all it is!"

A second later the door slammed shut and I laid in the dark hotel room. Feeling oddly empty.

Chapter 14 ~ Ty

Joy? No. Elation? No. Bliss? No. Even that word didn't sound right.

I couldn't think of the right word to describe the level of happiness that I was feeling today. I'd watched Liv walk out of the nightclub last night with a chip on her shoulder and anger in her eyes. And I knew that it wouldn't be long until her and Gabe were finished.

I also knew where she'd be – right now. Because I saw her huff out of the hotel lobby a few minutes ago, toting her back pack. And I knew, more than anything else, that I shouldn't follow her.

I definitely shouldn't follow her.

But that's exactly what I was going to do. Just as soon as I finished confirming the details for tonight's concert with Allison.

• • • • •

"Trouble in paradise?" I asked taking the seat beside Liv, our legs pressed together in the tight space.

I was seriously starting to love Starbucks. The tiny tables that forced you to almost sit on top of each other, the intimate feel of the place and, of course, the aroma of coffee.

All good in my books.

With a giant, and definitely exaggerated sigh, Liv looked over at me. "I'm seriously not in the mood for any of your shit today, Benson," she warned.

"Someone's grumpy. Wanna talk about it?"

"You'd just love that. Wouldn't you?" Liv hissed.

"Your wonderful mood wouldn't have anything to do with Gabe and

Piper, now would it?" I asked, watching Liv's eyes narrow.

"What about Gabe and Piper?"

"Exactly. What about Gabe and Piper?" I echoed, stretching my arm across the back of Liv's chair, leaning into her a little more.

"Nothing," she returned, but the look in her eyes read anger and hurt. Or, possibly, annoyance.

Possibly for me.

"Hmm, I just thought you might be upset that Gabe and Piper spent the night dancing, then hanging out in Piper's hotel room while you were stuck in your room. Alone and suffering. How's the headache, by the way?" I added, doing my best not to smirk.

Liv leaned in, putting her lips against my ear. "Fuck you," she whispered, her voice pure venom.

A chuckle ripped from my throat.

God, I loved her.

"Well, I know how to turn that frown upside down," I promised using my index fingers to push up the sides of Liv's mouth.

"Seriously?" she muttered as my fingers pressed into her skin. But her 'I may reach over and kill you at any moment' expression, softened. Slightly.

"I'll be right back," I said, planting a quick kiss on her cheek before heading towards the till.

Liv watched me the entire time. As I ordered. As I paid. As I waited. As I sauntered back to our table.

It made me think of the way she watched my face in the bus. When she was giving me head. Her eyes were filled with possessiveness and longing then. Just like they were now.

And I relished it. I needed it.

"Your order me lady," I said with a horrible English accent, setting down a plate filled with every type of baked good that Starbucks offered.

A tiny smile crept across Liv's face as she eyed the treats. "Do you think things are so bad between Gabe and I - that I need to eat my feelings?"

I had to laugh.

Even when she was pissy, my girl still had a great sense of humor.

"Unless there's something else you'd prefer to put in your mouth?" I made a fist, pumping it back and forth by my lips while I pushed my cheek out in time with the thrust of my hand.

"You're sick," Liv deadpanned, shoving half a cupcake into her mouth.

"Mmmm."

And there it was. That wonderful, erotic mmmm sound Liv made every time that she ate. It always made me completely horny. And today was no exception. Although now, I didn't care if Liv realized that she gave me a raging hard on. Because I wanted her.

I'd always want her.

"Actually, you're the sick one," I rallied. "I was just trying to get something out of my tooth." Liv grinned at me. "It's been stuck there for days. You wouldn't want to help a friend out? Maybe try to get it unstuck? Using your tongue or other parts of your body that, would perhaps, provide some lubrication."

Liv spewed little chucks of cupcake on to the table as she laughed. A big, hearty belly laugh.

"You're gross," I teased, handing her a napkin.

"So are you. Guess that's why we get along so well."

"That's the sweetest thing any woman has ever said to me," I replied putting my fingers together to make a heart shape. "Almost makes me want to kiss you."

Liv rolled her eyes. "You always want to kiss me. Among other things."

"I said - almost."

"Really?" Liv asked leaning in closer.

So close that I could smell her perfume and the herbal shampoo that she always used. I curled my fingers around the sides of the chair to keep from fisting my hands in her hair and pressing my mouth to hers.

"Really." I replied, my voice coming out a little deeper than usual.

A slow, knowing smile crept across Liv's face.

"So, if I said that you could kiss me. Right here. Right now. You wouldn't be interested?"

She was flat out flirting with me. YES!

"No." I barely managed to squeak that one word out. The woman was torturing me.

And I loved it. From the elated look on Liv's face, I guessed that she did too.

"I think that you should kiss me," she challenged. "But make it good. Make it count."

Oh my God, she really was torturing me!

"Not yet Darlin', but soon. When you're ready to be with me. And only me. I'll make it count. I'll make every kiss count," I promised.

· · · · ·

Three hours later, Liv and I headed into the hotel. Her back pack slung over one of my arms while the other wrapped around her waist. A hundred more things left to tell each other. And a hundred more things left to laugh about.

Half way through the lobby, I saw them. To my left, Gabe and Piper were in the common area, snuggled together on one of the leather couches, staring at an iPad. Gabe's arm was stretched out on the couch behind Piper's head while she leaned into his body. Her hand resting on his forearm. They looked like a couple. A happy couple.

And I couldn't have asked for anything more.

I knew that pointing them out would hurt Liv. Maybe even crush her a little. But I'd be there to pick up the pieces. And, it was for the greater good.

Our greater good.

"Liv," I said, stopping, nodding towards the seating area.

"What?" she asked with a smile. And I almost felt like an ass for ruining her good mood.

Almost.

I could tell the instant that she spotted them because the smile fell from her face and a look, somewhere between disbelief and rage, set in. I stood still, waiting to see what she was going to do. Happy that I wasn't on the receiving end of her anger – for a change.

Several seconds ticked by as we stood there, watching them. And I started to wonder if Liv was waiting for them to notice us. I sincerely hoped not, because I didn't see that happening anytime soon. They were too engrossed in each other.

Finally, she glanced up at me.

"Hmmm." Was all that I dared to say.

"Hmmm! What's that supposed to mean?" Liv asked, her tone sharp, her eyes hard.

Apparently even a hmmm was too much.

Realizing that anything I said right now would be wrong, I decided to push it. Anger the raging bull as the saying goes.

"Don't be pissy with me, Darlin'." I held my hands up, taking a step back. "Your boyfriend is the one making nice with another woman. I'm the innocent party here."

"Innocent is not a word that I would use to describe you. Ever," Liv returned, her expression miraculously evening out.

Making me wonder how she did that. She went from angry to teasing in a matter of seconds. Even after spending three months with this woman, she still baffled me.

"Ouch! Why are you always so mean to me?" I asked, pretending to be hurt.

"Why are you such a drama queen all of time," Liv retaliated. "Come on," she demanded grabbing my hand. Practically dragging me over to the couch where Gabe and Piper were cuddled up.

"Hi," she said, as we stood in front of the coffee table across from them.

But neither Gabe nor Piper looked up. They were oblivious to everything and everyone else.

It was funny – sort of.

"Hello, Gabe and Piper," Liv greeted in a much louder voice, drawing the attention of everyone nearby. Although I got the feeling that she couldn't have cared less.

That's my girl! Let them watch the show. Who gives a fuck?

Gabe glanced up. "Liv!" he exclaimed. An 'oh shit' expression replacing the grin on his face.

I watched Gabe shift away from Piper, pulling his arm from behind her head. Then his eyes narrowed on me, honing in on our entwined hands.

"What are you two doing?" he asked, his eyes moving from Liv's. To mine. To our hands. And then back to Liv again.

"Ty was helping me with my thesis," Liv replied, tightening her grip on my hand. Although, I had no intention of letting her go anyway. "I thought you were at the concert hall setting up? With the guys," she fired back.

"We just got back," Piper cut in, her voice as acidic as the expression on her face. "And Gabe was just showing me the video he took of us during sound check."

Piper looked at me with clear disapproval in her navy blue eyes. But that was nothing new. I'd known Piper for four years and, so far, she rarely approved of anything I did when it came to women. She absolutely hated my ex-fiance. And made no bones about telling both Mindy and me that. Then, when I was single again, she hated the one-night-stand thing I did. And had no qualm about letting me know that either.

So, I fully expected to be getting an earful about Liv. But that was Piper. You always knew where you stood with her. And I respected her for that. Which made me wonder what this Gabe thing was about. Because she had a boyfriend. Actually she'd been with him for the entire time that I'd known her. And I was pretty sure that nothing had changed on that front.

"That was super nice of him. To video you," Liv replied dryly, not fazed by Piper's bitchy attitude at all. Her eyes swung back to Gabe. "We'll let you two get back to whatever you were doing. Let's go," she commanded, pushing me towards the front of the coffee table, her fingers digging into my palm.

"Liv," Gabe called as she pulled me towards the elevator. "Where are you going?" he demanded, catching up with us. "I think we need to talk." He looked at me, clearly wanting to be alone with Liv.

But that wasn't going to happen. Unless Liv ordered me to leave, I was staying put.

"We'll talk later. Ty and I are going out for supper." Liv turned around, storming through the lobby with me in tow.

But I wasn't complaining. Apparently we were having supper together. Just her. Just me. If a guilty feeling hadn't started to eat at my insides, this would have been one of the best days ever.

· · · · ·

Liv

"Hey, Baby Doll," Gabe greeted as he crept into our hotel room several hours after the concert had ended. "You still pissed at me?"

"I'm not sure," I replied turning the volume on the television down.

Gabe kicked off his shoes then sank down on the bed beside me, an apologetic look on his face. "I'm sorry about this afternoon. But, just for the record, nothing happened. Nothing is happening between me and Piper." He waited, looking at me. Obviously wanting me to say the same about me and Ty.

And nothing had happened. Ty and I went out for supper, then hung out in his hotel room until he left for the concert hall. Once I was sure that Gabe had left too, I went back to our room. Going to watch the guys had zero appeal for me tonight. And, with the weird mood I was in, I knew that there was a good chance Piper and I would get into it. I hadn't missed the way that she stuck up for Gabe. Or shot daggers at me. And I had zero intention of taking any shit from her.

Even still, I had no beef with Piper. Gabe stuff aside, she seemed pretty decent.

Was that weird not to hate the woman who was obviously interested in my boyfriend? Who my boyfriend was obviously interested in?

I should probably get professional help.

"Hmmm," I replied shrugging my shoulders. Wanting him to sweat about Ty for a while. I felt vindictive tonight for some reason. "I'm surprised you're back so early. It's just past one o'clock."

The bands and crew had gone for a bite to eat after the show. To give him credit, Gabe had texted, asking if I wanted to join them. But I definitely didn't. Sitting through one meal, watching the Gabe and Piper show, had been more than enough.

Gabe rolled his eyes, his lips pressing together into a thin line. "Whatever. You could have gone with us." I could see him getting annoyed, and it was somehow satisfying.

Something was definitely wrong with me.

"So does this mean that you're in for the night?"

Gabe sighed. "Actually, I just wanted to stop in and check on you. We were thinking about grabbing a beer at the pub next door. I thought you might want to come," he added, eyeing me warily.

This was the first time in the history of our friendship where I wondered if Gabe actually wanted me to go with him. A lump formed in my throat as the realization that – we – were – broken, set in.

"Gabe, we can't go on like this," I said quietly. "I don't want to fight with you anymore."

Relief flooded his face. Gabe leaned in pressing his lips to mine. "I don't want to fight with you anymore either, Baby Doll," he agreed, obviously misunderstanding the depth of what I was saying. "Why don't we just stay in for the rest of the night?"

"You really don't want to go out?" I asked skeptically.

"No, I'd rather just hang out with you."

"What about Piper? And I'm not asking to be mean or pissy," I clarified.

Gabe shrugged. "Piper had to call her boyfriend so I'm not even sure that she's going."

And there it was.

I'd bet my right arm THAT was the reason Gabe didn't mind staying in for the rest of the night. It was probably the reason he'd come back to 'check on me' too.

"Her boyfriend is hyper needy," Gabe continued, running his fingers through my hair. "He must have called her at least five times during supper. Then another dozen times after supper. It was even starting to drive me crazy."

"He must have really needed to talk to her. Maybe something important happened?" I rationalized, wondering if Gabe realized how jealous he sounded.

And it had nothing to do with me. Ah, the irony.

"No," Gabe replied rolling his eyes. "Piper said that he always calls her a million times a day when she's on the road. I don't understand why she just doesn't break up with him?"

"Maybe she loves him?" I watched Gabe's face cloud over.

"I don't think so," he quickly denied. "You should see her expression when they talk. It's closer to annoyance than love. And she doesn't answer his calls most of the time either. No, she definitely isn't in love with him," Gabe said with conviction, but I wasn't sure if he was trying to convince himself or me. "I just don't get it. Why would she stay with him?"

"People stay together for all sorts of reasons Gabe," I answered, seeing my chance to turn the conversation back to us. To our relationship.

I'd tried to make it work. I really did. But there was no way that could happen when I felt the way I did about Ty. And when Gabe obviously felt the way that he did about Piper. If Gabe and I were truly meant for each other, neither of those feelings would have materialized.

Now I just needed to make Gabe realize that.

"What's wrong, Baby Doll?" he asked tentatively, studying my face.

"Gabe, you know that I love you with all of my heart," I began. My heart pumping double time in anticipation of what might happen.

I drew in a deep breath, mustering up the courage to do what I should have done days ago.

Break up with Gabe.

"You know that I'd do anything for you. You'll always be my brother from another mother." I forced a grin but it felt more like a lopsided frown.

A pained expression crossed Gabe's face and I suddenly felt like chickening out. Like not telling him how I really felt.

"Your brother?" Gabe echoed. I nodded, a giant lump forming in my throat. My resolve dissipating with each passing second. "Liv, I'm NOT like your brother. I'm your boyfriend. We, we were going to make love." His hand fisted into my hair while his face crumpled. "We made out. Seriously made out. And you only do that with guys you're interested in – romantically."

"I know, but," I choked out, my voice already raw with emotion.

This was so much harder than I ever imagined.

"That's it Baby Doll!" Gabe exclaimed with hope in his eyes. "I know how to make us work as a couple. I mean really work." He paused, looking at me with such intensity that I worried about what he was going to say next. "We need to make love," Gabe stated with absolute certainty and elation.

Make love! I could barely make out with Gabe. That was definitely not the answer to our problems.

"Gabe, I"

"I know what you're going to say," he interrupted.

Doubtful. Very doubtful.

"But, just think about it Baby Doll. We all know that you have this romantic ideal of making love." A grin spread across his lips.

"Romantic ideal? At least that's nicer than saying I have a warped sense of sex," I replied.

"Well, I've always been nicer than my sister."

So true. Laina rarely sugar coated things. Piper reminded me of her – in that way.

"It's no secret that your heart and body are connected," Gabe continued. "That's one of the things I love most about you. We're kind of alike in that way."

That was also true. Unlike most of the guys I knew, Gabe never slept around. He had to seriously like a woman before having sex with her. And he hadn't liked many women.

But he loved me. And I was about to crush what he thought we had.

"So, the way I see it, making love just makes sense for us Baby Doll. It's going to cement the way we feel about each other. Take our relationship to the next level."

Gabe waited expectantly for me to say something. To agree with him, but I couldn't. Because I couldn't make love with someone that I wasn't in love with. No matter how perfect we seemed for each other.

"Gabe," I whispered, running my fingers over the stubble on his chin. "I love you so much." I watched Gabe's face harden and his eyes narrow.

"But you're not in love with me," he cut in. "You're in love with HIM. Just say it, Liv," Gabe demanded, rolling off the bed. "Say the goddamn words!" he shouted, standing beside me. His entire body vibrating with anger. "I'm so sick of HIM coming between us. Ruining things for us," he roared, his fists clenching into tight balls.

I drew in a deep breath, sitting up. Knowing that this was our moment of truth. I couldn't hide from it or wish it away any longer.

"Ty's not the only one between us, Gabe," I reasoned, hoping to soften the blow. Hoping that he'd see what everyone else already saw. "Piper is standing right there next to him. Admit it. If Piper was single, you'd be with her right now. Be honest with me, Gabe."

"That's so not true!" he seethed, his cheeks turning from pink to red. "You can lie to yourself about Ty and about my feelings for Piper, but don't lie to me. You never wanted to be with me. Did you? You were never GOING to be with me. Were you?"

"I can't help the way that I feel Gabe. I wish I could because then I would choose you every second of every day."

I wished he knew just how true that was.

"Ty's never going to love you the way that I do. He'll never treat you as good as I do."

"I know that. You're absolutely right. And I know that Ty and I probably wouldn't work out anyway, but it doesn't stop the way that I feel. I truly wish it did. And being with me won't stop you from wanting to be with Piper. I wish it worked that way, but it doesn't. Trust me."

"I don't give a shit about Piper," Gabe fumed although the look in his eyes clearly said otherwise. "Maybe if my girlfriend showed me a tiny bit of love, I wouldn't be attracted to Piper at all," he fired. "I'm not the one with the loyalty problem, Liv." Gabe stared at me, his eyes hard and unyielding. "I know what would solve both of our problems. And so do you."

Like lightening, Gabe moved towards me. Pulling me against him, crushing his mouth against mine like he had in the hotel hallway.

Taking me by complete surprise. Again.

I pushed hard against Gabe's shoulders and he lifted his mouth from mine, our eyes locking. The anguish on his face was absolutely heart breaking. But then, I probably was breaking his heart.

"You always fall hard for a guy once you sleep with him. Fall for me," he pleaded, his face softening. "We'd be so good together. You know we would. It would fix everything for both of us."

"Gabe," I said quietly, reaching up to cup the side of his face. "I'm not in love with you. I really want to be. I tried to be."

God, this was so hard.

"But us making love isn't going to change that," I added gently.

"Let's try," he whispered, a glimmer of hope still flickering in his eyes.

I shook my head. "Gabe, please, this is wrong. You're not in love with me either. I think you're in love with the idea of me. On paper, we're the perfect couple. But in real life, we're perfect friends. Best friends."

"Fuck you and fuck Ty!" Gabe exploded, letting me go, taking a step backward. He reached over, ripping the alarm clock out of the wall, throwing it against the opposite wall with such force that it shattered, spewing pieces of jagged plastic throughout the room. "I'm so fucking done with you. Go be with that womanizing scum bag. I hope he breaks your heart. I never want to see you again!"

Gabe jammed his feet into his sneakers then stormed out of the room, slamming the door shut behind him.

I'd hurt Gabe. Really hurt him. But we didn't belong together.

I just hoped that with a little time and some space, he'd be able to see that. And somehow forgive me.

Now I needed to leave. I needed to go back to Vancouver and give Gabe some time. I also needed to give myself some time. To put things into perspective.

Within minutes I'd checked the bus schedule and shoved all of my belongings into my duffle. After scribbling a please-forgive-me note for Gabe, I hurried into the hallway, eager to put some distance between me and this place.

But, apparently, that wasn't going to be so easy.

Leaning against the wall outside of my room, looking straight at me, was Ty.

"Whoa there, Darlin'. Where are you going?" he asked as I strode past, heading towards the elevator bank.

"Home," I replied, not bothering to stop. There was a bus leaving in an hour and I intended to be on it.

"It's almost two o'clock in the morning, Liv," Ty called from behind me. "Liv, just a minute," he huffed, catching up. "What's wrong?"

"I'm not in the mood, Ty. Just leave me alone," I warned, quickening my pace, desperate to escape. The realization of what I'd done to Gabe. How deeply I'd hurt him. Had began to sink in and I didn't know how long I'd be able to hold it together.

With one long stride Ty stepped in front of me, turning around so that we were face to face again. My bag dropping to the carpeted floor as I slammed into his chest.

"Why are you leaving, in the middle of the night?" he demanded, leaning down to pick up my bag. Slinging it over his shoulder.

A giant sigh escaped my lips as I fought to hold myself together. "Gabe and I just had a huge fight. I'm so done with everything. My bag please." I grabbed the strap, attempting to yank it from Ty's shoulder - but he held on.

One corner of Ty's mouth turned up before he corrected it. But I saw that smirk. Or at least the start of it.

Ass-wipe.

"So that's what the door slamming was about. Look Liv, I'm sorry that you and Gabe are fighting," he said, although his voice was too cheerful to sound believable. "But it's too late to be wandering around alone."

"Thanks for the tip, Dad. My bag, please," I demanded, holding my hand out.

"You're going back to Vancouver?"

I nodded. "There's a bus that leaves right away so I NEED to get going." I didn't have the time or energy for our usual cat and mouse game right now. Grabbing the strap of my bag, I pulled again - hard.

"There's no way that I'm letting you go to the bus station alone, at this time of night," Ty reiterated, easily holding my bag in place. "I can't believe that Gabe would either. He's usually over the top protective of you. What did you guys fight about?" He stared at me expectantly. "Must have been serious if you're leaving and he's not trying to stop you," he added when I didn't offer an explanation.

"My bag!" I demanded again holding my hand out. Anger starting to mix with the wretchedness that was already coursing through my system.

"I'm not letting you leave, Liv."

Fuck! I didn't need this right now.

"I'm a grown ass woman!" I fumed. "You know what. Just keep the fricken bag, you love looking through my things anyway. Enjoy yourself." I stepped around him, taking as long a stride as my legs would allow. I took another before Ty's fingers closed around my wrist. With fire raging in my belly, I swung around. "Let me go!" I seethed using my free hand to try to pry Ty's fingers from my arm.

"Owe, that hurts," he protested grabbing my hand. Holding that one hostage as well. "What are you fighting with Gabe about anyways?"

I shot him my best 'go to hell' look, still struggling to free my hands.

"Liv, I can't let you go. Not in the middle of the night," Ty reasoned, his voice suddenly soft and cajoling. "You can sleep in my room, then leave in the morning if you want." I opened my mouth to tell him to fuck off. But before I could get a word out, he added, "I'll sleep on the floor. I promise."

We stared at each other in silence, waiting to see who would break first. "I'm not letting you leave, Liv," Ty repeated in a firm voice. "You can either go back and spend the night with Gabe or stay with me. Your choice."

The irony of Ty saying that my only options were to sleep with Gabe or him, hit me like a ton of bricks. Squashing my anger and setting my grief free.

"If it wasn't for you then I might be able to 'spend' the night with Gabe and there wouldn't be a problem," I muttered under my breath. "Please, Ty, let me go," I cried, my emotions churning like an oncoming storm.

"Wait. You're leaving because of me?" Ty asked, his eyes sweeping across my stricken face.

"Not exactly. You're only part of the problem."

"Oh shit," Ty exclaimed, his eyes lighting up. "I get it! You can't have sex with Gabe - because of me. Because you're in love with me," he added, a look of absolute elation on his face.

I couldn't do this right now.

"Let me go," I pleaded, coming undone. Big, fat tears began to roll down my cheeks as I stared at Ty's fingers wrapped around my wrists.

"Oh, Darlin', I'm so sorry," he whispered, pulling me into a tight hug. "I didn't mean to make things worse. Just talk to me. We can figure everything out."

Familiar laughter floated down the hallway.

"Sounds like Dave and Farah. Let's go before they see you like this."

I nodded weakly, letting Ty guide me to his room. He unlocked the door and we stepped inside as their voices neared. Without looking back, I moved further into the room, collapsing on the bed, burying my head into the crook of one arm. This summer was supposed to be the most amazing experience of my life. Instead my life was collapsing around me.

The bed dipped as Ty laid down beside me, gently stroking my hair. "Talk to me, Liv," he pleaded, his voice soft and low.

I rolled over, staring into Ty's deep brown eyes for a moment before shifting closer to him. Resting my head against his shoulder. He wrapped his arms around me, pulling our bodies together. A comfortable silence enveloping us as we laid together.

"Liv," Ty finally whispered. "Look at me, please."

Shifting back, I looked at Ty, his face filled with concern. And love.

And that was it. Suddenly, I knew that I needed him. Like I needed air.

Reaching up, I traced the line of Ty's bottom lip with my forefinger. Watching his expression change from worry to longing. Intensity building between us like a slow burn. Softly, I pressed my lips against his, our breath mixing together.

"Are you and Gabe still together?" Ty asked, his voice already ragged.

"I ended it tonight."

"Oh," he breathed, a range of emotions flickering across his face like a roulette wheel.

Apparently, tonight had been emotionally draining for both of us.

And now, all I wanted to do was forget - everything. Except for the way that Ty made me feel.

I ran my hand down Ty's back, cupping his ass, pushing my pelvis suggestively against his cock. And like magic, it came to life - growing, hardening. For me. The ache between my legs began to grow too as I planted slow, wet kisses along Ty's neck.

And I needed more. I needed to feel Ty's hands on my body.

Pushing him back, I climbed on top, pulling my t-shirt off. Watching his eyes grow dark with desire as they raked over my naked skin.

"Make me feel good Ty," I pleaded, undoing my bra, then pulling his hands up to my breasts. My body already vibrating with anticipation of having Ty touch me.

His hands covered my boobs. His fingers pinching and tugging my nipples as we stared into each other's eyes.

"Yes, that's so good," I muttered, rocking against his cock, feeling a gush of wetness between my legs. Pulling me down, Ty's lips replaced his fingers, sucking on my swollen nipples. Making them deliciously sore.

And I wanted harder. I wanted more.

Like he was inside my head, Ty sucked on my nipple harder, using his teeth to bite and scrape against it. Making my stomach tighten, and the ache between my legs intensify. A giant moan escaped from my lips. Needing to touch him, to please him, I reached down undoing his pants, freeing his dick. My hands ran up and down his long shaft, then over the already wet head.

"I love the way you smell. I love the way you taste," Ty mumbled against my tits.

"I want to taste you," I replied starting to move down so that I could take his cock into my mouth.

"My turn first," Ty replied holding me in place. "Take your shorts off then put your pussy on my face. I want to lick you."

"But I'm already really wet," I mumbled as Ty dragged my shorts down.

"I can feel that," he agreed, running two long fingers in between the folds of my pussy. "But I'm going to make you so wet that you drip down the sides of your legs."

With one fluid motion, Ty shimmied my shorts off while sliding down between my parted legs. I reached out, gripping the headboard as Ty pushed two fingers deep inside of me. Watching as they plunged in and out of my entrance.

"I could stare at your pussy all night," he shared. "I love the way you open up wider and wider as you get wetter and wetter. For me."

He worked a third finger inside and I gasped with the pressure. And the pleasure.

"Fuck," I hissed moving my hips against his fingers, wanting to feel them even deeper.

Then Ty's tongue grazed my clit. And my insides turned into molten lava. Hot and thick and running.

"That's my girl, come for me. Come on me," Ty encouraged before he sucked my clit into his mouth. His tongue swirled around and around my sensitive nub, pulling it in and out of his hot mouth while his fingers plunged ruthlessly in and out of my throbbing pussy.

I was on fire for him. And nothing in the world ever felt better.

A giant shudder racked my body as I came. Long and hard. Wave after wave of pleasure rushing through me.

When I finally stilled, Ty pulled his fingers out of my pussy but continued to lick and suck on my swollen clit.

"Baby, wait," I said, flipping around so that we were in the sixty-nine position.

"Fuck, I love you," Ty hissed as I bent over taking his cock deep in my mouth while I spread my legs, pressing my pussy on his face again.

I sucked him, just the way I knew he liked – deep so that the tip of his cock touched the back of my throat. Again and again, I slid his cock in and out of my mouth while I caressed his balls, running my fingers along the sensitive area in between his legs.

Again and again, Ty licked my pussy, muttering incomprehensible words against the wetness.

"Darlin', I'm so close," Ty breathed, "you need to stop."

"Come," I urged, sucking harder.

All of sudden I was laying on my back while Ty hovered over me, our eyes locking. I watched as he ran the back of one hand across his mouth, wiping my wetness away.

Gradually, the predatory look in Ty's eyes melted away into something else. Something soft and sweet and loving. Making my heart clench.

"Darlin'," Ty said, his voice low and tentative, "I want to come inside of you this time. I want to make love to you?"

He was telling me what he wanted. But he was also asking me.

This was it. Our moment of truth. Once we made love, there'd be no turning back. We both knew it. And I wanted it.

Wrapping my legs around his waist, I moved my hips up, waiting for Ty to push inside of me. Pure happiness shone from his face as he realized what I was doing.

"Are you sure Liv? We can wait. If you're not ready," Ty said but I knew that he didn't want to wait any more.

Neither did I.

"I'm ready. Make love to me, Ty."

He lowered his body. Slowly pushing inside of me. Our eyes focused on each other. Our hands entwined.

"You're so beautiful Liv," he breathed, moving down so that our lips brushed. Softly and sweetly, Ty kissed me like we had all the time in the world.

And I wished that we could stay just like this – forever.

Gradually – very gradually - he began moving. Sliding his cock in and out. Each stroke pulling out a bit further, then pushing in a bit deeper than the last. While his tongue did the same to my mouth. Sampling. Tasting. Devouring.

"I want to make love to you all night," Ty breathed in my ear.

"Yes, this is so good," I said feeling like a spring that was being wound so tight, it might snap at any moment.

"I'm going to make you come all night long," Ty promised as his hand pushed in between our bodies.

My lips stilled and my breathing hitched as Ty's thumb began to rub against my throbbing clit.

"Does that feel good, Darlin'?" he asked.

"Oh God, yes, fuck me harder Ty," I moaned against his neck. "I'm almost there."

Ty rocked into me harder and faster, bringing me to the edge of oblivion. Again.

"Liv," Ty rasped weaving his hands into the back of my hair, holding our faces together as we came.

When our breathing calmed, Ty rolled us onto our sides still joined together. Pulling my leg up onto his hip, he drew me even closer, planting gentle kisses on my lips.

"Tell me that was real," he mumbled against my mouth.

"It was real," I returned, feeling like I was in heaven. "We're real."

Chapter 15 ~ Ty

I barely slept last night, but woke up feeling better than I had in my entire life. Liv and I made love all night. Over and over again. And I was ready to be inside of her. Again. Actually I'd been awake and ready for almost an hour, but the feel of Liv sleeping naked in my arms was just too good. I couldn't wake her. Instead, I reveled in the feel of her soft, warm skin pressing against mine.

She was mine now. And I was never going to let her go.

A sigh escaped Liv's lips as she stretched.

"Morning sunshine," I greeted when her eyes opened, finding me watching her. "I was wondering when you were going to get up."

She planted a slow kiss on my lips. "Morning." A smile lit up her face. "How long have you been up?"

She was so beautiful. I was the luckiest bastard in the entire world.

"Almost an hour." I pressed my lips to hers again, sliding my hand around to cup her breast. Running my thumb over her nipple.

"Why didn't you wake me?" she mumbled against my mouth, wrapping her leg around my waist. Pushing against my hard-on.

"I wanted to," I admitted, moving my head back so that I could see her again. "But you were so peaceful and it felt good just to hold you." I paused, trying find the courage to tell Liv how I was feeling. Knowing that we needed to be open, if this was going to work. "Honestly, I'm afraid that this is a dream and I'll wake up alone. That you won't want to be with me."

There, I'd said it. I put my fear out there. Now, the ball was in Liv's court.

"Baby, it's not a dream," she assured me, maneuvering so that my cock pushed into her already wet pussy. "I'll always want to be with you. I love you."

Fuck, she was everything that I ever wanted. And more. So much more.

"I love you too," I returned, with a smile so wide that my face hurt.

I slid my fingers between us, finding her clit. She sucked in a huge breath as I started rubbing it, up and down, while I pushed my cock, in and out of her entrance. Our eyes fixed on each other.

"We still have some things to work out, but nothing is going to keep us apart now," she breathed as I pushed harder on her sensitive nub. Her wetness spreading, making both of us damp.

"Are you sure, Liv?" I rasped, wanting to hear her say it again. My fingers still rubbing back and forth against the exact spot that I knew turned Liv's insides into liquid. "Because I can't bear to think that this is real. That you're mine. That I can touch you like this whenever I want. And then lose you. If you're not one hundred percent sure that you want to be with me. Please just tell me now."

Liv moaned softly as she worked her hips against mine. Pushing my cock deeper and faster into her tight center.

"I'm one hundred and ten percent sure, Ty. I'm going to show you how much I want to be with you, every day." Her lips crashed against mine with a hunger so raw that it sent shivers down my spine.

"You're all that I've ever wanted Liv. I'm going to make you so happy," I promised as she came apart and then, so did I.

• • • • •

After, we just laid there, still joined together, our lips brushing, our hands exploring. And it was perfect. But I knew that there was more we needed to talk about.

Gabe, for starters.

Although I didn't want to bring him up. I had to. Because I had to know if Liv was going to stay with me for the rest of the tour or go back to Vancouver.

I desperately wanted her to stay.

But I also realized how hard that might be, given Gabe's feelings for her. Regardless of his attraction to Piper, there was still something special between him and Liv. And I'd already helped to hurt Gabe enough.

Fuck, I was the orchestrator behind hurting Gabe. Using Piper to cause that huge fight between him and Liv last night. And, even though it worked out in my favor - hopefully in everyone's favor, eventually - I still felt like shit because of it.

Because of all of it.

Gabe was a genuinely good guy. He just didn't belong with Liv.

I did.

Our kisses slowed and I lifted my head, meeting Liv's eyes. A smile spreading across her lips.

"What now?" she asked, and I wondered if she could actually read my mind.

I wished that I could read hers because she still surprised the hell out of me most of the time.

"That's exactly what I'm wondering. I want you to stay and finish the tour off. As my girlfriend. But I get that it might be weird, and difficult, given your relationship with Gabe."

"Oh. I hadn't thought that far yet." Liv's eyebrows pulled together. "I think I should probably go back to Vancouver today. I just can't stay and do that to Gabe. It's still too raw between us."

"While I hate the thought of being away from you. Now that we're finally together. We are together – right?" I needed confirmation.

Just once more.

"Yes," Liv answered with a grin. "We're together."

"Just checking." I returned her grin. "Well, it's only a couple of weeks. Then, when I get back to Van, we can figure everything out. You should probably move in with me," I tried, "it would make everything a lot easier."

"Really?"

I nodded, a perma-grin fixed to my face. Having Liv move in with me would be like the icing on my cake. I knew that she wasn't ready for it. But I sure was.

"Can we back up the commitment bus a few spaces please?" Liv suggested.

"Can't blame a guy for trying when he's got the world's most amazing girlfriend. Just so you know, I plan to have you married and knocked up within a year."

Liv chuckled. "And who are you planning on marrying me to?"

I rolled on top of her, tickling her sides until she was panting with laughter. "Very funny," I huffed. Then I kissed her, tenderly, sweetly. Pouring all of my feelings into that one moment. "Darlin'," I muttered against her lips, "I love you."

Liv pushed me back and I thought that was it. I'd gone too far. I looked down at her, expecting to see fear or anger on her face, but instead, there was love. Pure love.

"I love you too," she said and my heart exploded with happiness.

. . . . .

Liv

I knocked on the hotel room door, holding my breath as I waited for someone to answer. Ty had gone to get us something to eat. Giving me the opportunity to – hopefully - start mending fences. I had a few hours until my bus left for Vancouver and I intended to make the most of them.

"Liv," Piper said dryly, her eyes narrowing as she stood in the doorway. It was almost noon and she was still in her pj's. Her eyes smudged with the remnants of black liner. Her short fushia hair sticking up every which way. "If you're looking for Gabe, he's not here." She pushed the door wide open so that I could see inside. "Maybe try Liam and Will's room."

"I'm not looking for Gabe, I came to see you actually," I explained, trying to hold my resolve in place. Piper was the first stop on my road to redemption.

She made a sweeping motion with her hand, inviting me in. "Guess I shouldn't be surprised about that." She closed the door, shuffling behind me into the room. "Look Liv, I know it was super late or super early, I guess, when Gabe got back to your room this morning. But we were just talking. He was upset about the fight you guys had and needed to talk it through. THAT was it. Despite what you think, nothing is happening between us."

"Gabe came here last night?" I asked, completely surprised. I never even considered that he'd confide in Piper. Although given the situation, it made total sense.

"To talk – yes," Piper reiterated plopping down on the bed. Eyeing me like I was about to steal something. Or maybe attack her.

"So Gabe talked to you about our relationship?" I asked, wondering how much he had actually told Piper. She nodded. "Hmm, what did he tell you?"

"That he loves you and thinks the world of you. That he hoped you two could make it work."

"COULD make it work?" I asked, not missing the past tense. Another nod. "And," I pushed, trying to gain some insight into what she was thinking and what exactly Gabe had said to her. Piper merely shrugged.

Ugh, this was like pulling teeth. She wasn't giving me anything.

"Was Gabe OK when he left?" I tried again.

"If you want to know something about Gabe. You should ask Gabe. Not me."

We stared at each other for a moment, clearly sizing one another up.

"Good advice, but that's a bit difficult right now," I shared. "I think Gabe needs a bit of time to cool off before we talk." Piper rolled her eyes.

And I wanted to smack her. This was like talking to a three year old.

"It's a Gabe thing Piper, trust me," I explained, trying to make her understand. Working to keep my temper in check. "He needs space to work things out. He's always been this way."

"Gabe thinks that you're in love with Ty," Piper spit out, her voice hard and judgmental. "I told him you'd be nuts to want Ty instead of him. Don't get me wrong, I love Ty. He's a great guy and a good friend, but relationship-wise, he's damaged. His ex screwed him over big time and he's busy making every other woman pay for it. Word of advice, Liv, don't get involved with Ty. You'll regret it."

I stared at Piper, unsure of what to say. I hadn't expected us to have a heart-to-heart chat about Ty.

"Gabe, on the other hand," Piper continued leaning forward, staring daggers at me, "is amazing. He's the kind of guy who'd do anything for you. He loves you and you're breaking his heart," she hissed getting up from the bed. Moving directly in front of me. "The worse thing is that you can't even fathom just how lucky you are to have Gabe. You so don't deserve him." Her eyes bore into mine as we stood toe to toe.

And I wondered if she was going to punch me. It looked like she wanted to. Big time.

"I agree," I said quietly. "I don't deserve Gabe." I watched a look of surprise sweep across Piper's pretty face. "He's the most incredible guy I know. He's honest and loving and smart and beautiful. Inside and out. He's my best friend, or at least I hope he still is." I paused, swallowing the lump that had lodged in my throat. "And he deserves way more than I can ever give him. Gabe deserves a woman who loves him with all of her heart. Who's madly in love with him." Pause. "But that's not me."

"You're not in love with Gabe?" Piper said slowly, skeptically. "You don't want to be with him?"

I shook my head. "Gabe's right. I'm in love with Ty." I held up my hand as Piper opened her mouth. "I know that Ty's a work in progress and, trust me, I've tried to fight my feelings for him. Let's face it, Gabe would be the perfect choice for me. But I just can't make myself feel, or in Ty's case not feel, something." I shrugged my shoulders, not knowing how else to explain it.

Ty and I were like a hurricane. Wild, oddly beautiful – and a force of nature beyond anyone's control.

"Did Gabe tell you that he's not in love with me either?"

Sheer surprise swept over Piper's face again. "You're so wrong Liv. Gabe said that he loves you with all of his heart," she asserted. "That you two are perfect for each other."

"We are perfect for each other and he does love me, he's just not in love with me," I clarified. Feeling my resolve strengthen.

"Are you sure about that?"

"Positive. Ask him."

"Then why are you two together? If you aren't in love with Gabe and he's not in love with you. Then what the fuck?" Piper stared at me expectantly.

"You said it, sister." I cracked a grin. "Gabe's gonna kill me for telling you all this, but you need to know."

"I need to know why?" Piper asked slowly, but I got the distinct impression that she knew exactly what I was about to say.

"Because I see the way that you two look at each other. There's something there, Piper."

"You're wrong Liv," she said vehemently. "I have a boyfriend. It's sort of serious."

"Sort of serious," I reiterated with a nod. "Well, you can deny your feelings for Gabe all you want. But it won't make them go away. Trust me. I'm the queen of denial." I turned, heading towards the door. "Thanks for the talk Piper, and for being there for Gabe last night," I said over my shoulder.

"Liv," Piper called as I reached the door.

"You never told me why you and Gabe were together in the first place."

"Ask Gabe," I replied, before slipping back into the hallway. Hoping to get back to the room before Ty did. I wanted to be naked when he walked in.

I decided to take the stairs, sprinting up them two at a time. Feeling good about my talk with Piper. It was obvious that she and Gabe had a lot to work out, but at least they could start with a clean slate.

As I yanked opened the stairwell door, I heard Ty's melodic voice. Apparently, I wasn't going to beat him to the room.

Guess we'd just have to get naked together.

"Don't worry, sweetheart, everything will be OK," Ty said, his voice soft and soothing.

Sweetheart?

I stopped cold. Slowly, I slid the door almost shut again, leaving just a crack so that I could hear what Ty was saying. Piper's warning blared in my mind like a fog horn, unleashing my worst fear.

He was playing me.

"What am I going to do?" a feminine voice moaned. "Richard called off the wedding. He cancelled my credit cards and closed our joint bank account. And took away everything! I'm broke and homeless!" A feminine sob echoed down the hallway.

Richard? Wedding? Relief flooded my body. This woman definitely wasn't with Ty. I was an idiot.

I opened the door just enough so that I could peek out. Ty and a tall, very thin, very pretty, blond woman stood a few feet down the hallway facing each other. From this angle I could only see her face and the back of Ty's head. Tears streamed from her eyes as she held onto his arm.

"Go back to Richard and work it out," he suggested.

Good idea. There were only a few hours left until my bus boarded. And there were still things that I wanted to do with Ty. To Ty.

"He'll never take me back!" she wailed, falling against Ty's chest as another sob racked her body. She leaned into him, her arms snaking around his waist.

Interesting.

"Don't say that. I'm sure you can work it out," he soothed, lightly patting her back with one hand while tucking the other into his front pocket.

After a moment Ty stepped back and the woman looked up. "He, he," she stuttered, "found out that I'm pregnant."

"You're pregnant?" Ty returned and I didn't have to see his face to know just how surprised he was.

This sort of felt like watching a soap opera.

The lady nodded as more tears ran down her cheeks. "Two months. I just found out."

"Two months ago?" Ty asked, his voice higher than I'd ever heard it before.

Weird.

"Ty, we both know where I was two months ago." She paused, drawing in a deep breath. "Richard knows that the baby isn't his and so do you," she said slowly, meaningfully.

I watched her reach for Ty's hand, placing it against her belly as my stomach heaved.

Or maybe I was watching a horror show.

"Oh fuck!" Ty exclaimed clearly shocked, his hand still pressed against the woman's flat torso.

"I need you, Ty," she pleaded. "The baby needs you. You're not going to walk away from me again. Are you?" I watched the lady's lip quiver as she stared up at him. "Really, this is all your fault. I mean this," she rubbed her non-existent belly, "wouldn't have happened if it wasn't for you. If I didn't love you so much. If you would have just..."

"Liv." Piper's voice called from a few stairs down, drowning out the woman's words.

"Shit," I muttered, easing the door shut. I turned around to find Piper standing right behind me.

She glanced at the door, then back at me. "What's up?" Piper asked slowly.

I could only imagine what expression was on my face. Because I felt like a wreck.

And a fool.

My first thought was to lie, so that I wouldn't look as pathetic as I felt right now. But I'd lied enough already. To everyone. And, apparently, to myself.

"Ty's in the hallway talking to some woman," I confessed, my voice wavering. "I'm pretty sure that they know each other. Really well," I added.

I wanted to scream that she was having Ty's baby and I was a complete moron for believing that he loved me. But those words stuck - like a chicken bone lodged in my throat - threatening to choke off my airway.

Piper pulled me away from the door so that she could peek out.

"Oh my God!" she exclaimed, easing the door shut again. "That's Mindy, his ex! What the fuck is she doing here?"

I shrugged, even though I knew exactly why she was here. She was telling Ty about their baby.

Piper leaned over, hugging me tightly. "I told you he was a bastard when it came to women." She drew back, her eyes scanning my face. "What are you going to do?"

"Go back to Vancouver," I muttered. "I was going to leave this afternoon anyhow."

"Are you going to talk to Ty? Give him a chance to explain? I'm sure he'll come up with a good excuse about why Mindy is here. He always does," she shared raising one eyebrow. Watching me. "Not that it's going to make a difference anyhow. She's here with her tears and a sob story like always. He's just going to crumble and take her back. Like always."

Piper's expression hardened as she looked at the door again.

"What do you mean by - like always?" I asked, feeling my entire body tense.

I probably didn't want to hear this.

Piper sighed. "It's just that Mindy has a revolving door to Ty's heart. She treats him like shit, leaves him, then comes back. And he always lets her. Dave said that the last time was different. That he's really done with her. I almost believed it after talking to you," she added shaking her head. "I'm really sorry, Liv, but it looks like Ty was just dicking around with you."

I forced a thin smile onto my suddenly dry lips. "Don't worry about it. Really, it's not the end of my world," I reasoned, trying to convince both of us. "No harm, no foul – right?" I paused, trying to draw strength from some unknown source and failing miserably. I desperately wanted to tell her about the baby, but it would only make me seem even more wretched. So I kept Ty's secret to myself. It would be coming out in seven months anyhow.

"You sure?" Piper asked, her face filled with concern.

"Yes." My voice broke, along with my heart.

"What can I do Liv?" she asked. "Should I go and get Gabe for you?"

"Definitely not!" I almost shouted. "Please Piper, don't tell Gabe any of this. It's better if he just thinks that I left last night. He doesn't need to be on bad terms with Ty. They still have to get through the next few weeks together."

She nodded, although something in her eyes made me worry. "What are you going to do?"

"I'm going to get my stuff from Ty's room and go home."

Piper cracked the door open and peeked out. "And how are you going to get your things?" she asked, sliding the door shut again. "They're still in the hallway. You'll have to walk right by them to get to Ty's room." She raised her eyebrows inquisitively.

I sucked in a deep breath, pulling the door wide open. "Then, that's what I'll do. Thanks for the talk, Piper, I appreciate it. Please take care of Gabe."

I stepped out into the hallway, watching Ty and Mindy as I walked towards them. Feeling completely surreal. Like I really was watching a movie.

I watched her lean towards him. I watched her run her hand over his chest while her eyes overflowed with tears. I watched her take his hand.

But what I really wanted to watch, was Ty's face. I wanted to see his exact expression, but the angle was wrong. Which was probably a good thing.

Because seeing his face would probably break me.

Just ten more steps. Then I'd be past them and could turn into the hallway where Ty's room was. Nine, eight, seven - I counted in my head as I got closer and closer - six, five, four,

"Liv. Oh shit, Liv!" Ty exclaimed as I passed by.

I put on my best poker face, turning around to face him. "Yes?"

He dropped Mindy's hand, taking a tentative step towards me. She also took a step, snaking her arm possessively around his waist while she eyed me.

I could have sworn that a smile crept across Mindy's lips for just a moment before a huge sob racked her thin body. Instantly, Ty's arm wrapped around her shoulders, gently rubbing her upper arm.

"Um," he stuttered as I stood staring at him. Hoping my expression echoed nothing that my heart felt. "What, what are you doing here? I thought you were still in the room?" He glanced at Mindy with wide eyes.

"Nope," I returned, using every ounce of strength that I had to keep my face from crumbling.

"I'll, um, I just need ten minutes," Ty said motioning to Mindy, his face a mixture of conflicted emotions.

Another sob racked Mindy's body and more tears spilled down her cheeks as she clung to him.

"Sure, no problem," I replied dryly.

Turning, I covered the last few steps to the hallway junction. Then sprinted the rest of the way to Ty's room. Rushing inside before I disintegrated into a gushing mess. Just like Mindy.

I glanced at my phone. It was twelve twenty. Ty said that he needed ten minutes and that's what I'd give him. Although I had no idea what he could possibly say to make this better.

Mindy was clearly back in his life. Which – from what everyone had continually said – meant that I wasn't. Not that I wanted to be anymore.

Everything had just changed.

I spent the next fifteen minutes arranging, then rearranging, the things in my duffle bag. I checked the bus schedule six times, the weather twice, and texted Laina that I'd be coming home. Pick me up from the station tomorrow night.

Thirty minutes passed. And still no Ty.

Why was I waiting here, knowing that he was just going to break my heart? He could just send me a piss off, I'm back with my ex text, for fuck sake.

Gathering up what was left of my pathetic self-esteem, I heaved the duffle bag onto my shoulder and stepped out into the hallway. Praying that Ty and Mindy hadn't migrated closer to the elevator bank.

And they hadn't. In fact, I couldn't see or hear them at all.

Without looking back, I made my way out of the hotel. Every step taking me further away from Ty.

And breaking me a little more.

Chapter 16 ~ Ty

After sending Mindy packing. Which wasn't easy. At all. I ran – full out – down the hallway towards my hotel room. Praying that Liv was still there.

I knew that it had taken longer. Way longer. Than ten minutes. But I wanted to be crystal clear with Mindy. I needed her to know, absolutely, that I was with Liv now. That I loved Liv with all of my heart and soul. And that Mindy would never, ever, be getting anything from me. Again.

That revelation clearly threw Mindy. Especially now that Richard, my ex-manager, had tossed her out. Not that I could blame Richard for what he did. If I didn't hate the guy so much, I probably would have congratulated him. After all, Mindy had cheated on him and was pregnant with another man's baby. His business partner's baby.

The sweet irony in this whole fucked up situation was that Mindy had cheated on me – with Richard. When I finally figured that out, Richard became my ex-record producer and Mindy became my ex-fiance.

And now, being her typical conniving self, she was trying to blame me. For her cheating on Richard. And getting knocked up by Bill. Because I was the one who introduced her - to both of them.

Which made total sense. If I was a complete idiot.

But fortunately, I was a recovered idiot.

Mindy cried and pulled out all of her usual tricks. But none of them worked this time. Because I didn't care about her anymore. The only woman I cared about was Liv.

I pushed the hotel room door open, in a complete state of panic. "Liv!" I screamed rushing in.

She was gone.

I looked in the bathroom and the closet. Her things were gone too.

Everything Liv, was gone.

I'd completely fucked up. I should have told Mindy to kiss off, right then – with Liv standing beside me. Holding my hand. Listening to me declare my love for her. Sharing that she was the woman I planned to marry and have children with. That she was the only woman for me.

The only bright spot was that I knew where Liv had gone. Maybe, I could make it to the bus station in time and beg her for forgiveness. I glanced at my watch.

If I had wings. Fuuuucccckkkk. The bus left twenty minutes ago!

My hands shook as I pressed the buttons on my cell phone. My favorite picture of me and Liv in New York popping onto the screen.

Please answer, Darlin'. PLEASE.

Three rings later, Liv's voice-message played. I dialed again. And again. And again. Leaving a message. A plea. Each time, for her to call me back.

But twenty hours, one concert, zero sleep, a hundred voice messages, and a thousand texts later – still nothing from Liv.

And I was officially losing it.

·　·　·　·　·

I'd been walking around in a drunken stupor for the past few days. But hadn't drunk a drop. I wanted to. Really wanted to. But it would dull the pain I felt inside. And I didn't deserve that. Because it was all my fault that Liv left. Thinking I'd betrayed her.

I hadn't quite figured out how I was going to get her back yet. So, until that happened, I'd live with the constant pain. And the shredded heart. Because for some insane reason, while it hurt, it also made me feel better.

A loud bang rattled the door of my latest hotel room. Then another bang. And another.

"Fuck Dave!" I shouted, hauling myself off the bed.

He'd been on me ever since Liv left and I started to fall. I knew that he was worried I was going down the same, deep, dark hole I'd been in after Mindy and I had disintegrated. But he was wrong. This was so much worse. With Mindy I drank and whored around. With Liv, I couldn't eat. I couldn't sleep. I was barely functioning. And I knew that seeing me this way made Dave worry. A lot.

Another bang rattled my door. Threatening to take it off the hinges.

"I said I'm coming Dave!" I seethed as I yanked open the door.

"You bastard," Gabe hissed, stepping toward me with his fist ready.

The next thing I knew, I was lying on the floor with blood gushing from my mouth.

"Get up!" Gabe demanded, standing over me. "Get up and fight. I'm gonna kick your God damn ass."

I laid there, looking up at Gabe. Trying to make sense of what was happening. While my head pounded and my mouth oozed.

"Wh, what?" I asked, attempting to sit up. And failing. I laid back down, the room spinning in quick circles. Gabe had obviously hit me good and hard.

"You slept with her, didn't you?" Gabe grabbed my shirt, hauling me to my feet. Making my stomach lurch. Making me almost vomit. "Tell me!" he screamed in my face.

"Yes," I admitted, my voice sounding like I'd just swallowed a handful of rocks.

Gabe let go of my shirt and I stumbled backwards, slamming against the desk. "Then you fucking got back together with your ex? You're a piece of shit Benson. I should kill you. I want to kill you," Gabe raged.

"What?" I asked.

I never even considered that Liv knew who Mindy was. Which was obviously stupid. We'd been photographed together a million times - at least.

No wonder Liv wouldn't talk to me.

"How could you sleep with Liv, then turn around and dump her like yesterday's trash?" Gabe's eyes burned into mine.

"You're completely wrong," I said quietly, hanging my head. "Mindy and I are not getting back together. I told her to fuck off and never come back. I just took too long doing it. And Liv left to go back to Vancouver." I wiped at the blood dripping from my chin, my eyes creeping up to meet Gabe's. "I love her, with everything I am."

Regret raged through me again. If only I could turn back the clock.

If only.

"Say that again," Gabe demanded, the anger from his face slowly draining.

"I love Liv – with all of my heart. I know that you do too and I'm really sorry about that. About everything Gabe. But Liv and I belong together." I sat down on the edge of the desk, drawing in a breath. "And I fuckin blew it." Tears started to form in the corners of my eyes, but I didn't care.

Let Gabe see me falling apart. I didn't give a shit.

"You poor bastard. I thought I had it bad." Gabe plunked down on the edge of the bed opposite from me. "Have you told Liv what happened? That you sent Mindy away?"

I looked up, surprised that Gabe wasn't about to finish me off. Almost sorry that he wasn't. The throbbing pain in my lip was oddly comforting. At least it was a tangible pain.

"She won't talk to me."

Gabe laughed. "That's not surprising. Liv's the most stubborn person I know. Just give her a bit. She'll come around."

"What?"

It sounded like Gabe was giving me his approval to be with Liv. What the fuck?

"You look like shit," he commented.

A grin pulled at my lips, ripping the skin open even wider. Blood ran like a river down my chin and neck, soaking into my favorite shirt. But I didn't care. "I think shit probably feels better than I do."

"As much as it tears me up, I know that you and Liv belong together. You're both the most intelligent idiots I know."

Say what? Gabe must have hit me hard. Really hard. Because I had to be hallucinating.

"What about you and Liv?" I asked tentatively, afraid that my head was as fucked up as my life right now.

Gabe sighed. "I love Liv. I'm pretty sure that I'll always love her. But we don't work. Not like you two do. Piper clued me in to a few things."

"Piper." I nodded, everything suddenly making sense. "You told Piper what's going on."

At least that wasn't surprising.

"Actually Liv told her."

"Get the fuck out!" There's no way, even in an alternate world, that I could see Liv and Piper having a heart-to-heart.

Gabe chuckled. "Yeah I know. Those two seem like oil and water, but apparently they worked everything out. Liv went to see Piper the morning after..." Gabe paused, a pained expression crossing his face for just a moment. "After we had that giant fight and then you two got together."

"Oh," I said. My guts twisting for what I'd done to Gabe. He didn't deserve that. And I obviously didn't deserve Liv.

But I wasn't sure if I could live without her.

"Liv and Piper saw you in the hallway with your ex. And," Gabe hesitated, "Piper told Liv all about Mindy. About how you always take her back. And may have implied that you were just dicking around with Liv. Like you did with all those other women."

"Fuck! This is even worse than I thought it was," I said standing, starting to pace back and forth. "Until today, I didn't even realize that Liv knew it was Mindy. Let alone all that other shit."

"Yeah, she's knows all about Mindy now. Piper said that she was absolutely crushed."

"She won't talk to me!" I yelled, on the verge of hysterics. "She's blocked my calls and texts. What am I going to do? I need to tell her that I'm not getting back together with Mindy." I stared at Gabe. He was my only hope. "I know this a lot to ask, but can you. Do you think that you can talk to her – for me?"

It was a long shot. But waiting another two weeks to let Liv know that I wasn't with Mindy - was completely incomprehensible.

The idea of cancelling the rest of the tour floated through my mind.

Gabe's face clouded over. "Ty, I feel for you. But I'm not ready to talk to Liv yet. It's still too fresh."

"But you said that Liv and I are meant for each other," I pleaded, ready to get down on my knees and beg if it would help.

"I know," Gabe agreed with a nod. "And, as much as it kills me, you are. But don't ask me to advocate for you. At least not right now. Give me some time. Then, maybe, I'll see what I can do. No promises though," he added.

"Thanks man. I'll take whatever I can get." A tiny spark of hope ignited in my heart. "For what it's worth, I really am sorry."

Gabe nodded, standing up, studying me. "Look," he said with a sigh. "I'll tell Laina that you're not getting back together with your ex. That Liv has nothing to worry about. That's the best I can do. For now."

"I could seriously kiss you man!" I exclaimed.

"Save that for Liv," Gabe returned with a slight grin, before heading for the door.

Leaving me with a huge, bloody lip and a bit of hope.

Chapter 17~ Liv

It had been an excruciatingly long two weeks waiting for Gabe to get home. Trying not to think about Ty. And trying to hold it together while Laina watched me as if I was a ticking time bomb.

I'd called and texted Gabe continually. But nothing. Not that I had expected anything else. He was hurt. And I was the one who'd hurt him.

Ty, on the other hand, had been calling and texting me non-stop. Until I blocked his number.

Pure self-preservation.

Because I couldn't listen to his voice or see his picture pop up on my cell anymore. He'd left apology after apology, begging me to call him back and let him explain. That nothing was going on. He loved me and only me.

Sure.

That might be the way he felt now. But wait until the baby came. Because I knew Ty. He was a good guy. And I couldn't see him not doing everything possible for his child.

So, if Mindy had him wrapped around her finger before, then no matter how good his intentions were now, once his baby came - he'd be hers again. And I'd be left, broken and alone.

Not that I wasn't already.

· · · · ·

"Hey, Baby Doll, can I come in for a minute?" Gabe asked from the doorway of the bedroom that Laina and I shared.

I'd been waiting for this moment ever since Gabe came back to Vancouver two days ago. We'd been tip-toeing around each other.

Exchanging a polite hello here and there but nothing more.

Making living together - painful.

Although I'd rehearsed what I wanted to say to Gabe twenty million times over, my stomach still twisted into knots as he stared at me. Waiting.

"Sure," I agreed patting the space beside me on my twin bed.

Gabe meandered across the room, looking as awkward as I felt. Plunking down next to me, he wrapped my hand in his.

Suddenly, I had the overpowering urge to crawl onto Gabe's lap, wrap my arms around his neck, and never let go. My thoughts had been so divided between him and Ty, that I hadn't realized just how much I missed Gabe.

And it made me sick that I'd let some guy come between us. Ruin what we had.

"I'm really sorry about what happened between us this summer," he began, staring at an invisible spot on my quilt. "It's just that I've had feelings for you for so long. And then we were together. I mean sleeping together, touching, kissing." He shrugged. "And it felt right. Really right. And I started thinking that you felt the same." Gabe paused, drawing in a deep breath, glancing at me. "But then I realized that Ty was interested in you. And you were interested in him. And I kind of went off the deep end." Another pause. "I forgot that I'm supposed to protect you. Not hurt you. I'm so sorry, Baby Doll."

I stared at him in complete shock. "Is this a joke?"

Gabe shook his head slowly. "No, Baby Doll, it isn't a joke. I mean it. I'm sorry. Please forgive me. I promised you a summer to remember but it ended up being memorable for all of the wrong reasons." He looked at me, chuckling nervously.

"But you have nothing to be sorry for," I protested. Watching Gabe's face for some sign that this was a colossal joke. I'd prepared myself for Gabe to hate me. To never want to speak to me again and probably demand that I move out. But I never, ever, considered that he'd be accepting the blame for what happened between us. Leaning in, I hugged Gabe as tears rolled down my cheeks.

"I have everything to be sorry for. When I realized that you were falling for Ty, I went crazy. It hurt." Pausing, Gabe shifted back finding my eyes. "But I know that's not who we really are. You're my sister from another mister." He cocked a half smile. "I pushed things too far. And I'm sorry."

"Oh, Gabe," I wheezed. "You love me and I was a giant bitch. I'm so sorry about everything. I wanted to be with you. I really did. I just couldn't make – it just didn't," I stuttered trying to find the right words. And failing.

"I know Baby Doll, I know," Gabe said pulling me against him again. "Can we just put this behind us?"

"Yes," I blurted out, before he could change his mind. Relief and happiness starting to creep its way through the haze in my brain.

"What made you change your mind about – everything?" I asked, although I was pretty sure that I already knew the answer.

Piper.

"Actually, I thought about what you said – about me being in love with the idea of you. And about my attraction to Piper. And – OK, this is really painful to admit – but, you were right. On both accounts. I'm not saying that I still don't love you, because I do. And we do make a great couple. But if we were meant to be together, then Ty and Piper wouldn't have mattered. They wouldn't have come between us."

"So where are things with Piper now?" I asked, feeling like a giant weight had just been lifted from my shoulders.

Gabe shrugged. "I don't know. She has a boyfriend." He shrugged again. "We'll see. I mean we talk or text almost everyday. We're friends, but who knows."

"Oh Gabe, that's great," I enthused giving him a quick hug.

Gabe leaned in, pressing his lips briefly against mine.

"Guess I shouldn't kiss you anymore."

"You can kiss me anytime you'd like. I'll always love you Gabe. Please don't ever forget that."

We stared at each other for a moment, an odd feeling settling between us. Something had changed. Subtly, but undeniably.

"So everything is OK with us now?" I confirmed.

"We're fine," he said nodding. "But I'd like you to do one thing for me."

"Anything," I readily agreed. "Want to have sex 'cause I can be naked in two seconds flat," I joked.

"Although that's very tempting," Gabe began, a genuine smile stretching across his lips. "That's not what I was going to ask. I want you to talk to Ty."

I shook my head in disbelief. "Get out!"

This had to be a joke. Gabe had zero love for Ty. He could barely stand Ty most of the time.

"Please, Liv," Gabe begged, "for me. I can't live with myself knowing that I'm the one responsible for ruining things between you two."

"You didn't ruin anything," I replied, shaking my head back and forth so quickly that it made me dizzy. "You were completely right. I didn't mean anything to him. I saw Ty with is ex."

"I know." He paused.

"Piper told you, didn't she? I asked her not to!" I fumed.

Nice! And I'd been thinking what a sweet person she was.

"Did she run and tell Ty too? What a bitch!"

"Easy, Baby Doll. Don't blame Piper. She was just worried about you and it took me days to pry it out of her." Gabe sighed. "I'm the one who told Ty that you knew it was Mindy. Right after I punched him in the face." A grimace pulled at Gabe's mouth.

"You punched Ty! In the face! Gabe!" I exclaimed, a smile stretching across my lips.

"Split his mouth wide open. I don't think he could chew properly for a week."

"Oh, my God!" I punched Gabe lightly in the arm. "Why did you do that? He could have kicked you off the tour."

"Are you kidding, the only thing he cared about was talking to you. Explaining what had happened."

"Explaining!" I let out a bitter laugh. "Not much to explain. I heard more than enough for myself."

"Are you really sure about what you heard?" Gabe probed.

"I heard enough to know that she's never going to be out of his life."

Understatement of the year.

The sound of Mindy's high-pitched voice telling Ty that she was pregnant had been replaying over and over in my head, ever since I got back. It was like having a horrible commercial jingle or a mini-pops' song lodged in my brain. Making me crazy.

"Ty told me what happened and I think you're wrong about that. It was just a big mistake. You walked into the middle of the conversation, Liv. He's not getting back together with Mindy. Really," Gabe added when I rolled my eyes. "Just talk to Ty. Let him explain. The guy is seriously in love with you."

"Since when are you a fan of Ty's? I'm pretty sure you're the guy who referred to him as a womanizing scum bag," I countered.

Gabe grimaced. "Yeah," he said, "I was mistaken about that too. Don't get me wrong," he added as I eyed him skeptically. "Ty did his share of, umm, playing around, but that was well before he met you. His feelings for you are genuine. Don't punish Ty and yourself for a stupid mistake, Liv," he implored.

Not surprisingly, Ty had missed telling Gabe one minor detail. That Mindy was pregnant with his baby! And even if Ty was telling the truth and not getting back together with Mindy, it didn't change the fact that they were having a baby. And instead of taking two minutes to come and talk to me, to be honest with me, he stayed with her. Expecting that I'd just sit there like an idiot waiting for him. But I was no man's idiot.

At least not twice.

"So based on the fact that you're defending him, I'm guessing you and Ty are BFFs now?"

Gabe shrugged. "After I punched him, we talked. Got everything out in the open. We started hanging out a bit here and there. Turns out he's a really great guy. I consider him to be a good friend now."

Say what?

My mouth dropped open in astonishment. Gabe reached over, pushing my jaw up with his fingertips. A grin fixed to his lips.

"I must be dreaming," I muttered. "So to recap, you were hanging out with Ty while I was writhing in misery here? You even refused to talk to Laina about what had happened." I shook my head in disbelief.

"Yeah, I'm deeply sorry about that." Gabe frowned. "You know me, I just needed a little time to cool down. Sort my feelings out." Gabe placed a kiss on my cheek before standing up. "Just think about what I said. Please."

I laughed bitterly. "So Ty screwed me over, literally, and you want me to call him? What did they do to you after I left?"

"I can't believe you're going to throw away your chance to have a great relationship. With a great guy. And be really happy because of your stupid stubborn streak. Baby Doll, most of us would kill for even the possibility of what you can have with Ty." Gabe shook his head as he walked out of the room.

Knowing that he was referring to his relationship – or lack thereof - with Piper, my heart sank. Life just wasn't fair sometimes.

"Call Ty," Gabe added, peeking his head around the corner.

I threw a pillow at him. "Yeah, sure, I'll get right on it," I called back sarcastically.

When hell freezes over.

Needing something comforting, like a giant bowl of Sugar Crisp cereal, I dragged myself off the bed. As I rounded the corner to our little kitchenette, I spotted Gabe with his head stuck in the refrigerator.

"I tried man, no luck," he said into his cell phone as he pushed containers around. Pause. "No, she's still really upset." Pause. "I don't think she intends to talk to you - ever." Pause. "I know, I told her that, but she's stubborn. Really stubborn. No, definitely don't come over. That'll make things even worse. Just give me some time and I'll work on her. See if I can get her to talk to you." Pause. "Kay, I'll catch up with you in a bit."

"Who's stubborn?" I asked, pulling a seat up at our breakfast bar.

Gabe jumped, cracking his head on the top shelf in the fridge. "Ouch," he complained, rubbing his head. He shoved the cell phone into his front pocket. "What?"

"I asked who's stubborn?"

"What are you talking about?" Gabe questioned, shaking his head back and forth. Reaching over me, he grabbed a banana from the fruit basket. "Want one?"

"No, thanks."

"So what have you been up to since you came back? Ah, remind me to tell you a great story later. It'll crack you up Baby Doll. Oh crap, look at the time, I need to get moving," Gabe rambled, before hurrying out of the kitchen and down our entrance hallway.

I followed.

"Where are you going?" I asked, my spidey senses tingling. Gabe had deliberately avoided answering my question and was acting completely weird.

And I wanted to know why.

"Umm, out with the guys. You know, guys' night," he explained shoving his feet into a pair of Converse sneakers.

"Who were you talking to?" I demanded, putting my hand on his arm as he grabbed for the doorknob.

"Umm, Brian," he muttered, stuffing a large piece of banana into his mouth.

"Who were you talking about? Who's stubborn?"

"Umm, Laina," Gabe muttered again, shoving the rest of the banana into his mouth. He handed me the peel. "Can you throw this out please? Thanks, babe," he mumbled yanking open our front door. "I'm late, catch you later," he added, hurrying through the doorway.

· · · · ·

The next day both Laina and Gabe stood in the doorway of our bedroom watching as I picked through research articles.

"See, I told you," Laina said to Gabe. "She's been like this ever since she came home. She's either in bed or on that fricken computer. I think she's only left the apartment twice in the past two weeks and that was to buy food," Laina shared, her voice filled with disdain. "She's turning into a recluse right before our eyes. It's very sad."

They paused, probably waiting for me to turn around - but I didn't. There was no way I was going to give them the satisfaction of acknowledging their taunts about my recent studious, and perhaps slightly reclusive, behavior.

"Very sad indeed," Gabe agreed after another moment. "What are we going to do?"

"Hold an intervention," Laina suggested enthusiastically.

This didn't sound good.

"An intervention. That sounds like a great idea. What do we do?" Gabe asked, and I could tell that he was trying not to laugh.

"Drinks and dancing!" Laina exclaimed.

"Club 89!" Laina and Gabe shouted in unison. "You go and call everyone. I'll get our princess up and mobile. Tell them we'll meet there at eight o'clock."

A giant sigh escaped my lips as I turned around, taking in Laina's elated expression. "You guys go without me. I'm not in the mood tonight."

"You need to shake this. Whatever this is – off. Starting right now," Laina demanded. "Liv, get your ass ready 'cause you're coming out tonight. No excuses accepted. You've barely left this apartment since you got back," she accused.

And your point is?

"I have a thesis due," I justified, not in the mood for this. At all. I just wanted her and Gabe to go out and leave me alone. "And Purdon gave me a class to teach this year so I need to prepare. You know what a hard-ass he is,"

I added as Laina raised her eyebrows, clearly not buying a word I'd just said.

"Forty minutes, Liv, and we're leaving," Laina warned, picking up her hair straightener then heading into our bathroom.

"Awesome," I yelled.

. . . . .

Club 89 was vibrating with people and eighties tunes. Decked out with strobe lights and a giant disco ball, this retro-club was THE place to be for returning UBC students.

With his new found wealth from the summer tour, Gabe had kept our table loaded with drinks. So only two hours in, I was feeling no pain. After dancing like maniacs, Laina, Liam, and I made our way through the crowd towards the table. Laughing about how I had almost wiped out trying to do the actions to the YMCA song.

Not my finest moment. But so fun.

We squeezed in by our table and Laina wrapped her arm around my neck. "I'm so glad the real Liv is back," she yelled into my ear. "I missed her."

"Me too," I agreed with a chuckle. "Thanks for dragging me out tonight."

"That's what best friends are for."

I watched the grin on Laina's face fade as she stared over my shoulder.

"Oh shit," she muttered.

"Oh shit - what?" I asked, turning to see what she was looking at. My grin disappeared along with my buzz. "What are you doing here!?" I demanded, coming face to chest with Ty.

"I live in Van. Did you forget that?" Ty answered, his deep voice sending a shock wave through my body.

Laina's arms wrapped around my torso in a tight hug. Her head resting on my shoulder, giving me strength.

Ty nodded at Laina. "Hi Laina, nice to see you again."

"Ty," Laina returned, her voice flat and anything but welcoming.

She was the only person who knew the entire truth about what I'd heard in the hallway. About Ty's impending arrival. That had been more than enough to thwart Gabe's attempts to get Laina on his side. And help convince me to talk to Ty.

God, I loved her.

"You think I can get a minute alone with Liv?" Ty asked, his eyes trained on me. Burning a hole into my soul.

Or maybe that was the alcohol.

"I don't think that's a good idea," she declined, moving in front of me like a shield. "Are you planning on staying?"

"I guess that depends on whether I'm welcome to stay or not."

I drew in a deep breath, stepping out from behind Laina. "Stay," I said to Ty, watching happiness replace the apprehension on his face. Making me want to crumble into a million pieces at his feet.

He was beautiful and smart and sweet and sexy. So sexy.

And, not mine. Smarten up, Liv!

"Thanks, Liv, you don't know how much I appreciate that. Can we talk? Please?" he asked, his big brown eyes pleading with me to say yes.

And I wanted to. Actually, I wanted to take him home and take off all his cloths and -

Fuck! Being so close to him wasn't helping. I needed to put some space in between us. Now.

I turned to Laina. "I'm going home. Tell everyone that I'll see them later." Drawing in a deep breath, I looked at Ty. "Don't follow me," I directed, feeling my determination to stay away from him already starting to wane.

In record time I worked my way through the crowd and into the fresh sea air. Inhaling deeply, I tried to calm my stomach. The sickening surprise of seeing Ty, combined with the copious amounts of alcohol that I'd already drank, was wreaking havoc on my insides.

I headed back towards our apartment, not in any particular hurry. Everyone would still be out for hours and the long walk would do me good. So would some alone time.

My jean's pocket vibrated. I pulled my cell phone out and Gabe's face flashed on the screen.

"Hey, Gabe."

"Baby Doll, where are you!?"

"Heading home. I told Laina to let everyone know that I left."

"She told me. Then we went to find you but you'd already vanished. You can't just take off on your own, Liv," Gabe chastised. "Van is a huge city and it's getting late. Tell me where you are and I'll come get you."

"Ty was at Club 89!" I exclaimed. "He's back in Van."

"I know. I've seen him a few times," Gabe admitted. "He really wants to talk to you Baby Doll. Can't you find it in your heart to just talk to the guy?" Gabe cajoled. "It'd be great if you two could at least smooth things over. I like Ty. I want to be able to hang out with him. And you."

"You're asking for too much Gabe. Gotta go. I'll see you at home."

I pressed end, shoving the phone back into my pocket. Within seconds it started to vibrate again. But I ignored it. And I continued to ignore it for the next hour and a half as I made my way back to our apartment.

·   ·   ·   ·   ·

Feeling a million times better, I climbed the stairs to the second floor of our building. The heavy thump of base getting louder with each step. Gabe and Laina were obviously home already. And having a party.

Perfect. Just what I wasn't in the mood for tonight.

Pushing the door open I surveyed the numerous pairs of sandals and sneakers stacked in our tiny entryway. Adding my own sandals to the pile, I made my way into the living room.

"Liv!" several voices cried out as I turned the corner into a mass of bodies and pumping music.

Before I even had time to respond, Gabe was in front of me. "Can I talk to you for a minute?" he asked, pushing me back into my bedroom, closing the door behind us. "You scared the shit out of me tonight!" he reprimanded. "Where've you been and why haven't you been answering your phone? I've been trying to call you for almost two hours. We were just debating about whether to go out and look for you."

"Sorry, Gabe," I apologized feeling awful for making everyone worry. I'd been in my own world. Caught up in my own misery. "I just needed some space. And I stopped for a frozen yogurt – and a donair." I grimaced as Gabe grinned.

"And there's my girl. I should have known." He pulled me against him for a quick hug. "I need to tell you something. And please try not to get mad." I nodded. He sucked in a deep breath, making me worry. "Please don't kill me. Not that Laina left much life in me after she found out what I did," he added. "I just did it because I love you and I want you to be happy."

I looked at him, unsure where this conversation was heading. "OK," I agreed - tentatively.

"I invited Ty to come to Club 89 tonight." Gabe scrunched up his face, obviously waiting for me to explode.

"What?! How could you blindside me like that Gabe?" I demanded, glaring at him.

"I thought, well I hoped, that once you saw Ty again, that, -" Gabe inhaled deeply. "That maybe you'd see him and..."

"And what, Gabe?" I asked, my cheeks becoming hotter by the second. "Forget that Mindy's always going to come first for him? That he left me sitting in the hotel room – alone - while he comforted her. That's just shit! You don't do that to someone you love," I ranted. "I'd be an absolute fool to think that Mindy wasn't an issue. And I'm not interested in being any man's second choice."

"Baby Doll," he said softly, taking my hand in his. Massaging the pressure point between my thumb and index finger, just like I loved. "Look, I don't expect you to be with Ty or to even be friends with him again. All I'm asking is that you let him explain. That's it." He looked at me expectantly. A flicker of hope in his eyes.

"He's here. Isn't he?" I hissed, pulling my hand back. My eyes narrowing.

Fuck! I didn't need this right now. I barely made it out of Club 89 without falling apart. Being trapped in our tiny apartment with Ty would be too much.

It already felt like too much.

"Yeah. He was worried about you too."

"You invited him over. To our home?!" I exclaimed, my words coming out fast and squeaky. I sucked in a deep breath, willing myself not to freak out. "And Laina let you?"

"She was a hard sell – trust me on that. But even Laina realized that you and Ty need to talk. That he'd never do anything to deliberately hurt you."

"She's drunk, so this doesn't count," I disagreed.

"Look Baby Doll, Ty's my friend and now that he's in Van, I'm going to be hanging out with him. I want him to be welcome in our home. PLEASE, for me, just talk to him. PLEASE, Baby Doll?" Gabe beseeched.

"Fine," I said, "I get that you're friends with Ty now and that you two are going to be hanging out. But, I won't be. So please don't ask me to sit down and have a heart to heart with him. Because it's never going to happen."

My heart couldn't take it.

I looked into Gabe's eyes, wondering if I should just tell him everything. Tell him Ty's secret. If Gabe knew, there was no way in Hell that he'd want me to be with Ty. Or even be around him.

I opened my mouth, ready to spill everything, but the words wouldn't come out. Maybe because this wasn't my news to share. It was Ty's. Everything would come out in a few months anyway. I'd just have to wait.

And stay away from Ty in the meantime.

Gabe kissed the top of my head. "Fair enough, but I still think you're making a horrendous mistake."

A wry smile spread across my lips. "You know, this whole thing is kind of funny. You're the one who was so adamant that I stay away from Ty. And now you're the one trying to get us together."

Gabe cracked a smile. "OK, I guess it's sort of funny. Come on, let's go out. Say a quick hello to everyone."

"To everyone, hey?" I confirmed, eyeing Gabe. "Don't push it, pretty boy."

"Pretty boy, is it?"

"Well, you are pretty. And a pretty good kisser too, if I do say so myself. Maybe we made a mistake. Maybe we should give it another try," I suggested nodding towards my bed.

This idea was seeming better and better.

"Nice try, Baby Doll. But I don't think you really want to open up that can of worms again," he said raising his eyebrows. "Come on, it won't be so bad. Besides, soon you're going to be seeing Ty all of the time. Might as well get used to it."

"Why would I be seeing him all of the time?" I questioned. "In a few days I'll be spending most of my time at the University again. Purdon's already packed my schedule so full that I might have to start sleeping in my office. Ty could probably move in here and I'd barely notice." I paused, looking at Gabe with apprehension. Wondering if he knew something I didn't. Ever since Ty entered our lives, we'd both been keeping secrets from each other.

"Sure. Sure. Sleep in your office, that's a good one," Gabe chuckled nervously, making me even more suspicious. "Well, let's get this show on the road," he encouraged taking my hand.

"Gabe," I said, pulling back. "I'm done for the night. You go without me. I'm heading to bed."

Gabe looked at me and I could feel 'a pep talk' coming on.

"Baby Doll, you know that you're only delaying the inevitable. You're going to have to face Ty sooner or later. Why don't you just get it out of the way?"

Later sounded great. Or possibly never.

"This is the best time. It's late so he won't stay long. And you're surrounded by all of your friends. Come say a few hellos then you can sneak off." He took my hand again, nodding towards the door. "No time like the present. Right?"

Fuck no! But I followed Gabe anyway.

· · · · ·

Ty

I knew the second that she walked into the room. I could sense her. And, I wondered if she could sense me.

Turning, I watched Liv and Gabe move into the crowded living room holding hands. Her face filled with anxiety. Her eyes scanning the room. For me. Except that when our eyes met, she turned away. And never looked back.

We spent the next hour circling around each other, but not talking. I couldn't keep my eyes off her and she didn't even glance at me.

Absolutely killing me. Slowly and painfully.

Being so close to Liv, but not being able to touch her or talk to her was agony. But I'd promised Laina – with my life. That I wouldn't go near Liv. She had to come to me. It was the only way that Laina would agree to let me come to the apartment. And, right now, I'd take what I could get.

Laina also told me that she'd taken the liberty of throwing out all of the flowers, and chocolates, and balloons, and leopard print thongs that I'd sent to Liv over the past few weeks.

Given our past, and Liv's quirky sense of humor, I was hoping that she'd find the underwear funny. And then, of course, call me and I'd explain about Mindy. And we'd laugh - and everything would be fine again.

But Liv never even knew about the thongs. Or any of the other gifts.

So much for plan A.

But I was here now, in the same room with her. And no matter how long it took, or what I had to do, I was going to get her back.

On to plan B – insert myself into Liv's life, in every possible way. Making it impossible for her to ignore me.

I hoped.

·   ·   ·   ·   ·

The next morning, I woke up with a terrible crick in my neck. Which didn't surprise me after sleeping – or trying to sleep - on Gabe's couch. It was the first time in years that I'd crashed at someone's place after a party. And I sincerely hoped that it was the last time. Because I was way too old for this shit. But staying, meant that I was near Liv.

And would see her this morning. Or more specifically, right now.

I watched Liv paddle into the kitchenette, already dressed in shorts and a tank top. Oblivious to the fact that I was only twenty feet away. Starting at her like she was my own personal sun.

Apparently paralyzing the upper part of my body had paid off.

She poured a bowl of Raisin Bran, then settled onto a stool at the breakfast bar, leafing through a magazine as she ate.

"Morning, Gabe," she called as I moved up behind her.

"Um, it's not Gabe but good morning, sunshine," I greeted, stepping into the kitchen, shooting her a grin. Her eyes widened while her mouth dropped open. "I slept on the couch last night. Wasn't in the best shape to drive," I explained.

"What, you forgot how to call a cab or did your fortune run dry, rock star?" she quipped. A sour expression contorting her beautiful face.

"And there's the Liv that I know and love," I replied, moving over to the coffee maker. Needing to do something so that I wouldn't touch her.

Because I really, really wanted to touch her. And beg her to forgive me. But she clearly wasn't ready for that – yet.

I pulled out the used filter, dumping it into the garbage. "Would you like a coffee?" I asked, methodically rinsing out the plastic filter holder.

"No - thanks," she said, focusing all of her attention on the magazine.

"I hate to interrupt when you're reading such a stimulating article," I teased, glancing at the page describing how to achieve the perfect eyebrow arch. "But where do you keep the coffee and filters?"

"Cabinet right above the coffee maker. Cups are in the far left-hand cupboard on the top," she answered, keeping her eyes fixed on the magazine.

Liv shoveled in the last spoonful of cereal as I measured out the coffee then started the machine. Picking up her empty bowl, she moved into the kitchen. Almost pressing her body against the counter in an obvious effort to keep as much space between us as possible. I watched her give the bowl and spoon a quick wash before placing them into the dish rack to dry.

"Liv," I said softly, only inches away from her.

We were so close, yet felt so fucking far away from each other.

Slowly, she turned around meeting my eyes. Unable to hold back, I stepped closer, feeling my heart squeeze as her face hardened. She pressed back into the counter, trying to get away from me.

Shit! I needed to go slower. Keep my distance. Even if it killed me.

"What?" she barked.

"Are we playing nice today kids?" Gabe asked as he shuffled into the kitchen behind us. "Mmm coffee," he muttered going over to the cupboard and taking down two cups. "I'm assuming you don't want any, Baby Doll?"

Liv shook her head, her eyes warily trained on me. Like she was waiting for me to attack her or do something equally horrible. Like touch her.

"How 'bout some eggs and toast, Liv? Ty?" Gabe asked, placing a cup under the still running coffee maker.

I stepped to the left, leaning against the end of the counter. Angling my body so that it was impossible for Liv to leave the kitchen without crawling over me.

It was a dirty move, but I couldn't let her leave. She needed to be near me. That was only way I could wear her down. And we both knew it.

"I was going to take you all out for breakfast. As a thanks for letting me stay over last night," I offered. "Don't worry, Liv. I'm pretty sure that my meager bank account will cover it," I added with a smirk while she glared at me.

Gabe shook his head as he looked from Liv to me.

"What time does Laina usually get up?" I asked.

Gabe snorted. "If we wait for Laina, it'll be lunch not breakfast. I'll just bring her something back. Liv, you ready to go?"

"Already ate," she said dryly, motioning to the still wet bowl in the dish-dryer.

"As if you can't force down a few eggs and bacon," Gabe joked.

"I need to get to the University to do some work. And I'm meeting Marcie later," she explained, glancing at the narrow kitchen entrance. Which was now entirely blocked – by me. I couldn't help it. A grin tugged at my lips.

Antagonizing Liv was still fun. So was getting naked with her. But first things first.

Gabe finished filling the second cup of coffee, handing it to me. "Milk or sugar?"

"He likes milk, not sugar," Liv blurted, making both Gabe and I look at her. "It's in the fridge. Help yourself," she added as her cheeks turned pink.

I straightened up, reaching over to open the fridge door. While I grabbed for the milk, Liv slipped by, heading into the hallway and away from me.

I followed.

"Liv," I called, watching her slip on a pair of sandals as I rounded the corner.

"What?" she asked, her voice and face filled with irritation.

"I think you have on Laina's sandals."

She held her arm out, preventing me from moving any closer, as she glanced down at her feet. They almost floated in the flip flops.

"Sure you don't want to come for breakfast?" I cajoled, wondering how bad she'd freak out if I pressed her against the door, then kissed her. Hard and deep.

Based on her expression, out of a ten-point scale, her freak out would probably be a fifteen.

"I need to buy a new chair for my loft. And was hoping that you'd come shopping with me afterwards?" I continued as she yanked the door open. "You have great taste and we shop together really well. Maybe we can make a day of it like last time? Grab some supper afterwards?" I was hoping to dredge up some good memories of the time we'd spent together in New York.

The biggest, brightest smile took over Liv's face as she looked at me. "I'd be happy to."

No way, the New York thing worked! Thank you psych degree.

"As soon as pigs fly," she hissed, stepping out in the hallway, shutting the door in my face.

Chapter 18 ~ Liv

I had been absolutely dreading the next hour. It was my hour from hell. Actually, it was going to be my hour from hell three times a week, for the next four months.

I pushed my way through the crowded University hallway towards my assigned classroom, trying not to panic as each step brought me closer to my worst nightmare. Teaching the research component of an intro Psych class for Purdon.

He expected a lot from his students and even more from his graduate students. So not performing well in this class would mean dire consequences for my academic life.

No pressure – at all.

Adding to that already overwhelming stress, was my fear of public speaking. I figured that standing up in front of an entire class while trying to sound intelligent, and not throw up, was either going to do wonders for my stage fright. Or kill me.

Drawing in a deep breath I pulled the door to my classroom open. Hoping that I'd get a few minutes to prepare before students started to file in. As soon as I moved through the doorway, however, my eyes honed in on Dr. Purdon and some tall guy talking on the far side of the room.

Purdon was probably here to watch my first class. Perfect. Just perfect.

My anxiety level jacked up by a hundred. I was seriously going to need a miracle to get through the next hour.

Quietly, I slunk over to the front desk and set my notes down, praying that they wouldn't notice me.

"Ms. Madison," Purdon beckoned from across the room, motioning for me to join them.

"Shit," I muttered to myself.

Fixing a smile on my face, I nodded to Dr. Purdon. Giving the other guy a quick once over as I crossed the room. Although I couldn't see his face, his cargo pants and collared t-shirt, told me that he was a new grad student. Purdon was infamous for passing new grads, especially those new to the University, off on his existing students.

With my luck, he was probably going to saddle me with this guy.

"Dr. Purdon," I greeted, hoping that my voice didn't sound as shaky as I felt.

"Liv Madison, I want you to meet our new PhD student," Purdon began as the guy – as Ty – turned to face me.

I'd wished for a miracle, but got a tragedy instead. A fucking tragedy!

"This is Ty Benson. Mr. Benson, this is Liv Madison," Dr. Purdon introduced.

Ty stuck his hand out towards me as I stood staring at him with my mouth hanging open.

"Hey Liv," Ty greeted casually. He glanced at Dr. Purdon, his hand still poised in the air between us. "Liv and I know each other already."

"Oh," Dr. Purdon replied looking inquisitively at me. Then at Ty. Then at Ty's outstretched hand. "I wasn't aware that you two had a prior relationship. Will that be a problem Ms. Madison?"

Ty dropped his hand as I snapped my mouth shut, my senses returning. I plastered the brightest smile possible onto my lips, nodding cordially at Ty before meeting Purdon's laser sharp stare. "Absolutely not, sir."

Dr. Purdon looked at me skeptically, studying my face for a moment before turning towards Ty. "Is that right, Mr. Benson?"

"No problem at all. In fact, I'm looking forward to working with Liv over the next few months.

Months! Shoot me now! There was no way that I could be around Ty for a few hours. Let alone months. I was so screwed.

"We spoke about her Master's thesis this summer," Ty continued, his deep voice chipping away at my defenses. "And it really interested me. There's good potential if she researches it and combines the information properly."

"Hmm," Dr. Purdon mused, tapping one stubby finger to his chin. "I'm glad you feel that way." He glanced at me. "Ms. Madison, I think that Mr. Benson has a lot to offer you."

A huge smirk spread across Ty's lips as he eyed me. And it didn't require a PhD to figure out what he was thinking.

Ass wipe.

"Mr. Benson, how would you feel about mentoring Ms. Madison? Your PhD project is along the same line of thought. I think it would be beneficial if you two collaborated. Starting with this class." Dr. Purdon turned towards me as I entered panic mode.

This was a horrible joke. Right?

"Ms. Madison, I think you can learn a lot from Mr. Benson. His Masters' thesis was one of the best I've ever seen. I was worried about not being able to support you as much as I'd like with the current course load and my latest book going into publication. This looks like a gift from the Gods." Dr. Purdon's thin lips curled upwards revealing more gum than teeth.

Bile churned in my stomach while Ty looked like he'd just won the lottery.

"You two are a match made in heaven," Purdon continued enthusiastically. "Well, I'll give you the next five minutes to get Mr. Benson up to speed Ms. Madison. I'd like to start meeting with you both every other Friday at two pm to discuss the class and review the progress you've made on your work. Let's start next Friday, see you both in my office at two pm sharp." Dr. Purdon nodded to each of us then took a few steps towards the door before swinging back around. "Ms. Madison, how many desks are in the office that you share with Ms. Holston?" he inquired.

Nooooo!

"Um, there are three desks in the office." I had to force the words out of my mouth because I knew exactly where Purdon was going with this. Brad had just finished his masters. Leaving a vacant desk.

"Perfect!" Dr. Purdon exclaimed with a single clap of his hands. "Mr. Benson still needs a space. He can use the spare desk in your office. Please be so kind as to show Mr. Benson where that is and provide him with the key code. Good day." He nodded before scurrying out of the classroom.

I wanted to drop to the floor and cry. But that would blow the new, 'you really don't affect me' cover, I'd put into action.

Just now.

So, instead, I turned away from Ty walking purposefully towards the desk. Deliberately keeping my back to him while I organized the handouts as students started to trickle in.

I could feel Ty watching me, but my new, 'not giving a shit attitude,' said that I didn't care.

Or, at least, I hoped that it did.

.   .   .   .   .

Turns out that Ty was a gift after all. His mere presence ignited something deep inside of me. I channeled all of my feelings and rage for him into teaching. And, miraculously, was able to make it through the entire hour without noticeably stumbling or, more importantly, having a panic attack. Or fainting. Or vomiting. Or making a complete jackass out of myself.

It was a true life miracle! Seriously.

Now I only had to do this again another forty or so times. I jammed the remaining handouts into my bag trying not to think about that, or the fact that Ty was standing by the door, watching me. Obviously waiting for me.

"Baby Doll," Gabe's voice called over the din of the students' chatter. "Ty! Hey man, what're you doing here? Don't tell me that Purdon's making you teach a class, too?" Gabe chuckled.

Crap. I totally forgot that Gabe was coming to take me for lunch.

I picked up my bag, turning to see Gabe and Ty shaking hands. After their intense dislike of each other all summer, this new-found comradery was hard to get used to.

"Purdon wants me and Liv to co-teach for his Psych 104 class. We're supposed to collaborate on her thesis too." Both Gabe and Ty turned to look at me. A grin lighting up Ty's face, while a weird expression contorted Gabe's.

"Lucky me," I replied with exaggerated enthusiasm, moving over next to Gabe. Wondering what was up with him.

And then it dawned on me.

"Hey, wait a minute," I said, my eyes trained on Gabe. "You've known that Purdon is Ty's advisor too and didn't say a word to me. Didn't you?"

Gabe glanced at Ty, his eyes widening. His lips pressing into a thin, worried line.

"I asked him not to. I didn't want you to freak out," Ty answered.

Gabe just nodded, looking from me to Ty.

"Nice," I returned dryly, not bothering to mask my anger. "Traitor," I muttered.

"Hey Ty, I'm gonna take Liv out for a celebratory lunch. Why don't you join us?" Gabe invited, ignoring my jab. And dumping a pile of manure on top of my already shitty day.

"What are we celebrating?" Ty asked, watching me closely. Like he thought that I was about to bolt.

And I was.

Gabe chuckled, his deep voice filling the entire classroom. "The fact that Liv didn't faint or throw up. You didn't, did you?" he confirmed, a goofy grin fixed to his lips.

"Ha ha, very funny," I retorted, still pissed off at him - and Purdon. It seemed like they were working together to make my life as miserable as possible.

"Actually she did incredible," Ty enthused. "You'd think she was a seasoned pro."

I stared at Ty in amazement. The guy just didn't quit.

"I'd love to go to lunch with you two," Ty accepted.

Of course you would. But I wouldn't.

"Great, we can tell Liv about all of the things she missed during the last bit of the tour. Vegas was pretty amazing. Remember that club we went to after the concert?" Gabe grinned, playfully punching Ty in the shoulder.

Did I just step into an episode of the Brady Bunch? This entire situation felt completely surreal. And wrong. So wrong.

Ty laughed. "Maybe we should give Liv the PG version of that night?"

"Agreed," Gabe returned wrapping his arm around my shoulder. "This guy is wild!" He shook his head in awe. "Baby Doll you missed some good times."

"Awesome," I deadpanned. I'd spent the last hour stuck in a room with Ty. And there was no way in hell that I was going to – voluntarily - spend another hour having lunch with him.

I needed space. Now.

"Well, let's get going – I'm starving," Gabe said, guiding me towards the door.

We stepped out into the hallway. Gabe and Ty turned one way, while I slipped out of Gabe's arm, heading the other.

"I need to go to the library," I called over my shoulder, continuing to put more distance between us. "You guys go on without me."

I headed towards the library anxious to get away before Gabe or Ty could object. Six long strides was the exact distance that I covered before someone grabbed my arm. Turning around, I came face to chest with Ty.

"Why don't you come to lunch, then we can go to the library together afterwards? We have a lot to discuss, co-teaching the class - among other things," Ty added. His innuendo crystal clear. "I'm sure Purdon will want to know exactly how we plan to work things out." He paused, looking at me hopefully.

I stood there, staring at him. A million thoughts and feelings shuffling through me at the same time.

"You know how anal he is," Ty continued when I said nothing. "And you still have to show me where our new office is." Although he managed to keep a grin from reaching his lips, his eyes shone with happiness.

Share an office with Ty. For the entire year. I wasn't going to make it. I'd crumble and get back together with him. And then he'd break my heart all over again when the baby came.

His baby. With Mindy. Fuck me, this really sucked. Bad.

My heart squeezed so tight that my entire chest suddenly ached.

"You and Liv are sharing an office?" Gabe asked, grinning from ear to ear as he closed the short distance between us. Ty returned his grin with an even bigger one, along with a nod. "Holy shit, this just keeps getting better. And just for the record, I had nothing to do with that," he added, looking at me.

I glared at Gabe, wishing that I'd told him everything. Then he wouldn't be so eager to push me and Ty together. Not that it really mattered anymore. Purdon had basically handcuffed us together for the next four months.

"Actually, Lindsay, Ty, and I are sharing an office," I corrected. I glanced at Ty. "I'd rather not wait to put the books on reserve. You guys go have lunch and I'll see you at home later - Gabe. Ty," I added, "I'll e-mail you with the course information and a lesson plan. Just pick which units you want to cover and we'll take turns teaching, that should be easy enough. The office Lindsay and I share is in the basement of this building, room twenty-one.

The door code is seven, four, seven, five pound. The desk on the far left hand side is yours. DO NOT touch anything else. You think that Purdon is anal, wait until you meet Lindsay," I warned.

I turned and strode away without looking back. Fear clawing its way up my spine.

I wasn't going to make it.

•   •   •   •   •

The next day I headed down the hallway to my office with new resolve. I could. No, I would. Work with Ty and keep things strictly professional. All I had to do, was not look at or speak to him, unless absolutely necessary. Or, at least, until I could get my feelings in check. Which should only take a year or so.

Piece of cake.

I entered the office to find Ty and Lindsay chatting as if they were old friends. Ty was perched on the side of Lindsay's desk, playing with her favorite bobble head, while she stared at him with open adoration.

Just great. Another awesome start to another shit-filled day.

I'd been counting on quiet, studious and overtly uptight Lindsay to keep things in our office professional. But that obviously wasn't going to happen. Not only was she letting Ty sit on her desk - she was letting him touch her things.

This was bad. So bad.

Because I'd learned within the first week of sharing an office with Lindsay that she hated chit-chatting, talking about anything personal – hers or yours - and people touching her things. Period.

"Hi Liv," Lindsay greeted. "We have a new office mate. Ty, this is Liv, Liv, Ty," she introduced, two hundred percent more bubbly than usual. Making my stomach heave.

Ugh.

"We've already met," I said dryly, moving past her desk towards the back of the room. "Purdon's making us teach 104 together."

I dropped my bag on to the floor, sinking down on my chair, eyeing Ty's desk to the left of mine. It was already filled with papers, books and miscellaneous writing utensils. He obviously hadn't wasted any time moving in.

Lindsay's high pitched laughter filled the room. And I thought about working from home today.

And possibly for the rest of the semester.

But that would only delay the inevitable. And let Ty know exactly how much he affected me.

Doing my best to ignore the terrible twosome cackling behind me, I pulled out my laptop, plugging it in and firing it up. Making a mental note to bring earplugs with me tomorrow.

"So," Ty said, sneaking up beside me, making me jump. He chuckled, pulling his chair next to mine. "I went over your lesson plan last night. For the most part it looks good, but I think we can tweak it a bit. Maybe split some of the teaching up so that we both contribute each class?" Ty stared at me expectantly, his gorgeous eyes working my insides into a blob of jelly.

I shot him a big, toothy grin. "That sounds great. Just e-mail me your new lesson plan and I'll have a look over it as soon as I find time." I tore my eyes away from his, staring down at my laptop.

Conversation over. Short and sweet. Good job, Liv.

Ty sat, staring at me for a few moments before getting up. "Lindsay, I'm going for a coffee run – my treat. What can I get you?" he asked.

"Oh, that's super sweet of you Ty," she enthused. "I'll have a chai latte please."

"You got it. Back in a minute."

I heard the door click shut as Ty left. Pulling out my phone, I texted Laina.

```
Me:
Officially in hell. Ty is already here and
Lindsay is drooling. Is anything right in the
world anymore?
```

Laina:
LOL. Can't believe Ty has the ice queen worked up. World must be ending. Come home and we'll go for drinks.

Me:
It's only 8:30 in the morning!!

Laina:
Exactly☺ No time like the present.

Me:
We better wait until a respectable hour to start drinking. See you at lunch. Margaritas are on me!

"Oh my God, Liv," Lindsay exclaimed leaning against the corner of my desk a few seconds later. "Do you know who he is?"

I glanced over, amazed at the change in my usually half-dead inside office-mate. Lindsay's cheeks were flushed and her blue eyes almost glistened as she waited for me to respond.

"Ty Benson," I answered slowly, surprised that Lindsay had the ability to name any of the current bands, let alone be gaga over them. She didn't seem like the groupie type. At all.

"YES!" Lindsay shouted. "Ty Benson from Raincheck! Holy Moses, I almost peed my pants when he walked in this morning. This is the best day of my life!"

At least someone was happy.

She reached over shaking my shoulders. This was the first time she'd ever touched me. And we'd been sharing an office for an entire year already. A smile spread across my lips in response to Lindsay's excitement. It was fun to see this side of her. She seemed almost human.

"I take it you're a fan?"

"Oh my God! That's an understatement Liv. I'm their biggest fan!" She looked at me skeptically. "How come you're not excited?"

I shrugged. "I don't know, Ty's just Ty to me."

"Ladies," Ty interrupted, making us both jump.

"Hi Ty, sorry we didn't hear you come in," Lindsay explained, her cheeks getting redder by the second.

Ty grinned at her, then me. "Must have been some conversation. Hope I didn't interrupt anything important. Lindsay, here's your chai latte," he said, wiggling a paper cup out of the beverage holder. "Liv, a peppermint tea with honey for you." He held the paper cup out to me.

"Thanks," I said, taking it from his hands, trying not to react as our fingers brushed. "You didn't have to."

"But I wanted to," Ty said, looking at me intently.

"How do you know what Liv likes to drink?" Lindsay asked, looking at me then Ty. "You actually know each other, don't you? Are you, are you together?" Her eyes narrowed as she stared at me.

"Definitely not," I blurted out, pretending not to notice Ty's face tighten.

"We met this summer. Gabe's band opened for us on tour," he explained patting Lindsay's shoulder, his features smoothing out again.

"Gabe your room-mate?" Lindsay asked, visibly relaxing.

"Remember, I mentioned that Gabe and his band Diesel were going on tour this summer and I was tagging along? That's why I've been gone for the past four months," I added sarcastically although it was obviously lost on Lindsay. Ty had her complete attention. I rolled my eyes, looking back at my computer as Lindsay gushed over him.

"Oh yes, right," she replied. "So did you and Liv hang out all summer?"

"A little here and there. We spent a great day together in New York. Another in Santa Monica," he added.

Of course he had to mention the place where we spent the night together. Where we had the best sex of my entire life.

"That was my favorite. What place was your favorite, Liv? Santa Monica maybe?" Ty stared at me with a stupid, hopeful expression on his face, tearing my heart out.

He was trying to kill me. I could feel it.

"Your girlfriend didn't mind you spending time with Liv?" Lindsay cut in, much to my delight.

"I don't have a girlfriend. I'm currently single," Ty answered putting a hand on each of my shoulders, lightly kneading my tense muscles. "Unless Liv has anything to say about that?"

"I'm pretty sure that I don't have the right to say anything about that," I replied with extreme annoyance and just a hint of hurt.

"Maybe, if you would stop being so pig headed and let me explain, you would," Ty fired back.

"There's nothing to explain. Gabe told me everything already," I hissed.

"Then there's no harm in letting me tell you too."

"Sure, just as soon as pigs fly."

Lindsay looked from Ty to me, then back at Ty again. A look of confusion on her face.

"Liv's got a great sense of humor," Ty said to Lindsay. He squeezed my shoulders tightly, making me squeal like a pig. "Your shoulders are so tight, Darlin'. I'll have to start working in a daily massage for you. Maybe if you loosen up a bit your mood will improve," Ty recommended, his voice pure sarcasm.

"Thanks, but if you want to help ease my tension maybe you could talk to Purdon about making some changes?" I suggested, pushing Ty's hands off my body.

A wry smile played across Ty's lips. "I have no idea what you mean," he said with exaggerated innocence. "I'm pretty happy with the way things have worked out – academically speaking. Hopefully every else will fall into place too."

"I have a ton to do today," I replied between gritted teeth, willing myself to let it go. We didn't need to get into anything in front of Lindsay. "Do you two mind chatting at Lindsay's desk?"

Lindsay looked at me as if I was crazy. "Sure," she readily agreed. "Maybe we should take our drinks out to the seating area so that Liv can get some work done?"

"Super idea!" I faux enthused. "Take your time getting to know each other. By the way Ty, Lindsay's single too." A wry smile crept across my lips as Ty shot me a wicked look.

· · · · ·

The following Monday I entered our shared office to a replay of what I had walked in to every morning last week. Lindsay was perched on the corner of Ty's desk giggling like a school girl as Ty picked through his emails. I squeezed past them, dropping my bag on to the floor.

"Happy Monday, Liv," Lindsay greeted cheerfully. "I put a peppermint tea - with honey - on your desk."

I spied the paper cup by my pop-up Calvin and Hobbs calendar. "Thanks, Lindsay that was really nice of you. Great hair," I complimented. Lindsay's usual tight ponytail was gone today. Instead her light brown hair hung in loose waves around her shoulders. "You should wear your hair down more often."

"Thanks, Liv," Lindsay said shooting me a giant smile. "I think I will. I have some amazing news," she shared with cheerleader-level enthusiasm. "Ty's agreed to surprise my little sister at her birthday party!" she exclaimed.

"Oh wow, that is amazing! Very nice of you Ty," I commented glancing at him.

Ty grinned at me, shrugging his shoulders. "How could I say no to my new office buddy and biggest fan." He shot me a look.

"Office buddy," I returned with a smirk. "Nice."

"I can't believe that I'm friends with Ty Benson!" Lindsay gushed.

"You're a lucky girl," I said sarcastically. "Better watch out or the rumors are going to start flying about you two."

"Be nice," Ty mouthed.

I rolled my eyes, knowing he was right. It wasn't Lindsay's fault that Ty and I had - issues. I pulled the laptop out of my bag and booted it up.

"Oh, Liv, before I forget, Dr. Purdon came by this morning looking for you. He wants you to e-mail him your teaching outline again. I think he misplaced it or something."

"It's only ten minutes after eight! What time was Purdon here?" I asked, annoyed that I'd missed him. Now he'd probably give me the gears for not being dedicated enough to my academic responsibilities. That was the speech I'd over heard Purdon giving to Brad last year after the poor guy requested two days off to help with his sister's wedding.

"Umm, seven-twenty I think," Lindsay replied rearranging the pens in Ty's desktop organizer.

"Were you in yet?" I asked Ty.

"No, I got here just before eight. You have a chance to look over my suggestions for the course yet?"" he asked, watching me intently. I hated when he looked at me like that. It felt so intimate. Like there was no else in the world except for the two of us.

"Sorry, not yet. I'll try to get to it this afternoon."

"So what are you going to e-mail to Purdon?" Ty asked, using his long legs to propel his chair over to my desk.

"I guess I should get some work done," Lindsay interrupted, looking hopefully at Ty.

"Sounds good," Ty replied still focused on me.

"We should go to that new sushi place for lunch today," she suggested, obviously not ready to vacate her spot near Ty yet.

"Great idea, the three of us should all go. Get to know each other better since we'll be spending so much time together this year," Ty returned. "Right, Liv?"

I gave him the evil eye before looking back at my laptop.

"Fantastic, I'll tell you when it's noon, Ty. Actually, let's go at eleven forty-five to beat the rush."

Lindsay slowly sauntered back to her own desk as I started an e-mail to Purdon.

"I asked what you're going to send to Purdon, Liv," Ty demanded placing his hand on top of mine.

"Ty," I hissed, "I'm in the middle of something. Don't you have anything better to do than bother me? Besides there's nothing wrong with my outline. I worked really hard on it."

"Liv, do NOT send Purdon the same teaching outline that you gave to me! It needs to be amended so that we are co-teaching. Not just taking turns," he warned, spinning my chair to face his, inching so close that our knees interlocked between the seats.

The smell of Ty's cologne and feel of his thighs pressing tightly against mine, brought back memories of when we'd made love. My gaze moved from his dark eyes to his perfect lips, then back again as my pulse thumped quicker and quicker. Being so close to Ty was like torture.

All I had to do was lean forward, just a few inches, and my lips would press against his.

"Have a look at what I sent you then we'll go over it and decide – together - what to send Purdon. I mean it, Liv. Don't make me tell him that you're not being cooperative," Ty threatened, dragging me back to reality.

My eyes narrowed. "You wouldn't," I replied through gritted teeth. My temper heating up, killing my desire to molest him.

"Oh, wouldn't I? Which reminds me, we need to spend some time going over your thesis too. I have some ideas for gathering statistical data that'll be applicable for both of our topics." Ty stared at me expectantly, waiting for me to agree.

"I've already gathered a bunch of data," I argued. Not willing to let Ty bully me into spending any more time with him.

"Fine, then we'll go over it this afternoon," he ordered.

"I'm busy." I stared at him defiantly.

"OK, then you can come over tonight. I'll make us supper and we can discuss your thesis while we eat." A wry smile spread across Ty's lips.

"When pigs fly," I seethed, my eyes shooting daggers at him.

"I never knew that you liked pigs so much," he mocked. "Six o'clock sharp, Liv, or I'm talking to Purdon tomorrow." With one push, Ty rolled back to his desk.

"I hate you," I muttered under my breath.

"What's that, Liv? No, you don't have to bring anything, just yourself," Ty replied cheerfully, antagonizing me to the fullest.

My fingers flew over the keyboard pecking out an e-mail to Purdon, then attaching the course outline that I had already done. I glanced over at Ty, watching for a moment as he leafed through a resource book, before pressing send.

· · · · ·

Ty

It was exactly five thirty as I stood outside of Liv's place. Waiting for someone to answer the door. Hoping that she was home.

"Hey man, what're you doing here?" Gabe asked as he pulled the door open. "And what do you have in your hands that smells like heaven?"

"Liv and I have some work to do, so I thought I'd bring over supper for everyone." I handed Gabe a giant brown paper bag just as Liv stepped out of her bedroom.

"Ty brought us supper!" Gabe enthused, racing by Liv as he headed for the kitchen.

Must be something about living in this apartment, because everyone here really enjoyed food.

Liv's eyes narrowed as she watched me close the distance between us.

"I realized that you don't know where I live," I explained, stopping just inches away from her.

Just inches away from touching her. Kissing her. Running my tongue along her smooth neck.

Shit! Thinking this way wasn't going to help.

"So I thought that I'd come to you," I continued, working to pull it together before I did something that would make Liv freak out. "It's been a good month since we talked about your thesis. I can't wait to see what you've got so far. From the sound of it, you've made some real progress." Unable to help myself, I inched forward. Drinking in her scent and her warmth.

"Ty," she said, her voice barely above a whisper, our eyes locked together.

And that was it.

Leaning in, I brushed my lips against hers. Slowly. Lightly. Trying not to push it too fast or too far. Until Liv ran her tongue along my bottom lip.

And I completely lost it.

I pushed her against the wall, fisting both hands in her hair, kissing her. Deep and demanding. Trying to devour every last bit of her.

"Ty, Liv, get your asses in here, we're all set. Liv, Ty brought Chinese food – your favorite!" Gabe called from the living room.

"Fuck," I breathed against Liv's mouth as she stiffened.

Shoving me away, Liv headed into the living room without uttering a single word. Bringing me crashing down.

After taking a few seconds to get *everything* under control, I followed her.

"Thanks, Ty," Laina mumbled with a mouth full of noodles as I entered the living room. "This was super nice of you. Maybe you should come over more often." She grinned at Liv, then me.

'Traitor,' Liv mouthed as she plunked down beside Laina. Her plate already heaping.

"Glad you're enjoying it, Laina," I replied, filling my own plate from the makeshift buffet on their coffee table. I sat down beside Gabe on the floor, stretching my legs out. "So I was thinking that we should get a foosball tourney going Thursday night? I'll order pizza and get some beer. What'da you think?"

"I'm totally in!" Gabe enthused.

"Oh, me too," Laina chimed. "Unless it's a guys' only night."

"Girls are always invited to my place," I returned with a grin, looking at Liv. "Liv, you coming too?"

"I have plans for Thursday," she said before shoving an entire spring roll into her mouth, slowly chewing.

OK?

"What plans do you have?" Gabe asked, shooting her a look. "We were just talking about hitting happy hour at The Pub on Thursday. You know, grabbing some pub grub and a beer."

Liv pointed to her jam packed mouth, clearly happy that she couldn't partake in the conversation.

Well played.

•　•　•　•　•

After finishing eating, we all helped to haul containers and plates into the kitchen.

"So what are you doing this Thursday?" I asked as Liv packed the remainder of the food into the fridge.

"Going out with some people that I used to work with at the Shoe Store. I haven't really had a chance to see them lately," she replied, looking anywhere but at me.

Damn. She was lying, right to my face. And not very well.

"Mmm," I said, leaning against the wall next to the fridge. "You should see if you can reschedule and come Thursday. You haven't been to my place yet."

"No, I haven't," Liv replied, moving over to the sink. A giant smirk spread across her face as she washed her hands. "You should ask Lindsay to come."

"Very funny. And don't you dare mention it to her," I said softly into Liv's ear as I reached an arm around either side of her waist, sliding my hands under the running water.

"You done yet?" she demanded. Her voice filled with annoyance, although her body leaned into mine.

"Not yet," I said resting my head on the top of hers, pressing into her even more. "This may take a while. My hands are really saucy."

"So is your mouth," she quipped.

"I can think of some interesting ways you can help to fix that."

"Looks like we've made up," Gabe commented as he stepped into the kitchen.

I dried my hands, giving the towel to Liv before shifting us to face Gabe. My arms wrapping tightly around her waist to prevent her from escaping.

"You'd think so," Liv hissed, attempting to move away. But I held her captive against my chest. Contemplating never letting her go again.

Gabe grinned at the two of us. "Think I'll let you two work this out on your own. Laina and I are heading over to Brian and Liam's, so the place is all yours. Have fun," he called, turning the corner into the hallway.

"Wait!" Liv called, pushing away from me, sprinting after Gabe. "You never said anything about going out."

Stepping into the hallway, I watched Liv glance from Laina to Gabe. Gabe just shrugged before grabbing Laina's hand and pulling her out the door.

I was developing a serious man-crush on that guy.

"Wanna go see a movie?" I asked as Liv stood, staring at the door. Probably wishing that she could leave too. Obviously afraid to be alone with me.

"What?!" she exclaimed, swinging around with fire in her eyes. "I thought you came over here to work?"

I couldn't help but grin. Making Liv angry reminded me of when we first started hanging out. Or whatever you'd call that.

"I did, but now I feel like going to see a show. We can work extra hard tomorrow. Come on, Liv, loosen up a little and enjoy yourself. I promise I'll behave if you say yes."

She stared at me with doubt written all over her face.

"Please, Liv? My treat," I cajoled. Fighting the urge to close the space between us and touch her. Everywhere. I jammed my hands into the pockets of my jeans as a safety measure. "I was thinking that, since we're going to be spending so much time together. With work and after-work activities. It'd be nice if we could at least be friends again."

"Friends?" Liv choked. "That kiss felt a little more than friendly." Her eyes fell on my lips and I jammed my hands further into my pockets.

I wanted to kiss her again. So bad.

"Really, I thought that it felt quite friendly," I countered with a grin. But instead of returning my smile, she shot me a look that would bring a raging bull to its knees.

OK, humor wasn't working, so let's try the truth.

"Look Darlin', I'm sorry about what happened in Santa Monica. I really am. I know that it looked bad. And that I should have told Mindy to fuck off with you standing right there, beside me." I sighed. "If I could go back, that's exactly what I would do."

"But you didn't. You left me sitting in that hotel room, while you comforted HER. Eating our time up. Knowing that I had to leave," Liv almost spit.

She was right. Completely right.

"I know," I agreed, "it was a stupid, shitty move. I was just so focused on making sure that Mindy knew I was in love with you. And that she meant absolutely nothing to me."

"You called her sweetheart," Liv said, her eyes filled with hurt.

"No. Did I?"

Did I? I didn't remember that.

"You definitely did."

"I'm sorry, it must have just come out. Old habits die hard, I guess."

Liv nodded. "That's what I was told."

Shit, I wasn't getting any where.

"Is there anything that I can say or do to make you forgive me? The whole Mindy thing was a giant, fucked up mistake. Please Liv. I can't live without you. You mean everything to me," I begged, wanting to break down right then and there. "I love you."

Liv's eyes softened and she took a tentative step towards me. "I love you too. But I, I just don't know." She moved away again.

She loves me! My heart pounded like a jack hammer inside of my chest. Oh, please.

"Just tell me how to fix this. I'll do anything Darlin'. I swear, I will."

Liv looked at me for a long moment. Probably the longest moment of my entire life. "Time," she finally muttered.

"Time?" I returned.

"I need some time. To make sure that you mean it. That things between you and Mindy aren't going to change. You broke my heart that day Ty, and I can't - I won't - put myself through that again."

I nodded, feeling a tiny bit lighter for the first time in weeks and weeks. "Time. I can do that, because nothing is going to change between me and Mindy. Ever."

A sharp laugh spewed from Liv's lips. "Of course it won't."

"I'm serious Liv. You're it for me. So if you don't take me back, I'm going to become an old lonely spinster."

"I think that spinsters are women," Liv deadpanned.

"Liv, we used to be friends. We used to hang out together. You know, talk and have fun. Do you think that, maybe, while we're taking a time out, we could attempt to be friends again? At least. I miss you," I tried. Willing to take whatever Liv would give me right now. I just needed to be around her. And I needed her to be around me.

"Friends?" she reiterated. "Just friends. No more kissing or touching?"

"Not even if you beg me to."

Oh, please beg me to touch you.

"Nice try Benson. I'm in psych too you know. Go use your reverse psychology on someone else."

"Fine," I sighed, "then how about we start with a movie? No kissing, no touching."

"A movie," Liv contemplated. "OK, I guess going to a movie never hurt anyone."

Really? Sitting beside Liv in a darkened theatre without touching her, may very well kill me.

Chapter 19 ~ Liv

Today was THE day. The unfortunate Friday we had our meeting with Dr. Purdon. Our very first meeting. And to say that I was terrified would be the biggest understatement. Ever. Because Purdon scared the crap out of me.

I'd been waiting for Ty to come back to the office for at least thirty minutes. So that we could go to Purdon's office together. But he never materialized. Which was odd, because things had been decent between us ever since we went to the movie. And agreed to try the friends thing.

So, I trudged towards Purdon's office – alone. Hoping Ty was going to show up so that I wouldn't have to face Purdon by myself.

"Come in," I heard Purdon call out through the thick wooden door as I knocked for the second time.

I turned the knob. As the door swung open, I spotted Ty sitting in front of Purdon's desk.

Thank God!

Ty nodded as I slipped into the room.

"Hi, Dr. Purdon," I greeted as brightly as I could manage while my stomach flip flopped like a fish out of water. I'd only been here a few moments and already felt like a basket case.

Purdon eyed me, a sour expression on his face. "Have a seat Ms. Madison. Mr. Benson and I were just going over the teaching outline for your course."

I glanced at Ty, and he shook his head - just a bit.

Oh shit! Not good.

"This outline looks exactly the same as the one that you submitted in August," Purdon continued. "I see no changes, other than assigning one topic to you and the next to Mr. Benson. I was pretty specific in my instructions to you both Ms. Madison. I pointedly said that I wanted you two to collaborate on teaching this class. NOT just take turns like well-behaved kindergarten children. What do you have to say about this Ms. Madison?"

I looked over at Ty, wondering what he'd told Purdon. Ty met my gaze, his eyes wide and wary.

"Mr. Benson already had his turn to explain. Now I want to hear what you have to say."

I drew in a deep breath. My stomach retching. "This is completely my fault, Dr. Purdon. Ty wanted to make some changes, but I thought that my teaching outline was good."

"Hmm, that's interesting. Apparently you two are in cahoots. I'm not sure who's covering for whom, but I want this situation rectified by Monday. I expect an improved co-teaching outline to be waiting in my inbox by five pm on Sunday. No excuses!"

"Dr. Purdon, Liv, honestly," Ty began.

"I've already heard more than enough from you, Mr. Benson," Purdon interrupted, staring at Ty with disappointment all over his face. "When you called me this summer to personally ask if I would take you on as a grad student I was honored. Up until now, your work has been exemplary. I expect great things from you, Mr. Benson, and this isn't even close to being good," he added, tapping my course outline with his stubby index finger.

What the fuck?!

I stared at Ty with my mouth hanging open. Like an idiot, I'd just assumed that he'd been assigned to Purdon the same way I had. Never. In a million years. Did I even consider that Ty had requested Purdon. On purpose!

He'd completely manipulated – everything! Setting this entire year up so that we'd be stuck together. Ass wipe.

Anger began to fester deep in my gut.

Purdon nodded to Ty, then me. "Good day Mr. Benson, Ms. Madison," he said dismissing us.

And I couldn't get out of there fast enough. I needed to get away from Purdon. And Ty.

Ty and I vacated Purdon's office, stepping into the hallway. And right into the midst of a large group of female students. To my extreme happiness, it took all of two seconds for one of them to recognize Ty.

"Oh my God, it's Ty Benson!" a girl exclaimed and the group closed in around him.

He grabbed for my hand, but I managed to wiggle in between the girls. *Escaping.*

Without looking back, I headed for home, where a nice glass of wine and giant piece of the chocolate cake waited to ease my angst.

• • • • •

The doorbell rang as I poured a generous class of wine to go with my generous piece of cake. Stepping into the hallway I yelled, "Go away, no one's home."

Before I had a chance to move, the door flung open and Ty stepped inside. His face echoing what I felt. Pure anger.

Shit, I forgot to lock the door.

"Thanks for waiting for me," he said sarcastically, slipping his sneakers off.

"I didn't want to come in between you and your female fans. I know how much you enjoy rubbing elbows and whatnot, with all of those young sorority girls," I called as I hurried into the kitchen. Wishing that Ty would just go away. But knowing that wasn't going to happen.

"Ha ha," Ty returned. An undeniable edge to his voice. "Don't walk away from me, Liv! We need to talk."

"You fed me to the wolves today," I accused, swinging around to face him.

"I did not feed you to the wolves!" Ty fired back. "Actually, I took most of the heat for this before you arrived. Although you're probably too pig-headed to realize it."

With one stride, he ate up the remaining space between us. I angled my head up, staring him right in the eye as we stood toe to toe. My temper raging.

Pig-headed? Ass-wipe. I'd show him pig-headed.

"I told Purdon it was my fault that your shitty teaching outline hadn't been fixed," Ty continued, "because I'd been busy getting settled in."

"So let me get this straight, you went to Purdon's office early. Without me. To..." I put my index fingers in the air, making quotes as I said, "take the heat for me."

"He caught me in the hall a half an hour earlier," Ty said with complete exasperation. "Don't you think that Purdon went easy on you, considering you deliberately disobeyed his orders?"

We stared at each other for a moment. My mind replaying the scene in Purdon's office. Admittedly, Purdon had been pretty decent. Which was totally out of character for him. Last year, he spent an entire hour berating another grad student for the improper use of a footnote.

"I told you that we needed to make some adjustments," Ty added, when I stood there. Mute. Starting to feel bad. "I e-mailed my suggestions to you, like you requested. But you didn't even bother to look at them. Did you?" he demanded. "You're so fricken stubborn, Liv. You screwed us both over by refusing to act like adults and work things out with me."

And my temper flared - again. No one else could push my buttons quite like Ty did.

Dick-head.

"Work things out with you?!" I stormed. "That's a good one, considering you didn't even give me the option to decide if I wanted to work things out with you. Did you?"

"Meaning?" Ty asked, his eyebrows pulling together in obvious frustration.

"You called Purdon to ask if he would be your advisor!" I fumed. "I can't believe you. Is there anything that you won't do to get what you want?"

Ty sighed. "I was desperate, Liv. You wouldn't talk to me. I figured that if you were forced to be around me, you'd eventually forgive me and we could work things out. And just for the record, I never said anything to Purdon about co-teaching." A grin pulled at the corners of Ty's mouth.

"You're a real piece of work, Benson."

Ty reached around, resting his hands against the countertop on either side of my waist. His eyes piercing mine.

"Move!" I demanded.

"Not until you agree to work things out like rational human beings," Ty returned, his voice low and deep. The warmth of his body permeating mine. Making me overheat.

"Well, I guess we're going to have a problem then because only one of us falls into that category," I retorted, clenching my teeth together. "Please MOVE," I hissed, starting to feel desperate. Like a caged animal.

"First promise me that we'll work it out," Ty asked and it was clear that he wasn't talking about the course outline. "This is getting ridiculous, Liv. I know that I've hurt you and I'm sorry. It wasn't intentional. I'm not getting back together with Mindy. I promise. Can't we get past this?" he pleaded, his voice breaking along with my heart. "Please Liv. I miss you so much."

Completely worn out, I leaned my head against Ty's chest, closing my eyes and inhaling deeply. It had been a long week, and I didn't have anything left in me. I was tired of fighting with Ty. And I was tired of constantly wanting him.

All of it was too much.

Ty wrapped his arms around me, pulling me tightly against his body. And I couldn't help it. I slid my arms around Ty's waist, hugging him back. Relishing the feel of being in his arms again.

I could stay like this all night. Or, possibly, forever.

Ty dipped his head, pressing his lips to mine.

Slowly and thoroughly he kissed me. Making my legs feel weak and turning my insides into complete mush.

"I miss you, Liv," he breathed against my mouth. "I miss you so much."

"I miss you, too," I whispered, pressing my lips to his again. Slowly, I slid my hands down his back then underneath his t-shirt as he kissed me senseless. "Let's go to my room," I suggested when the need to be with him had beaten down my better judgment.

Ty eyes met mine. "Does this mean that we're OK again?" he asked, hope evident on his face.

Making me feel like a bitch. Because I knew that we weren't OK. That we'd never be OK again. But I wanted him.

So much.

"Do you want to talk or do you want to get naked?" I replied kissing his neck, sliding one hand around to the inside of his leg.

He caught my hand in his, holding it still. "Get naked - more than you can possibly imagine." Ty pressed his lips against mine again. Softly. And so sweetly that it made me want to cry. "As long as it means that we'll be together from now on."

I studied Ty's face for a moment, caught between my overwhelming desire for him and the truth.

"I'm offering you sex. With no strings attached. Just this one time," I clarified. Knowing that this wasn't a good idea. But desperately wanting to, or maybe even needing to, be with Ty. Just once more.

"No relationship. No commitment. Just sex?" he confirmed, his eyes sweeping over my face.

"Yup, isn't that what every guy wants?" Slowly I ran my free hand over his butt.

"Not this guy and definitely not from you," he replied letting me go, taking a large step backwards.

"What?" I asked. "I thought that you wanted me?" I did my best to work my mouth into a pout like I'd seen Laina do a million times before. Guys were always putty in her hands when she did this.

"More than anything. But I don't want to just have sex with you Liv. I want to make love to you. I want to make love to you everyday for the rest of my life and I won't settle for anything less."

I sighed in frustration. Apparently, I wasn't very good at pouting so would have to go with my usual. The direct approach. "Making love isn't an option. Hot, sweaty sex is," I clarified looking at Ty expectantly almost salivating at the thought of running my hands over his naked body.

I took a step towards him.

"No thanks." He held his hand out to stop me from closing the remaining distance between us.

OK, this was a switch. Usually I was the one saying no.

"When you want me to make love to you, with piles of strings and a big, fat, long-term relationship attached. Just let me know."

Ty strode out of the kitchen, leaving me standing there feeling like a complete idiot.

Gabe walked into the apartment a few minutes later. Finding me in the same spot, still contemplating what had just happened with Ty.

"Liv, please tell me that you and Ty aren't fighting again?" he demanded moving across the kitchen towards me. "I just saw him leaving. He told me that he's not going out with everyone tonight. What'd you say to him?"

"Nothing," I protested. Gabe eyed me skeptically. "Fine. I offered to have hot, sweaty sex with him. So he left."

Laughter spewed from Gabe's mouth. "That's a good one, Liv," he snorted. "Seriously though, what did you say to make Ty take off like that? I thought you guys were friends, or at least friendly, again?"

"I already told you – true to life. Ask Ty yourself," I added as Gabe rolled his eyes.

"Oh Baby Doll, what am I going to do with you?" he mused. "I just don't get it. Ty's crazy about you and you're obviously crazy about him. Work it out so that the rest of us don't have to be crazy too. I'm begging you," he added holding his hands under his chin as if he was praying.

"Yeah, yeah," I replied, moving past Gabe and into my bedroom.

Feeling defeated and beat down, I flopped on my bed still reeling from the fact that Ty had walked away from me. He'd literally said no to having sex with me. Then walked away! I wouldn't have seen that coming in a million years.

On the bright side, maybe it was a good thing. Not having sex again would keep things simple between us.

Simple.

That's exactly what I needed right now. That and a big glass of wine. And maybe two pieces of chocolate cake.

Chapter 20 ~ Ty

Fear pounded through my body like a jack-hammer as I snuck into Liv and Laina's bedroom. Hoping that Laina didn't sleep naked. And that Liv wouldn't kill me after I woke her up.

We hadn't left things on a good note when I walked away from her yesterday. But I needed more than just sex from her. A lot more. And I might have figured out how to get it.

Fortunately, Gabe had agreed to get up and let me into their apartment this morning. So with fingers crossed, I crept over to Liv's bed, perching on the edge by her shoulders.

"Liv," I whispered into her ear. Her eyes fluttered open, meeting mine. "Wake up Darlin'. We need to get going."

"I must be dreaming," she muttered, her eyes drifting shut again.

"Liv," I whispered, "it's not a dream. Wake up," I cajoled, gently shaking her.

She reached up grabbing my t-shirt, pulling me down on to the bed next to her, snuggling into me.

We weren't going to get very far like this. But God, it felt good to hold her.

I wrapped my arms around her, pulling her even tighter. Stroking her hair and planting tiny kisses across her forehead. "Liv, we need to get going. Come on, Darlin', time to get up and moving," I coaxed, loosening my arms. Attempting to move away from her.

"Shhh," Liv hushed, pulling me close again. Wrapping her body around mine. "I'm not ready to wake up. I'm having the best dream."

"What are you dreaming about?" I asked quietly.

"That you're here. Holding me."

And, at that exact moment, I knew this had to work. Because we belonged together.

I pressed my lips to Liv's, smiling against her mouth. "You're not dreaming, Darlin'. I'd love to spend the day in bed with you, but we've got to go. It's getting late."

"Go where and what time is it?" she asked, opening her eyes.

"It's seven in the fricken morning! On a Saturday!" Laina hissed from across the room. "Time to shut the hell up!"

Liv and I grinned at each other.

"Sorry, Laina," I said quietly. "Liv, get ready and pack a small overnight bag. We won't be back until tomorrow evening."

I started to get up, but the sight of her laying there. Watching me. Hair a mess. Eyes wide. Did me in. I leaned down, kissing her. Slowly. Sensually. While her hands pushed underneath my t-shirt, running up and down my back.

"If you're gonna make out, get your own room for fuck sake!" Laina groaned from the other side of the room.

It was probably a good thing that Liv didn't have her own room right now. Because I didn't think that I'd be able to say no this time. And giving into Liv, without those agreed upon strings in place, wouldn't get me anywhere.

Or at least not where I wanted to be.

With a giant sigh and huge amount of effort, I tore myself away from Liv, heading towards the door.

"Hurry up, we're leaving in twenty minutes," I confirmed before stepping out of the room, closing the door behind me.

. . . . .

Twenty-five minutes later, we were in my silver SUV heading toward the docks. The shock that I felt from Liv agreeing to come with me – without a fight – was just wearing off. I expected to have to beg and cajole and then beg some more. But that didn't happen. She walked out of her bedroom with an overnight bag, put on her sandals. And away we went.

Talk about invasion of the body snatchers. Who was this? And what happened to the stubborn woman I fell in love with?

Not that I was complaining.

I glanced at Liv again, my stomach churning in anticipation of what might happen this weekend. I desperately wanted a miracle, yet knew that something worse might come from it.

But it was a gamble that I had to take.

"Why won't you tell me where we're going?" Liv asked for the twentieth time. Excitement evident on her face. Filling up my heart. Fueling my hope.

"All in good time, Darlin'," I answered with a grin. Reaching over I took her hand, threading our fingers together.

"Are we taking a ferry somewhere?" she probed as we headed toward the docks.

"We're going to the island. And that's the only thing I'm telling you. So just sit back and enjoy the ride."

• • • • •

Two hours and twenty-five minutes later we were on Vancouver Island, pulling up to a sprawling ocean front home, where the most important people in the world – to me – would be this weekend.

"This house is beautiful," Liv commented, studying the large A-frame structure filled with floor-to-roof windows.

I shot her a nervous grin before grabbing our bags out of the back seat. Taking Liv's hand, I led her towards the oversized front doors.

"After you, my lady," I said pushing a door open. Making a sweeping motion with my arm.

Wide-eyed and obviously curious, Liv stepped into vaulted ceiling foyer taking in the dark granite floors and contrasting light grey walls. Even though I'd been here thousands of times, I still had to admire how beautifully put together this house was.

"This is beyond gorgeous," Liv said quietly, her face filled with awe.

"Thank you," my mom replied, stepping around the corner with a welcoming smile.

"Mom," I greeted, scooping her up in a giant hug. "Liv, this is my mom, Marie. Mom, THIS is Liv."

Liv glanced at me for a moment before holding her hand out to my mom, sheer surprise on her face.

"Liv," Mom said, ignoring Liv's outstretched hand, leaning in to hug her instead.

And this was just one of the reasons why my mom was the absolute best.

Mom took Liv's hand, leading her into the adjacent living room with me trailing behind. "I've heard so much about you, sweetheart. It's wonderful that you and Ty could find the time to come and visit."

I gave my mom another hug before pulling Liv down beside me on the enormous black leather sectional. "We're so glad to be here," I replied, grinning like crazy. Having the two women that I loved most, in the same room together, was like my version of heaven.

I just knew that they were going to love each other.

"Yes, thank you for having us, Mrs. Benson," Liv added as I draped my arm around her shoulder, pulling her close. Reveling in the fact that she instantly snuggled into my side.

"Call me Marie, sweetheart," Mom invited. "Now what can I get you both to drink?"

"Tea would be great, Mom. Liv?" I asked.

"Tea is perfect. Can I help you?"

"No, thank you, Liv," Mom responded, clearly pleased and surprised by Liv's offer to help.

The few times that I'd brought Mindy home, she'd never offered to help. Not once. With anything.

"You two just sit and relax while I fix us a bite to eat and brew some tea. Caroline and Ian and the kids will be here this afternoon, so you better enjoy the peace while it lasts." Mom stood for a moment smiling at us before moving off to the kitchen.

"Mom? Caroline and Ian and the kids?" Liv questioned, eyeing me.

"This is my mom's house – obviously." I grimaced, watching her closely. Waiting to see if she was going to explode. Mindy definitely would have. "Caroline is my sister and Ian is her husband," I explained, intertwining my free hand with hers. My eyes never leaving her face.

"Why didn't you tell me that we were going to meet your family?" Liv asked in a hushed voice. "I would have at least dressed nicer," she said glancing down at her faded jeans and pink tie-dyed tank top.

I didn't think it was possible, but I loved her even more now.

She wasn't angry that I'd basically hijacked her into meeting my family. Nope, not my woman, she was worried that she wasn't dressed nice enough.

I was a lucky man.

"I didn't tell you, because I didn't think that you'd agree to come with me. And you look amazing." She did. She always did. "So, if I had asked you to come and meet my family, you would have said?"

Liv crinkled her nose, looking somehow adorable and sexy at the same time. "Probably no."

"Probably no?" I returned with a cocky grin.

"Fine. Definitely no," she admitted - reluctantly.

"Then I'm glad that I didn't ask you. Relax, you're going to love my family," I assured her. Leaning in, I pressed my lips softly against hers.

This was going to work. We were going to get back together. I could feel it.

· · · · ·

"Your house is beautiful, Mrs. Benson," Liv complimented, as the three of us sat down for lunch an hour later.

"Marie," Mom reminded her, smiling from across the table. Mom looked out of the large picture window at the immense back yard that eventually turned into ocean. "Thank you, Ty bought it for me after his father and I split up. He insisted that I didn't take anything from Phillip. That he'd look after me," Mom shared, her eyes misting up.

"Phillip can be a bit much," I elaborated, reaching across the table to pat Mom's hand. "It was just easier this way. He's a lawyer for a big corporation," I shared as Liv stared at me with wide eyes. "If Mom had asked for anything, although she deserved more than half of everything," I said nodding at her, "he would have made things hard on her. Fortunately, I was able to help out a bit. Guess my unfortunate career choice wasn't so unfortunate after all."

Liv shot me a grin and I wondered if she was remembering one of our first conversations. When I told her about Phillip's thoughts on my career choice.

God, it felt good to prove him wrong.

"Helped me a bit," Mom mused with a shake of her head. "My teacher's salary definitely wouldn't have bought this house. I keep telling Ty that it's too much for one person."

"True," I teased, shooting Mom a grin. "But with Caroline and Ian and their three little monkeys coming to visit all the time, you need the room." I pushed a forkful of quiche into my mouth and couldn't help but make a classic Liv mmm sound. My mom was the best cook. Ever.

"Hopefully there will be more grandchildren on the way soon. Ty is going to be a wonderful father," Mom said to Liv. And I choked on my quiche. "Wait till you see him with his nieces. It'll melt your heart."

"Thanks, Mom," I muttered. Watching Liv to see if she was going to freak out from Mom's – us having babies - innuendo.

Nope. Nothing, but a giant smile. Thank God!

"Are your parents still together, Liv?"

"Yes," Liv answered as she scooped another piece of quiche onto her plate. "And still amazingly happy together. It used to embarrass my sisters and me when they'd hold hands and kiss in public. But now I really appreciate that. You are an amazing cook, Mrs. – Marie," she complimented, making my mom's entire day. Or maybe week.

"Liv enjoys her food," I teased, putting my hand on Liv's knee.

"I like a girl who eats," Mom replied watching us intently. "I don't think I ever saw Mindy eat a thing. She was a real treat."

And here we go.

I rolled my eyes. "Water under the bridge, Mom."

"Well, Liv seems like a genuinely nice person. It's about time you found a nice girl. So what are your plans for the future sweetheart?" Mom asked Liv, and I couldn't help but hope that I was a part of them.

Although I was fairly certain that Liv realized my mom was, in essence, interviewing her, she didn't seem to mind. She happily answered questions about her life and future desires. While asking a ton of questions of her own. About Mom and our family, and what I was like as a child – which was slightly embarrassing.

"Look at the time," Mom gasped, glancing at the clock on the wall almost two hours later. "This was such a wonderful conversation. I didn't realize how fast the time went."

Neither did I. Sitting here with Liv, chatting with Mom, felt so normal. Like Liv and I had been together - forever. And were just over for a visit.

My heart swelled. This was turning out even better than I hoped it would.

"The kids will be here in a few more hours," Mom said, getting up and patting me on the shoulder. "I should get started on supper. I hope you like salmon wellington with creamy dill potatoes, Liv? It's Ty's favorite meal."

"That sounds incredible. Do you need any help?" Liv asked, stacking our lunch dishes together.

"Please leave those," Mom insisted. "I know that you two have some school work to do. Go and get that done so we can enjoy the evening together." She kissed my cheek before shooing us out of the kitchen.

"You heard the boss lady," I said, taking Liv's hand. Leading her into the dining room. "Why don't you get settled and look over the outline that I sent you for Purdon? I'm just going to take our bags upstairs. Then we can go over everything together." I kissed Liv, nice and long, before heading towards the foyer where we'd left our things this morning.

"So what do you think?" I asked a few minutes later, sitting down beside Liv at the enormous mahogany dining table.

"OK, I hate to admit it, but I like your course outline better." Liv rolled her eyes as a giant grin spread across my lips.

"What's that?" I returned, holding a hand to my ear.

"Very funny, Benson. Fine," Liv said drawing in a deep breath. "I'm only going to say this once so you better listen." Pause. "You were right and I was wrong. I'm really sorry that I got you in crap with Purdon."

A smirk played across my lips. "So, we're good?"

"We're good," Liv agreed. "Let's send this off to Purdon, then I'll show you the research I've done so far for my thesis."

The next few hours flew by as we discussed our work and made an outline for additional research.

. . . . .

"Hello everybody, we're here!" a tiny voice hollered from the foyer.

"Looks like the monkeys have descended," I said, winking at Liv. Taking her hand, I led her out of the dining room towards the foyer.

"Uncle Ty!" my three little monkeys screamed in unison, running over to me, jumping up and down with their hands high above their heads. I bent over, scooping all of them into my arms, planting a kiss on each little pink cheek.

"Liv," I said turning towards her with a bundle of joy times three stowed in my arms. "This little monkey is Maddy," I said looking at the biggest girl, "she's six. This little monkey is Sadie." I nibbled the middle girl's ear. She giggled, pressing a wet kiss on my cheek. "She's four. And the littlest monkey is Jessie, she's two."

"I'm almost three!" Jessie corrected in an authoritarian voice, looking at me with a stern expression.

"So sorry, Jess." I grinned sheepishly. "I stand corrected. Jessie is almost three. This is Caroline, my sister, and Ian, my brother in law. Everyone, this is Liv."

Liv smiled at the five faces staring at her and I worried that she might feel overwhelmed.

"Nice to meet you all," she greeted, seeming fine. At ease even.

Jess wiggled out of my arms, marching over to Liv. Looking up with a tiny hand perched on each hip she asked, "Do you like red jello and cheerios?"

"Definitely," Liv replied, shooting me a look. I shrugged, not sure where this was going.

Jessie held her little arms up to Liv, waiting to be picked up. Once she was safely stowed in Liv's arms, the two studied each other. While the rest of us held our breath.

"I like you," Jess finally stated placing a chubby hand on each of Liv's cheeks.

"I'm glad. I like you too." Liv smiled at Jessie then at me.

Thank you, my little monkey.

. . . . .

The eight of us spent the remainder of the day eating, playing games and having the best time ever. Liv and I had even been nominated by the girls to get them ready for, and tucked into, bed. Which I always loved doing and was ecstatic that Liv enjoyed it too.

"Liv sweetheart, you look tired," Mom commented as we relaxed in the living room. Enjoying the peace and quiet that had settled in after the girls were asleep. "Those girls can wear you out. I think that Jessie is taken with you." Mom smiled at Liv.

"I'm definitely taken with her," Liv returned. "Your kids are so great," she said to Caroline and Ian.

"We're kind of fond of them. However, we are willing to lend them out," Ian joked.

"We might have to take you up on that for a weekend," I said glancing at Liv, loving the thought of playing house with her and my nieces. "The girls would have a blast in the city."

Liv grinned at me, letting her head fall against my shoulder. "That would be fun," she agreed.

And I think she honestly meant it. My love for her just kept growing. If this kept up, I'd have to convince Liv to fly to Vegas with me and get married before the weekend was over.

If only.

"OK sweetheart, you better get to bed or you're never going to make it through tomorrow's festivities. The girls have big plans before you two go back to the city. Ty, show Liv where you will be sleeping," Mom directed.

"I'd love to visit some more, but I think you're right Marie. I'm beat."

I stood, pulling Liv up off the couch. "Night everyone," I called as we sauntered out of the room.

"Your mom knows that we're not actually together. Right?" Liv asked when we reached the staircase. Her face suddenly serious.

"My mom chooses to believe what she wants."

"Meaning?" Liv probed, as we headed up the large, open staircase.

"I never keep anything from my mom. She knows what happened between us and how I feel about you. She also knows that we want different things."

"Different things?"

When we reached the landing I turned to face her. "I want to be with you and only you, in every way possible. And you only want one thing from me." I strode over to the first door, pushing it open. Disappearing inside while Liv stood with her jaw on the floor.

"Oh my God, Ty! You told your mom that I only want to have sex with you?!" she demanded trailing after me, closing the door behind us.

"Well, it's true. Isn't it?" I stated, trying to keep a smile from breaking loose. While Liv looked like she wanted to break certain parts of my body loose. Or maybe off. "Bathroom's there." I nodded towards the open door on the right hand side of the room.

I placed our bags on the padded grey bench at the foot of the bed, unzipping both.

"You want to put your clothes in a drawer or just leave them in the bag?" I asked pulling a pair of pajama pants and t-shirt out of my bag. Doing my best not to look at Liv. Because I knew that she wanted me to. And it clearly pissed her off that I wasn't.

God, it was fun riling her up.

Liv stepped closer to me. Staring right at me. Waiting for me to look over. "You seriously told your mom that I only want to have sex with you?"

she asked incredulously, when I finally glanced at her.

"Again, it's true isn't it? Or have you changed your mind about giving us a chance?" I turned, facing her. Waiting for her to either agree or explode.

Preferably the former. But, based on her expression, probably the latter.

"Have you changed your mind about having sex with me?" she replied instead. Her stubborn streak rearing its ugly head.

Gabe was so right about her.

"Not without those strings," I said firmly.

"Fine." She shrugged, watching my face as she slowly took off her clothes, laying them neatly on the bench beside me.

Fuck! She was playing dirty.

She pulled a small flowery bag out of her duffle. "I'm going to have a shower," she said smirking at me. Slowly, she made her way across the room heading towards the washroom.

While I stood there. Watching her. Suffering.

"Mind if I join you?" I asked a minute later. When the last of my willpower had deserted me.

"Not in the least," Liv invited, moving over to make room.

I stepped into the shower as Liv lathered her hair. A huge smile on her lips as she eyed me. Clearly thinking she'd won.

And maybe she had.

We soaped and rinsed without saying a word, our bodies brushing together intimately in the tight space.

"Want me to wash your back?" I asked, my voice husky, my need for her more than evident.

"That would be nice," Liv said, turning away from me. Pushing her ass against my erection.

Fuck! She was bad. But two could play at this game.

Slowly. Methodically. I washed Liv's back and shoulders, finally reaching around to soap her mid-section. My hands dipping lower with each stroke, moving down the fronts of her legs. Then running up the inside of her thighs, close to her pussy. So very close.

Liv leaned further back, spreading her legs wider.

And I knew exactly what she wanted. Lightly, I brushed the tips of my fingers over her clit.

A giant grown left Liv's lips, just before she pleaded, "oh, yes. Touch me, Ty. Make me feel good."

"Just admit that you love me. That you want to be with me and I'll make you a very happy woman. In every way possible," I breathed into her ear, pressing my fingertips against her clit, moving them up and down as she thrust against my hand. "Tell me," I demanded, sliding my other hand up to her tit. Pinching and tugging on her nipple while I worked her clit. Hard. Making her moan. "Just say it," I insisted again.

But Liv refused to give in. She refused to say the words that I needed to hear.

God she was stubborn.

Using super human strength, I took my hands off her. Just before she came.

Liv turned towards me running her hands up my wet chest, locking her fingers behind my neck. Her eyes dark with desire. Filled with frustration. "You know that I want you and it's obvious that you want me," she said pressing her pelvis against my throbbing cock. "So just shut up and fuck me already."

"Not until you say that you'll give us a chance. I need to hear those words Darlin'. Please," I begged, on the verge of losing complete control. "Once we're together again, there's no going back. You know it. We both know it."

"Sex is what I'm offering you. All that I'm offering you. And, given the circumstances, I don't think that you should be asking for anything more," she replied, her eyes hardening with each word.

Circumstances? I just didn't get it. I didn't get her. I told her that Mindy and I were over. Period. I'd apologized. Over and over again. And now, I was standing here – naked – offering her my heart on a silver platter. What the fuck more did she want?

Liv dropped her hands from around my neck, stepping out of the glass cubicle while I stood there. My mind reeling.

She toweled off then brushed her teeth while I stayed exactly where I was. Just watching her. As my plan - and my world - started to unravel. I was so sure that we were going to get back together. I would have bet my life on it this afternoon.

Liv left the bathroom without uttering a word. And I still hadn't moved.

Countless minutes later, I managed to pull myself together. Turning off the shower and getting ready for bed.

Summoning every bit of strength that I had, I opened the bathroom door. And knew that this was it. I'd apologize and explain everything just once more. Then I was done. My heart could only take so much rejection.

Slowly, I trudged across the carpet towards the bed where Liv lay with her back to me. "Liv?" I said, climbing into bed with her.

She didn't answer, her eyelids pressing together even tighter.

Just one more try.

I shifted closer, brushing the wet hair from Liv's shoulder. "Can we please talk about - us?"

"I don't have much to say," she responded quietly. Chipping a piece off my heart.

"Fine, then just listen. I was an incredible jerk to you for most of the summer and I apologize for that," I began, determined to lay everything out this time. "I was in a bad place when we first met. And it took me a while to realize that you're not like the other women. The women who just want to be with me, because of who they think I am, or what they think I can give them. You like me for me. The real me. Thorns, sarcasm, bad attitude and all." I paused, drawing in a breath. "Once we started spending time together, I realized how amazing you are. And I just couldn't help myself. I fell in love with you, Liv. Deep, crazy love. I did some things that I'm not proud of. Like throwing myself at you when I thought you were Gabe's girlfriend or making you wait while I told Mindy that I never wanted to see her again. That I'd finally found someone. Someone amazing. Please, Liv, look at me," I pleaded.

She turned over. Her face filled with as much pain as my heart felt. "If I could go back and do it over again, I would have told Mindy that with you by my side. I'm so sorry, Darlin.'"

"I know that Ty. Don't get me wrong. It really hurt when I thought that you were choosing Mindy over me. But I get it now." She paused, staring at me with such intensity that my breath hitched and my body tensed. "Is there anything else you'd like to tell me? Anything that we need to talk about?"

The naked woman in my hotel room? Fuck! That must be what's eating at her.

"Laina obviously told you about the, umm, woman in my hotel room. I know that it looked bad, but nothing happened. I swear."

Liv's eyes narrowed. "Laina never said anything about some woman in your hotel room."

Shit! That wasn't it.

"That's because nothing happened. I swear. It was right after we had that fight in the bus and Dave and I got wasted. Nothing happened, Liv," I insisted. "You're the only woman I want to be with. Honestly."

"OK, I believe you," she said slowly. "And even if something did happen, we weren't together anyway. You were free to do anyone you wanted."

"But I didn't," I argued. Cupping the side of her face, I pressed my lips to her forehead. "I swear."

"OK. Is there anything else that you'd like to tell me?" Liv asked. Making me afraid.

She had to know about Piper. That was even worse than the naked woman.

"Piper. You're talking about Piper, right?"

"You slept with Piper?" Liv gasped, her mouth dropping open.

"No!" I replied, taken aback. "Definitely not. Contrary to popular belief, I haven't slept with every woman that I've ever met. But thanks."

Liv grinned, her body relaxing. "Thank God! That would be completely weird if you had slept with Piper. Considering that she and Gabe are, well, whatever they are. So, what about Piper?"

Maybe, she didn't know?

I sucked in a deep breath, hoping that I wasn't about to start World War III. But there was no turning back.

Clean slate. Laying it all out. Right?

"I was the one who booked in Kismet," I confessed. "But you probably already knew that."

"Actually, I didn't know that," Liv replied, her eyebrows raising. "Allison specifically said that the event organizers had booked them in."

I shook my head, waiting for the wrath of Liv to rain down on me. "It was me. I booked Kismet in knowing how Gabe felt about Piper. Hoping that you guys would end up fighting. And it worked." I grimaced.

"Yeah it worked!" Liv hissed, sitting up, glaring at me. "Gabe refused to talk to me for weeks and weeks! You could have ruined our entire friendship! You just needed to give me some time, to figure things out."

"I know that I should have waited for you to sort it out," I agreed, sitting up, taking Liv's hands in mine. My anxiety growing exponentially as I watched her face harden. "But I was terrified that I was going to lose you to Gabe. And then I saw you in the elevator and realized that you hadn't slept with him yet. And I knew that I had to do something. Fast. I was desperate Liv," I pleaded, praying that she'd understand. "I just couldn't lose you. You mean everything to me. So I added Piper into the mix." I paused, drawing in a breath. "I'm deeply sorry for causing you and Gabe so much angst. Although I don't regret what happened because of it. Being together – really together - with you means more to me than I can ever explain."

Liv sighed, her face softening. Just a bit. "That was a shitty move Benson."

"I know. I panicked. I should have trusted you," I admitted.

"You should trust me. How do you expect to build a good relationship without trust?"

"Liv, I trust you with my life. You are my life. No more lies, no more secrets. From now on. I promise."

She looked at me skeptically. "I'd like that. And I'd like to believe you. So, I'm going to ask you one more time. Is there anything else that you need to tell me?"

I shook my head. "Nothing. That's it. I swear."

Thank, God.

"Are you sure?" Liv pushed.

What was she getting at? I racked my brain, but there was nothing else I'd kept from her.

"Of course, I'm sure."

Liv sighed in exasperation. "What about the baby, Ty?"

"What baby?" I asked slowly. Having no idea where this was going.

"Your baby," she said, clearly frustrated.

"My baby? Are you, are you pregnant Darlin'?" I asked, excitement starting to build in my stomach.

At least this would explain the mood swings. Although it was a really odd way to break the 'we're having a baby' news to me.

"Oh my God!" Liv hissed. "I'm not pregnant. Mindy is!"

Disappointment brought me crashing down. "How do you know that?"

"Fuck Ty! I heard her tell you. How can you sit there, asking me to be with you? To build a life with you. And not think it's important to tell me that another woman is having your baby?!" she asked incredulously.

A throaty chuckle left my lips.

This is the stupid, fucking, misunderstanding that she's been so upset about.

"I don't find it funny at all," Liv hissed, staring daggers at me.

"Mindy is pregnant with my ex-manager's, business partner's baby, Liv," I explained. "Not mine. There's no way in hell I'd ever get in bed with that bitch again." I laughed again. Loud. And it felt so good.

"But I heard her say..."

"That I knew who the father of her baby was?" I watched Liv with a huge smile fixed to my lips.

"But, Mindy said that it was your fault she was pregnant."

Somehow my already gigantic grin widened. "Mindy says that everything is my fault. It's part of her ploy to keep me where she wants me. Waiting on the sidelines, in case her current relationship doesn't work out. What she meant is that I introduced her to Richard, my previous manager and one of the many guys she cheated on me with. I also introduced her to Bill, Richard's business partner and the father of her unborn baby. So, of course, everything is my fault."

"Oh my God, she is a giant bitch! No wonder Marie hates her," Liv exclaimed.

"You have no idea how much my mom hates her." Lightly, I ran my fingertips down the side of Liv's face. "Can we put everything behind us and just start over?" I leaned in to kiss her, but she turned away.

"I don't know Ty," Liv replied, different emotions flickering across her face.

"You don't know what?" I asked, trying to hold it together. Not getting it. There was no baby. No Mindy. No Gabe. Just us.

What the fuck now?

"I don't know if I can take another chance on us. Too much has already happened. There are so many lies. And so much hurt. And it seems like every time that I turn around, there's more."

That was it. I lost it.

I got up, pulling on a pair of pajama bottoms and t-shirt before stomping to the door.

"I thought if we had some time alone, I could make you understand but that's obviously not going to happen," I fired back, rage and hurt burning me alive. "I've poured my heart out to you again and again, Liv. I honestly don't know how much more I can take. I've done some things that I'm not proud of. And I've owned up to them. I've apologized and sincerely meant it. If I could, I'd go back and change what I've done. But we both know that's not possible."

I yanked open the door, striding out of the room. Leaving Liv, and my hope for us, behind.

· · · · ·

Liv

I woke up the next morning alone. And feeling like I'd been on an all-night binge. My eyes hurt from crying and my soul ached for what I'd done to Ty. He'd laid his heart out for me. And I'd crushed it. To pieces.

But lies and misunderstandings seemed to permeate our relationship. As soon as we'd work through one thing, there seemed to be another, then another – waiting to mess us up. And I didn't want to live like that.

I couldn't live like that.

Slowly, and very reluctantly, I got ready then snuck downstairs wishing I could somehow escape. The thought of facing Ty, and his family, made me want to cry. Then throw up. Or maybe throw up and then cry. Because I was sure that they all hated me right now.

Lord knows that I hated myself.

As I neared the middle of the staircase I could see Ty on the living room floor with Maddy on his back, playing horsey.

"Giddy up Uncle Ty," she squealed in delight. Ty sat back on his knees pawing his hands in the air. A thin smile on his lips and dark purple circles under his eyes.

Apparently his night hadn't been any better than mine.

"Liv!" Jessie cried, running full tilt toward me. "You finally woke up." We met at the bottom of the stairs and she lifted her little arms towards me. I picked her up, shifting her weight onto my hip. "I wanted to wake you up but Uncle Ty wouldn't' let me. He said that you were really tired and needed to sleep."

"Oh Liv, perfect timing," Marie said coming out of the kitchen, a smile on her pretty face. For me.

What? I was a total bitch to her son and she was still smiling at me. Ty obviously hadn't told her what happened last night. He was such a good person.

A tiny bit of tension left my body. And remorse took its' place for the relationship that Ty and I might have had.

"Jessie, go and tell Mommy and Daddy that it's time to eat." Jessie wiggled out of my arms heading up the stairs as fast as her little legs would go. "Can you tell Ty and Maddy to come and eat please, Liv?"

"Sure, Marie." I crossed the hallway into the living room. "Time to eat guys."

"Yeah! Bacon!" Maddy cheered dismounting her uncle then taking off towards the dining room.

"You should have woken me up. I would have helped make breakfast."

"Like Mom would have let you," Ty said stretching his arms over his head. "She's getting heavy." A smile settled on his lips but didn't quite reach his eyes. "How did you sleep?"

"OK. Where did you sleep last night?" I asked, feeling horrible all over again.

Ty shrugged. "In one of the other bedrooms."

"I'm sorry," I said drawing in a deep breath. "I didn't mean to start anything last night. This isn't the time or place."

"I'm sorry too," Ty returned stepping over to me, circling his arms around my waist. "Last night, I thought that I could walk away. God, I wanted to walk away from you – permanently. But I can't. I love you too much. I know we can make this work."

"Ty," I sighed. "Can we not do this now?" I pleaded glancing at the kitchen, hoping that Marie – and everyone else - wouldn't have to witness this.

"Tell me that you'll seriously think about it. And I'll let this drop. For now. Because honestly I don't care if the entire world knows how I feel about you."

I nodded. "I barely slept last night thinking about what you said. Let's just enjoy the rest of the day with your family and we can talk on the ride home. OK?"

"OK." Ty leaned in, softly working his lips against mine. Making me want to cave. Again.

"Grandma said TIME TO EAT!" Maddy yelled from the dining room entrance.

Ty grinned at me. "Guess we'd better go eat before the boss lady gets mad."

• • • • •

"You know Liv, you and my son are very much alike," Marie said as she sat down next to me on the couch after breakfast. She glanced out the picture window at Ty, Ian and the two older girls playing in the back yard, before smiling at me.

Jessie crawled from my lap to hers with a giggle.

"I'm not too sure about that," I returned.

Marie chuckled and Jessie mimicked her, a giant grin stretching from ear to ear.

"You're both stubborn and like to get your own way," Marie countered patting my knee.

"Fair enough," I acquiesced. "Then maybe we're too much alike in all of the wrong ways."

"I wouldn't say that. I have a feeling that once you two get this misunderstanding sorted out, nothing will ever keep you apart again. That's where the stubbornness will work in your favor." Marie's expression turned serious as she studied my face. "I know that Ty has his faults, Liv. But he's a good man, with a good heart and he genuinely loves you. Fame has been hard on him. Did he ever tell you why he was in such a funk for the past two years?" I shook my head no and Marie continued. "His ex-fiancé. Thank the Lord they never actually got married. Did a number on him. She almost wiped out his bank account, buying clothes and an expensive car, going on trips with her friends." Marie shook her head, her eyes hard as she shared Ty's pain. "After they first broke up, she kept coming back to him. For money I'm guessing, although Ty would never talk to me about that. And he usually tells me everything." Marie paused, composing herself. "Don't get me wrong. Ty let that happen, but only because he thought that she loved him. And he loved her. Turns out she was only using him to get her singing career started. Broke my son's heart."

My mouth dropped open in surprise. This was the first time I'd heard the complete, and was sure unedited, version of what had happened between Ty and Mindy.

"That's terrible," I said. "Ty mentioned Mindy here and there but didn't tell me that part."

"Actually I'm surprised that he even mentioned Mindy to you at all. He doesn't like to talk about her. As a mother, it almost kills you to see your child go through something like that." Marie's voice was as somber as her expression. "But then he met you and he's Ty again. He's happy again." Marie looked at her son through the glass wall. "Well, mostly. But then I can see you're not exactly happy either, sweetheart. What's stopping you from giving it a chance with Ty? You two would be good together."

"Oh Marie, I honestly don't know," I confessed. "Ty is a wonderful man, but with everything that's happened – it's, it's -" I stumbled, searching for the right words.

"A bit scary?" Marie suggested.

"Exactly," I agreed, thankful that Marie understood where I was coming from. "My feelings for him are a bit scary too. I've been in love before but it's never been this intense. And complicated," I explained, relieved to confess my true feelings. Marie smiled, encouraging me to continue.

I'd sugar coated the truth for Laina and Gabe, not wanting them know the depth of my feelings for Ty. Not wanting them to feel sorry for me again. My last broken relationship was enough for both them and me to go through. And my feelings for Ty were already a hundred times stronger. So I'd been keeping everything bottled up inside. Hoping that bottle wasn't going to shatter.

"If Ty and I could work past this, there'd be no turning back, which is also a bit frightening. I don't know if I'm ready for that. In my past relationships I've always jumped in head first and ended up getting hurt. With us, Ty's ten steps ahead of me already."

Marriage. Kids. Yikes!

"Which means that we could both end up with -"

"- something wonderful," Marie finished for me.

"Maybe," I said skeptically.

We stared at each other for a minute, sharing an easy, yet solemn silence. Finally, Jessie reached over patting my hand.

"Why are you and Uncle Ty so sad today, Liv?" she asked.

I smiled at her brushing a light brown curl behind her ear.

"I think Liv just needs some time to sort things out, my girl," Marie answered placing a kiss on top of Jessie's small head.

"Don't worry Liv. You and Uncle Ty can still get married and have lots of babies. You just need to kiss and make up." Jessie looked at me, worry filling her big brown eyes.

"That's great advice Jess, thanks," I said, smiling at her.

"I agree," Ty's deep voice chimed in from behind.

"Uncle Ty!" Jessie cried, sliding off Marie's knee, running to him. He picked her up, hugging her tightly as our eyes met.

"Ty, come give me a hand in the kitchen for a moment," Marie directed as she stood up. "Think about what I said sweetheart." I nodded as she patted my shoulder before heading off.

Ty followed his mom with Jessie in tow. Leaving me to contemplate Marie's words of wisdom.

· · · · ·

An hour later we were on the road, heading back to Vancouver. Aside from a bit of chit chat, neither one of us said much. Both of us locked away in our own thoughts. Every once in a while Ty would glance over, but he never touched me like he had on our way to the island.

It was apparent that everything had changed between us in the space of a day. And not for the better.

"Do you want to come up for a bit?" I asked as we pulled in front of my apartment building. A part of me hoping that he would and another part hoping that he wouldn't.

Ty shook his head. "Thanks. But not tonight. I need to get some things done at home. You alright to go up alone?"

"I'll be fine," I replied getting out of the SUV, taking my duffle bag with me.

Hoping that was really true. That, somehow, I would be fine. Because I felt like an absolute mess right now.

"Thanks again for taking me to meet your family. They're all wonderful." I paused for a moment. A wave of sadness washing over me as the realization that I probably wouldn't be seeing Ty's family again, hit me. "So I guess I'll see you tomorrow at the office?"

I watched different emotions flicker across Ty's face. A thin smile finally settling on his lips as he nodded at me.

"Sure. Have a good night Liv."

I closed the door then watched Ty drive away, a feeling of heaviness overwhelming me.

· · · · ·

I trudged towards my office on Monday morning, feeling like shit. I'd barely slept last night thinking about Ty's heartfelt confession and my not-so-wonderful reaction to it. One minute, I wanted to call him and profess my love. Then, the next minute, I was glad that I hadn't.

Drawing in a huge breath, I opened the office door expecting to see Ty perched on the corner of Lindsay's desk (or vice versa) with that infectious grin on his face. Much to my surprise – and unexpected disappointment - he was nowhere in sight.

"Hi, Liv. How was your weekend?" Lindsay greeted as I shoved the door closed behind me.

"It was fine. How was yours?" I replied, heading past her to my desk. *Wishing that I'd stayed in bed today.*

"Good, thanks for asking," Lindsay said poking her head around the hutch of her desk. "You don't happen to know where Ty is. Do you?" She stared at me expectantly.

Ah, Ty. And there it was.

"No idea. I assumed he'd be here. He hasn't shown up yet?" I asked, surprised that Ty wasn't in the office already. He usually showed up by seven thirty. Eight at the latest.

"No, not yet. He must be running late." Lindsay paused, concern blossoming on her face. "You don't think that he's sick do you? Maybe we should phone him?" She looked at me, clearly excited about this idea. "Maybe he needs someone to bring him soup or something? You know, I make the best beef barley soup. Maybe I should run home and start a pot? What do you think, Liv?" Lindsay rambled.

Apparently Ty had messed her up too. Usually she got straight to the point.

"Wait! Do you have his phone number?" Lindsay asked, enthusiastically. "What am I saying? Of course you have his phone number. That was a silly question."

More rambling. Oh, Lindsay. Not good.

"It's only twenty after eight. He probably stopped for coffee or something. Let's give him a bit before we start to panic." I pulled the laptop out of my bag and proceeded to set it up as Lindsay watched me.

"That's reasonable, except that Ty's usually here by now. Aren't you worried? Even a little?" she questioned.

I swung my chair around to face her. "Not yet. I'm sure that Ty is fine. Maybe he slept in," I suggested.

Or, maybe, he was just avoiding me. If I was him, I'd avoid me.

• • • • •

Three hours and twenty-five minutes later, Ty still hadn't materialized. Lindsay was now fit to be tied and I was starting to think that something really was wrong.

"OK Liv, your class starts in fifteen minutes and Ty still isn't here. We need to phone him!" she demanded, shaking my arm, violating her rule of 'no physical contact,' with anyone other than Ty.

"Fine, you're right," I said, torn between calling Ty and doing something even worse - giving Lindsay his phone number. I stared at her for a moment - contemplating.

"I know that you have Ty's number, Liv! Either you call or let me call him. Something might be seriously wrong!" she shrieked.

"OK, OK, you're right Lindsay. I'll text him." Lindsay let out a giant humpf sound. "If he doesn't respond within the next few minutes, I'll call him," I added before she could protest. "And you can do the talking."

"That sounds reasonable."

I pulled out my cell and selected Ty's contact info.

```
Hey Ty. We haven't seen you this morning.
Everything OK? Lindsay is going nuts and trying
to take me with her.
```

• • • • •

I laid my phone on the edge of the desk, then began to collect the handouts we needed for today's class. Lindsay stared at the thin rectangular box in anticipation. Like it was going to spit out a genie or something equally magical – a rock star.

```
Hi Liv. Tell Lindsay that I'm still alive. See
you in class.
```

• • • • •

"He's fine Lindsay," I relayed.

"But where is he?" she demanded.

"I have no idea. He just said see you in class." Without waiting for

Lindsay's next bout of Ty-related questions, I stuffed the papers into my bag and headed for class.

Two minutes before class started, Ty sauntered into the room, a cordial smile fixed to his lips. Over the next hour, we whipped through the lesson plan that Ty had developed, easily playing off one another. Then, as soon as the class was done, so was Ty.

"See you later Liv," were his departing – and only – words to me.

• • • • •

Over the next two weeks, more of the same. Ty would materialize just before class, then vanish as soon as we were finished. Any communication that we needed to do was via e-mail and always to the point.

Outside of class, I never saw him. At all. Although I knew that he was still going out with Gabe and everyone else. Whenever I didn't.

Ouch!

I even tried to pry information out of Gabe and Laina, but whenever I mentioned Ty, they'd just tell me to "woman up" and talk to him myself.

Awesome.

The more Ty avoided me. The more I missed him.

Which sucked – immensely.

Chapter 21 ~ Liv

On Saturday night, I couldn't take it any longer. Ty had consumed my every thought over the past two weeks and I needed to do something about it. Just before Gabe, Laina and I were set to leave for Club 89, I faked feeling sick, gambling that Ty wouldn't go out at the last minute - now that I had bailed.

I also gambled that he'd be at home on a Saturday night - alone.

Fifty minutes later I stood outside the door of Ty's waterfront condo. A mixture of excitement and apprehension surging through my body as I rang the doorbell. Still debating about whether or not this was the stupidest idea I've ever had.

Before I'd reached a conclusion, the door swung open and Ty stood there. Looking at me with a puzzled expression on his face.

Conclusion now reached - this was definitely a stupid idea. What was I doing here?

"Liv, what are you doing here?" Ty asked, echoing my thought.

Good question. Think he'd believe that I was selling Girl Guide cookies?

"I came to talk to you," I confessed, deciding to woman up and get this over with. "I hope this isn't a bad time? Sorry, I should have called before coming over," I rambled, my nerves now on overload.

Instinctively, my fingers tightened around the handles of the paper shopping bag dangling from my hand.

"It's never a bad time for you to come over. Is everything alright?" he asked stepping back, motioning for me to come in.

"Everything is fine," I returned in a shaky voice, moving through the doorway.

'Please be alone,' I prayed as Ty shut the door behind us.

He eyed me for a second before starting down a long hallway dotted with red four doors and various pieces of colorful artwork. Under better circumstances, I would have loved to stop and look at each of the pictures.

"How did you know where I live?" Ty questioned.

"Gabe," I replied, trying to sound casual as we entered the living room. My heart beating so hard that it literally thumped in my ears.

"Gabe?" Ty confirmed with a skeptical look on his face.

I nodded.

It was sort of the truth. I did get Ty's address, from Gabe's cell phone, after I hacked into it this afternoon. Because if I'd asked Gabe for Ty's information, he would have told Ty. And I didn't want anyone to know about this.

In case I changed my mind and chickened out. Like I was considering doing. Right now.

I glanced around the room trying to muster up the courage to follow through with my plan. But even in my anxious state, I could appreciate how amazing the space was. It seemed like our entire apartment could fit into this one room. Half of the walls were exposed red brick while the other half were painted the same warm, cappuccino brown as the hallway. A bright red sectional sofa and black shelving unit took up the far end of the room, while a pinball machine, foosball table and old school Pac Man video game occupied the other end.

"Great place," I complimented, turning back towards Ty. Sucking in a huge breath, I tried to calm down.

"Thanks. I still want to get a chair to put in the corner next to the fireplace," he replied motioning towards the empty space. "But I have no idea what to get."

"Maybe we can go shopping later?" I offered.

If I made it to later.

"Sounds good," Ty agreed, his eyebrows lifting in surprise. "Can I take your bag and coat?"

"Are you alone?" I asked hesitantly.

"Yes," Ty slowly answered, looking at me as if I'd finally lost it.

And maybe I had. Or would – soon.

"OK," I stammered before handing Ty the paper shopping bag. He set it on the couch, eyeing me suspiciously as he waited for my coat. Slowly. So slowly. I unbuttoned the knee length black trench coat that I had on.

Ty's eyes widened as I slipped it off of my shoulders, holding it out to him.

"What, what, are you wearing?" he stammered, his eyes raking over my almost naked body.

"Strings. Lots of strings," I returned, feeling slightly more confident.

Through a lot of effort - and a ton of bad language - I had managed to wrap my torso in a pink ribbon. Barely covering the necessary parts.

"Oh – my – God – Liv! Are you trying to kill me?" Ty moaned, rubbing the six o'clock shadow on his chin while his eyes continued to take in my version of a human present.

Stepping closer to him, I ran my hand down his toned chest. "Think of me as an early Christmas gift," I suggested. Stretching up on my tiptoes, I pressed my lips against his.

A giant groan escaped Ty's lips as he took a step back. "I meant what I said, Liv. I don't just want to have sex with you. I want more." His eyes swept over the ribbon wrapped portion of my body again. "Although the thought of unwrapping you is seriously tempting. No!" he huffed, turning around, almost running into the adjoining kitchen. "No," he repeated as I followed him with the paper bag in my hand.

"Well, if you don't like this gift," I said motioning to my body. "Then maybe you'll like this one." I handed the bag to Ty.

"This is for me?" he asked. I nodded my head, almost vibrating with anticipation. "I'm kind of afraid to open it," he admitted, setting the bag onto the black granite countertop. "I'm still reeling from the last gift you just offered me." He glanced at my body again, a sigh escaping his lips. "I don't think I can take much more Liv."

"Open it," I urged running my hand down his bare arm. "You'll like it. I promise."

Ty looked at me, grimacing. "That's what I'm afraid of."

"Don't be such a baby. Open it," I urged.

With a huge sigh, Ty pulled the bag open, peering inside. He took out a bottle of chamomile shampoo and argon conditioner, opening the cap and smelling the contents of each.

"These are the shampoo and conditioner that you use," he said, his face filled with confusion.

"How do you know that?"

"Trust me, I know the way you smell," he said, leaning over to bury his face in my loose curls. "Mmm, I love the way you smell," he muttered, pulling away from me. With obvious effort. Making me smile.

He reached into the bag again, pulling out a pink toothbrush. "Pink, my favorite." He flashed me a grin. Reaching back into the bag, he took out a black, lacey thong. Holding it up, he looked at me, clearly confused. "Um, thanks, but I don't think this will fit."

I took the thong from his hand holding it up to my waist. "It fits perfectly," I returned.

"OK, now I'm totally confused. Darlin', what is all this?" He stared at me - waiting.

"This," I said, pointing to the ribbons crisscrossing my torso, "are strings. Lots of strings. And this," I said motioning to the items Ty had placed on the countertop, "is commitment. As your girlfriend," I said slowly, "who's in a big, fat, committed relationship with her amazing boyfriend, I'll be staying here a lot. So I thought I'd bring some things to keep here. You know, for convenience sake."

I watched the expression on Ty's face change from confusion to elation. He picked me up swinging me around and around. Hugging me tightly. As soon as he set me down, his lips crushed against mine while his hands raked over my back and hips.

"Before I unwrap my gift," he said looking deeply into my eyes. "I just want to make sure that I understand what you're saying. I need to know for certain that we're on the same page."

"Baby, I know it's taken a long time and that I've been stubborn – about everything. I'm so sorry."

Ty gently ran his finger tips along the side of my face. "Me too. But what made you change your mind?"

I sighed. "I missed you." Ty looked at me, confusion on his face. Again. "Over the past couple of weeks," I continued, "you haven't been around and I realized how much I looked forward to seeing you every day. Even when you were tormenting the crap out of me." He smirked. "I realized how much I NEED to see you every day. How much I want to be with you. I love you."

"I love you too." Ty pressed his lips to mine for a slow, sweet kiss. "Remind me to call my mom later and thank her."

"OK, why?" I asked planting tiny kisses along Ty's neck, breathing him in.

"She told me to give you some space. To stop pushing and let you come to me. Mom said that we're meant for each other. I just needed to be patient and give you time to realize it."

"Marie said that?" I asked meeting his eyes. Ty nodded. "She's a smart lady, no wonder I like her so much."

"That good because she's your future mother-in-law," Ty returned with a smirk.

"Don't you think you're getting a little ahead of yourself again, Benson?" I teased, my heart swelling with happiness.

"Absolutely not. There was something between us right from the start. Something that I've never felt with anyone before. Liv, you have my heart and my love. Always."

"You're my other half," I returned, my eyes misting up. "I love you Ty Benson more than I can ever say. Make love to me?" I asked, melting into his beautiful eyes.

"Darlin', I'm going to make love to you every day for the rest of our lives," he promised bringing his lips to mine. "I love you so much, Liv. Thanks for coming to your senses," Ty said lifting me into his arms, a huge grin on his lips. "Finally."

Chapter 22 - Liv

I'd moved in with Ty at the start of December. So, for our first Christmas together, we halved the time between Ty's family and mine. Making the holidays a whirlwind of driving and visiting. And, now, I was happy to be back at home.

Our home.

Waiting to ring in the New Year with all of our friends.

"Great party Baby Doll," Gabe complimented, planting a quick kiss on my cheek as he helped himself to another plate of food. "You guys really went all out. The food is amazing and the place looks like Christmas threw up in here."

I glanced around our living room, taking in the million twinkle lights that Ty had strung up and the colorful Christmas decorations I'd placed on every surface possible.

The place looked amazing. Even if I did say so myself.

"Thanks, Gabe," I replied with a grin. Pulling open the oven, I took out a cookie sheet full of mini quiches. "The pizza bites will be done in a minute if you wait."

"I'll circle back." Gabe grinned. "Piper's waiting for a drink and some food." He held up a plate piled high with snacks.

"Piper can have her own plate, you know," I teased, looking at the tenuous pile of tortilla chips stacked up on the side of Gabe's already overfilled plate.

He chuckled. "I don't mind sharing with her. I'm just glad she was able to make it tonight." He grabbed two bottles of beer out of the bright red ice tub on the kitchen table.

"Me too. It's a shame that her boyfriend wasn't able to come through," I said, doing my best not to smirk when Gabe's expression soured.

"Yeah, that's a real pity."

I eyed Gabe skeptically.

"What! I said it's a pity." He shot me a big grin. "Better not leave her waiting."

"Yep, turn on that infamous Gabe charm and get going," I teased. A grin tugged on my lips as I watched him weave through the crowd to where Piper was talking with Dave, Lindsay and Liam.

"Great party Darlin'," Ty said wrapping his arms around my waist. "I think you've set the bar a little too high though. Now people are going to expect THIS." He waved his arm in front of us. "Every time we have a party. In my bachelor days, they'd be lucky to get a piece of pizza and semi-cold beer."

A feeling of contentment settled over me as Ty and I looked around the room filled with our friends.

I was the luckiest woman in the entire world.

"I'm OK with that. All of the work was totally worth it," I replied, gazing into Ty's eyes. "Besides, your bachelor days are over."

Ty leaned down, kissing me slowly, making my stomach tighten. "Yes, they certainly are. Hopefully we'll make it official sooner than later."

He smirked as I raised an eyebrow.

It had been an ongoing joke with our friends ever since I'd moved in with Ty. They'd been relentlessly razzing us because of how fast we were moving. Betting that by next Christmas we'd be married with a baby on the way.

To be fair, Ty and I had been going out for less than three months before deciding to live together. But living together felt right. Everything about being with Ty felt right.

And, although I wasn't ready to admit it yet. Especially to Ty. The whole getting married and having a baby idea was starting to sound pretty good.

"Have you noticed the tension between Laina, Brian, and Dave tonight?" Ty asked. His eyes moving from where Laina and Brian were talking, to where Dave was standing twenty feet away, watching them.

"Yup, can't say that I'd want to be Laina right now."

I'd watched my best friend flit between the two guys for the past three hours as they vied for her attention. It was exhausting to watch. So I could only imagine how Laina was feeling. But, then again, she thrived on attention. And she was definitely getting that - to the max - tonight.

"I thought she was done with Dave?" Ty asked, trying to seem casual.

I shook my head, grinning at him. "Seriously Benson, I'm not giving you any intel for your buddy. He screwed things up with Laina, so he needs to make them right. If that's even possible."

"Yeah, that's what I told Dave. Although in his defense, Laina was the one who told HIM not to call her anymore."

"And the fact that he listened to her tells me that he doesn't know Laina at all," I returned.

"I know Darlin'. He's just wondering where Laina and Brian stand. Whether there's even a point to try to work things out with Laina?"

I sighed. "Honestly I don't know. She and Brian have been spending a lot of time together lately. And you know how he feels about her."

"Yes, but how does she feel about him?"

"That's the million-dollar question. Laina's been unusually tight-lipped about Brian, so I'm not too sure. Guess time will tell."

Ty worked his lips against mine. Making me wish that we were alone. And naked.

I just couldn't get enough of him.

"Ty!" Will shouted. "You're up next."

Ty held his thumb in the air as he straightened up. "Looks like it's my turn to conquer Pac Man. Don't forget that I get the first New Year's kiss."

"You get every New Year's kiss, babe." I watched Ty saunter over to the game, loving that he was mine.

"Hey Liv. I just wanted to thank you for inviting me," Piper said, taking Ty's place beside me.

"You've already thanked me," I returned shooting her a smile. "We're happy that you were able to make it."

"Fortunately, Seattle isn't too far away. You and Ty did a fabulous job decorating. Very festive." Piper paused, chewing on her bottom lip for a moment. "About what I said at the hotel – about Ty - I'm sorry. I was obviously wrong. I guess he just needed to meet the right woman." She glanced at me sheepishly.

I grinned, remembering that conversation and her warning to stay away from Ty. "Well, the right woman or man," I said glancing at Gabe. "Will do that to you."

Piper followed the direction of my gaze, landing on Gabe. "He's a great guy. I don't think I've ever met anyone like him before."

"Yep, Gabe's definitely one of a kind. You know, he's never really been in a serious relationship before," I shared, loving the look of surprise on Piper's pretty face.

"How's that possible?"

"I guess he just hasn't met the right woman. She'll have to be pretty amazing to turn his head." We looked at each other for a moment. Each of us thinking about that. "I know it's none of my business but why didn't you want to spend New Year's Eve with your boyfriend?"

Piper sighed running a hand up her tattooed arm.

"I just needed a break. Things have been pretty intense between us lately." She stared at the wall for a moment before continuing. "I told him that I was playing a gig tonight." Worry lines snaked across Piper's pale forehead as she bit her bottom lip again.

"Oh," I replied, shocked at her honesty. "If things are so intense between you two, why don't you just break up with him?"

"It's complicated Liv."

I nodded in understanding. "Gottcha, I'm the queen of complicated. Or at least I was before Ty forced me to sort things out between us." I watched Ty high-five Liam, a giant grin on his face.

God, I loved him.

"I'm really grateful that he didn't give up on me," I admitted, looking at Piper again. "If there's someone who has your heart, don't give up. Work it out."

A smirk settled on Piper's lips. "Could you be any more obvious or cliché, Liv?"

We both chuckled.

"Fair enough," I agreed. Watching Piper's face light up when Gabe smiled at her from across the room.

"Gabe's probably waiting for his pizza bites," she said, scooping some of the gooey triangles onto a plate.

"He sent you over for more food?" I asked, shaking my head. "I think he's trying to eat enough for a week."

Piper chuckled. "Yeah, I've never seen someone eat so much and still look so hot - I mean fit," she corrected, biting her lip.

"Hey everyone, it's almost time!" someone shouted. "Turn down the music."

Everyone turned towards Ty's giant flat screen, watching as the big apple began to descend.

"I'd better go and find Gabe," Piper said. "Happy New Year, Liv."

"Happy New Year to you too."

"Hey, Darlin'," Ty greeted, slipping in next to me, wrapping his arms around my waist, pulling me close.

"Three, two, one, Happy New Year!!" everyone yelled in unison.

"Happy New Year, my love," Ty whispered into my ear.

"Happy New Year, my love," I returned, pressing my lips to his. "May this be the first of many to come for us."

View other Black Rose Writing titles at www.blackrosewriting.com/books and use promo code **PRINT** to receive a **20% discount** when purchasing.

BLACK ROSE
writing™

CPSIA information can be obtained
at www.ICGtesting.com
Printed in the USA
LVOW08s0817200717
541871LV00002B/2/P